HERO

IS A FOUR LETTER WORD

SHORT STORIES BY

J.M. FREY

"The Once and Now-ish King" first published in *When The Hero Comes Home* (Dragon Moon Press, 2012)
"Zmeu" first published in *Gods, Memes, and Monsters* (Stone Skin Press, 2015)
"The Moral of the Story" first published in *Wrestling with Gods: Tesseracts 18* (EDGE Publications, 2015)
"The Twenty Seven Club" first published in *Expiration Date* (EDGE Publications, 2015)
The Dark Lord and the Seamstress first published by J.M. Frey (Here There Be 2014)
In, Two, Three, Four, Five first published by J.M. Frey (Wattpad, 2017)
"Another Four Letter Word" first published in *Hero is a Four Letter Word, second ed.* (Short Fuse, 2013)
"The Maddening Science" first published *When the Villain Comes Home* (Dragon Moon Press, 2013)
Ghosts, first published as part of The Accidental Turn Series (REUTS Publications, 2016)

www.jmfrey.net

ISBN-13: 978-1-7753402-3-2
eBook ISBN 13: 978-1-7753402-4-9

For Brienne Wright.

She's the first person to help me up when I stumble,
and the first person to pop the champagne
when I have something to celebrate.
I am so proud of her determination and so blessed by her kind friendship.

Contents

HERO

IS A
FOUR LETTER
WORD

The Once and Nowish King

The first thing that Arthur Pendragon, the Once and Future (well, *Now-ish*) King did upon his rebirth into the world at the moment of Albion's greatest need, was to open his shrivelled red mouth and squall out: "Oh *hell*, no."

Which startled his Mother quite badly, you'll understand, as she had just put him to her breast for his first little feeding. She shook her head and glared balefully at the IV needle in the bend of her elbow, ignored her new son's outburst, and went about her task.

The second thing that Arthur Pendragon, the Once and Now-ish King did upon his rebirth into the world at the moment of Albion's greatest need, was to consume his body weight in breast milk. After which, he soiled his nappy, burped quite dramatically, and took a wee bit of a nap.

Getting born was hard work, you know.

The next thing that Arthur Pendragon, the Once and Now-ish King, did upon his rebirth was to wake up and ask to where that good for nothing senile git of a wizard had gotten. Nobody else was in the hospital room with Arthur and his new mother, so he had to repeat it a few times to convince her that she was not, in fact, hearing things. "Great ancient sorcerer with the beard?"

"What, Gandalf?" his mother asked, trying to make her eyes the size of regular eyes again, rather than saucers. She wasn't quite succeeding. "Or, um, Merlin?"

"Yes, Merlin!" Arthur shrilled, then frowned because his voice hadn't been that high since, well, since the last time he was a baby. In a more sedate, and what he hoped was a more kingly tone, he went on to clarify: "Who the hell else would I mean?"

"I, uh, I'm sure I don't know, dearest," his mother said, and started to cry.

Arthur felt quite bad about that, because she seemed a nice lady, especially since she had just put up with him in her womb for nine months. He resolved to be a bit gentler with her thereafter.

Were Guinevere here, she would surely have clipped him round his ears already.

Arthur was quiet on the way home, watching with utter fascination as his new father manhandled the strange metal carriage in which they rode. The motion of the vehicle made him nod off, soothing and quite like being tucked up safe and sound in a caring person's arms. His only grievance with this was that he had hoped to see more of the strange and wonderful world outside of the vehicle's windows. There were tall buildings and everything was covered in glass. Some great king must have been very wealthy to afford to give his subjects a whole city of glass.

The thought caused his tiny tummy to burble with foreboding, because perhaps this wealthy king was the very person he had been brought back to defeat. Shoving thoughts of his destiny aside for now – it was not as if he had Excalibur, or was yet strong enough to even lift her – he let the rocking motion lull him into a doze.

Once they arrived home, Arthur made a point of vocally admiring the shade of green on the walls of his nursery, and complimented his mother on her pretty coming-home dress. He had, after all, promised himself to be nicer.

She started crying again, and Arthur, who had never really been all that good with girls and who probably wouldn't have ever been able to attract a wife had he not had a crown weighing on his forehead, looked at his father and said, "What did I do?" He *really* wished Guinevere was here. His father only plopped down into the rocking chair and stared in horror at his little face.

"What?" Arthur said.

"I... don't think this was in the baby books, hon," his father said, all the blood draining from his face. If the man was going to swoon, Arthur hoped to at least be set down somewhere first. But the man stayed upright. He gulped on the air for a bit, then when his colour had mostly come back, he stood and lay Arthur in the middle of the crib and grabbed his wife's wrist. They left. Arthur heard the footsteps pad across the carpeting, tracking them as they traversed the hallway and then descended the stairs and went out the front door.

Oh, dear.

For a long, long time, Arthur lay still, listening. There was no shouting, no noisy roar of an unhappy lynch mob or of the metal vehicles. There was only Arthur and the inadequate swaddling blanket and the boring white ceiling. There were also five fuzzy white sheep that kept going around and around above his head, hypnotic and really sort of ...marvellous.

Right around when his stomach started to cramp with hunger, but after the King of Albion had suffered the indignity of losing control of his own bowels and soiling his nappy, his mother came back.

She hovered in the doorway for a moment, and Arthur gummed his bottom lip and tried to decide if he should say anything. It was, after all, what had gotten him into this mess. Before he could, she darted across the floor like a war charger and scooped him close and pressed his cheek against her neck and said, "I'm sorry, I'm sorry, I'm so sorry. It doesn't matter, it doesn't, you're my son and you're perfect and I love you."

Arthur reached up and patted her cheek gently. "I understand," he said, and sort of thought that he did.

Then his mother offered him a bottle, and he tried not to be disappointed. He wouldn't want to nurse a baby with the thought processes and memories of an adult man either, really, but the bottle meant she was rejecting him, if only a little. Arthur's stomach swooped in fear, and he realized it was because he didn't want to lose those tender, affectionate moments when he was wrapped in his mother's arms, head against her breast and the sound of her heart soothing him. He supposed he couldn't blame her. It had to be weird, having a fully articulate, fully cognizant child latching to your breast.

***

Arthur was doing his damndest to stay asleep and not let the little hunger cramps or the haunting sense that he wasn't bundled up enough wake him every few hours. It was uncomfortable and odd, but he was determined. He was absolutely capable of letting his parents get a full night's sleep, and perhaps to do the same himself. Having always been a man of strong will, he managed to do just that.

Somewhere in the middle of all of it, Arthur also managed to dream.

He was standing on a battlefield and he knew Mordred was behind him, but he couldn't turn around fast enough. He hadn't been fast enough in real life, either. Then there was Guinevere's big liquid eyes, and Lancelot's guilty frown, and something Merlin whispered in his ear about coming back one day, about the future of the kingdom resting upon his soul, about being called forth again like the pagan gods from their barrows...

And then there was a shrill screaming, the likes of which Arthur hadn't heard since once of his horses had fallen into a pit dug in the road by his enemies and snapped its foreleg. He'd killed the stallion for pity. It wasn't until someone's big warm hands were on his back and he felt himself tucked protectively against his father's soft, sloping chest that he realized he was awake and the shrill, plaintive sounds were coming from him. He, the Once and Now-ish King, was sobbing hysterically.

"Shhhh, buddy," his father said, and jogged him a few times, bumping him closer to wakefulness. "You're safe, you're safe. Daddy's here."

Arthur snuffled closer and let himself cry out the rest of his residual fear, because what his father said was true. He *was* safe here. At least for now. There were no dragons to slay, no traitors to rout, no scheming and politics to navigate, no affair to untangle. There was only Arthur, and his father's warm assurance, the sound of his mother's soft snores in the other room, and the woolly sheep spinning in a calm, slow circle, blown by the cool breeze of the night time air slipping past the gap in the endearingly crooked windowsill.

"Daddy," Arthur said, curling chubby fists into the collar of the man's sleep shirt, and didn't feel ridiculous at all for using such a juvenile term. King Uther would have boxed young Arthur's ears for daring to utter it, but here, now, it felt right. "I'm Arthur," he breathed.

"I know," the man said, and dropped a soft, dry kiss on his son's cheek. "That *is* what we put on the birth certificate."

The open affection of the gesture shocked Arthur into more tears, though these ones were soft, quiet, and grateful.

***

A few days later, Arthur's father was comfortable enough with his verbosity to hold complete, if distracted, conversations. Which was good, because the nightmare of his death had been subtly shifting each time Arthur fell asleep; he still stood on a field, but instead of being behind him with a sword, Mordred now stood before him on a broad grassy plain, and unlike the battlefield of his memory it was free of blood and the fallen. Instead of being alone on that knoll, he now had the vague impression of being watched on all sides, and of the tension that crackled between him and his traitorous nephew. They both wanted—coveted—something, and Arthur wondered if it was a crown again, or something more vital. Something more dangerous.

He stood and stared at Mordred and Mordred stood and stared at him, hands out as if prepared to grapple, weaponless and ready to strike. Arthur wished he had Excalibur so he could wallop the whelp down before the ungrateful snake could do him in a second time.

But then the dream ended; it always ended before either of them made a move.

Arthur felt that it was perhaps a warning, a vision of the future or the battle to come, and Arthur wanted to be certain he knew what it meant when the time arrived. He needed to understand, and the only way he could do that was to ask questions, to discuss.

But he couldn't do that until his father, so far the only other person besides his mother he trusted enough with this information, understood what was at stake.

"I feel the need to clarify," Arthur said as his father closed the bedroom door behind them. Downstairs were his mother's parents and his father's sister, all of whom had come to coo at the new baby and who, Arthur's father had patiently explained that morning, probably didn't need to know that their shiny new grandson and nephew could speak like a functional adult. Arthur, therefore, had spent the morning making gurgling sounds and being as adorable as he could manage and was really starved for some honest *adult* interaction.

"Clarify what?" Arthur's father asked, holding Arthur away from his body as if to ensure that the slight smell wouldn't travel through the nappy and into his own clothes.

"My name," Arthur said. "I'm not just any old Arthur – though I am thrilled that the name has gained such popularity. I am Arthur, *King* of the Britons, Uniter and Ruler of the land of Albion. And put me down already, man, you look ridiculous. Honestly, it's not going to *explode*."

Arthur's father chuckled and put Arthur on the change table and began the lengthy process of preparing to change his nappy.

"You *do* know me, don't you?" Arthur asked worriedly, when his father hadn't immediately been shocked, or gone into raptures, or at least made a leg and called him "your majesty." Perhaps he was forgotten.

"Hm, what?" his father asked, rooting around under the table for the wet wipes and dry powder. "Right, yes, King Arthur, quest for the Holy Grail, Sean Connery, myths to make the Welsh feel better about themselves, all that."

Arthur furrowed his chubby brow as best he could. *All* of him was chubby right now and it actually was slightly annoying. It was hard to be taken seriously when one was so damnably *cute*. "Sean who?"

"Actor. Played King Arthur in the films."

The thought that he had passed into history had been certain to Arthur; he had already been a great historical figure while he had lived. That he would pass into legend was a possibility, though he didn't enjoy the idea that he might have been forgotten as a real person. To find that he had become a *myth* hurt in ways that Arthur couldn't directly pinpoint, but he thought that it might have something to do with the idea that all of his bloody and hard work had been reduced to the sphere of an epithet, and all the people he had known and loved had been distilled into archetypes and clichés, ghosts of themselves.

But to find that there had been a *film*...horrifying.

Arthur had already seen two films in his admittedly young life – one that made his mother weep and smile as the man declared his love for the unattractively thin woman with a wide face (arms like toothpicks, she'd never be able to raise a blade to defend herself or her children from invaders), and one filled with great balls of fire and fast chases in those metal vehicles he now knew were called "cars" – and wasn't sure he had any great love for this bastardization of the bardic tale-weaving he had known in his last life. Though, he had to admit, the television was a remarkable invention.

To take his mind off it, he asked, "What exactly is wrong with Albion, anyway?"

"Pardon?" his father asked again, concentrating on his task and perhaps watching Arthur's willy with more apprehension than was strictly polite. After all, Arthur hadn't weed on him on purpose, and he had apologised besides. "What's an Albion?"

"This land. I united it. I ruled the whole island once, you know. Don't tell me somebody let it get all split up into different kingdoms again after all the hard work I did."

"It was for, oh, a thousand or so years," his father said, reaching for the fresh nappies, eyes still on Arthur. "But then Scotland and Wales and part of Ireland got sucked back in, wars for a few centuries about all of that, too, and so it's all mostly united again. The United Kingdom of Great Britain and Northern Ireland. We just say the 'UK' now, son. Oh, but, uh, I guess there's the colonies, too, only they're not colonies any more as we've become a commonwealth state and --"

Arthur coughed and his father trailed off, concentrating on getting the nappy under his son. Not a Kingdom anymore but a whole *Empire*; Arthur felt overwhelming responsibility pressing strangely on his little shoulders. Perhaps it would mean that he would be less prepared when the hour of need came, but right now Arthur wished that he could have had a childhood like the last one: oblivious of his destiny and happy in his innocence.

After a short silence, Arthur prompted: "So, Albion's greatest hour of need?"

The man shrugged. "Rotter in Downing Street? War in the Middle East? Decline of social niceties in direct correlation with the rise of texting and tweens?"

"Maybe it hasn't happened yet," Arthur ventured. Then he sighed, because baby powder? Best. Feeling. Ever.

"You'd be born before the thing that would make you need to be born has happened?" his father said, and finally looked up.

"Magic works in strange ways; besides, Merlin lived his life backwards. He always knew what was going to happen before it did." Arthur wanted to grin, but a wave of melancholy swept over him instead. "It was always frustrating, though, because he never remembered the day before. It was...difficult. Having a friend who never shared the same memories, I mean. Who never...shared anything you loved. Except your friendship." Arthur swallowed. "And the in-jokes never worked. Anyway. He'd know when I had to be born again. So that means whatever it is, it probably hasn't happened yet."

"That's a comfort," his father allowed. "I guess. None of us can choose his destiny."

Arthur frowned. "No; but some of us have it chosen for them." Arthur let this percolate for a bit as his father tamped down the sticky tabs on the side of his new nappy and picked him up. "By the way... surprisingly insightful, old man," Arthur said, snuffling and burrowing close to his father's warmth and the comfortable, safe smell of his neck.

His father smiled. "Thanks, kiddo. You get your brains from me."

Arthur felt that a good gummy yawn was probably agreement enough, and proceeded to put thought into action.

***

Arthur dreamed again. He dreamt of the great grassy plain, and of thousands of millions pairs of eyes watching him from stands erected all around him, hemming him in. But it was getting more detailed, the more he experienced it; or maybe it was just that he was familiar enough with the skeleton of the dream that he could allow his mind to take in the other, seemingly less important details.

It was a tourney field of some sort, but it was bisected at its narrowest, rather than with a rail across the length. This was not a jousting field, nor did Arthur wear any mail or armour. That it was a place for fighting, he knew, but what kind escaped him.

Mordred just crouched before him, a flapping swatch of white suspended on a metal frame behind his head, smirking and horrible and waiting.

They were both dressed in a ridiculously flimsy pair of uniforms, with thin boots and shin guards. The material was so slight that it would not block any blade, and it was in a colour so bright and garish that they would never be able to hide from their enemies. Perhaps that was the point; to prove that the knight wearing it was firm enough of mettle and strong enough of arm to not require armour.

The people in the stands around him blasted their disproval of his inaction into short, obnoxious trumpets and the sound filled the grounds with the angry buzz of disturbed hornets. They looked at him with such eager *expectation*, and Arthur had no idea how to give them what they wanted. He had always feared not being able to satisfy his subjects, but their now gazes were positively hungry. Arthur wondered what could be at stake should he fail this test that would make them so desperate.

A golden club sat in the middle of the tourney field. It was cup-shaped and large, with a great ball cradled between the carven swaths of its base. Arthur knew it was not the Grail. Beyond that, he had no idea why it might be significant, and his ignorance annoyed him as much as the anxiety in the audience's eyes ate away at his confidence.

A sharp cry woke him and he was chagrined to discover that once more it had come from him. Imagine, King Arthur, the strongest arm at the Round Table and the firmest of grip on the crown, unable to contain his own whimpers. Or bowels, for that matter. He shifted once in the darkness, but no tell-tale dampness announced its presence and he sighed. He was getting better at controlling *that*, at least.

When his mother came into the room a few minutes later with his bottle, Arthur peered up at her from his crib and said, "I'm sorry, Mother."

"Babies are like ink cartridges; low capacity and need to be refilled often," his mother said with a strained smile. There were dark smudges under her eyes and Arthur felt so guilty that he couldn't help the involuntary squirm.

"I didn't mean the night feedings, though I appreciate that, too," Arthur admitted, waving his hands happily at the bottle as his mother held it in his direction. She didn't like to pick him up to feed him anymore. Arthur missed the feel of the beat of her heart next to his cheek, the soft warm milk-and-rose-water-smell she had, the gentleness of her long fingers on the back of his neck, but he didn't dare say as much. He felt he was imposing on the poor woman enough. "I meant for... well... everything else."

His mother let him latch onto the plastic nipple of the bottle and stayed silent as he sucked. The formula didn't taste as wonderful as the breast milk had, but the fake bottle also wasn't giving him strangely twisted feelings of both young security and old lasciviousness.

When he was done, his mother rubbed his full belly in gentle circles until the little burp of swallowed air bubbled out of his mouth. Kaye had always outdone him at banquets, but Arthur was becoming increasingly impressed with his own manful belches.

Normally after the bottle, Arthur's mother left his nursery immediately. She was never inattentive or neglectful, not after that first time, but she wasn't comfortable around her son, either. He left himself drift back in the direction of sleep. If she wanted to watch him do so, he was happy enough to oblige.

"Why don't you talk to me as much as your father?"

Arthur blinked his way back towards consciousness and debated what his answer should be, or if indeed he should answer at all. But then, he never had been all that good at keeping his mouth shut when he should have – the sword in his back in the middle of a battlefield from the man who should have been his heir was proof enough of that.

"It seemed to make you happy," Arthur replied softly.

His mother jerked back, then leaned over the rail of the cradle and pressed her lips to his forehead. "I have a son who is healthy and content. I am happy."

"Then why do you look so sad all the time?" Arthur asked as she pulled away. Her eyes were sparkling again, like she was about to cry, ready to prove him right.

"I didn't ask to have a son who is the reborn Rightwise King of All England," his mother said softly.

"I didn't ask to be reborn," Arthur replied softly. "So I guess we both got the short end of that stick."

"I'm scared," she admitted. "I'm scared of what this means for the world. I'm scared that you're going to be hurt. That you're going to die."

Arthur kicked his feet for a few moments, looking up in the darkness at his mother's sad, dark eyes, the halo of woolly sheep that circled her head obliviously.

"What's your name?" Arthur asked.

"Evangeline," she said. "My friends call me Iggy."

Arthur tried to smile, but all he managed was a gummy lip purse. "Iggy," he said. "I'm scared too, Iggy."

She put down the bottle and picked up her son and sat with him in the rocking chair and cuddled him close. "I'll protect you, for as long as I can," she whispered into the faint reddish wisps of his hair. "And I guess you should call me 'Mummy.'"

"Do *you* want me to?"

Iggy pulled Arthur away from her stomach and met his eyes seriously.

"Yes," she said softly, and smiled. It was tentative, but it also felt like a victory, if only a very small one.

"Very well," Arthur sighed, content for the moment. "Mummy."

She pulled him close again and rocked him slightly. She hummed a snatch of a lullaby that Arthur was surprised to realize he remembered from his first childhood. Then she told him a soft, sad story about the Lady of the Lake. Arthur didn't have the heart to point out to her that he already knew this story with a bit more familiarity than he really would have liked, considering how it ended.

***

Every night for the next few weeks, Arthur dreamt of the tourney grounds and the golden cup and the buzzing, expectant, hungry eyes of his audience. There were other knights with him. Though they, like him, wore new faces, he knew them for Owain, and Cai, Gwalchmai, Peredur, the golden Geraint, the frightened Trystan, bold Bedwyr, Cilhwch, Edeyrn, Cynon, and even that bastard Lancelot. They, like him, wore the flimsy white uniform quartered with red bands, the ineffectual shin armour, and the shoes with spiked bottoms. Opposite them stood other knights in fierce red, Mordred at their head with his customary, bloody smirk. Between them stood the gold cup, the new grail for which Arthur had realized across the course of his nightly dreams they fought on this flat, green battlefield.

"If you can make this kick," Lancelot said behind his shoulder, "it's ours. The whole world."

"No pressure, then," adult Arthur said in his dream. And then he began to run towards Mordred and the strange limp net that hung like a shredded battle flag behind him.

He could feel himself wind up for something, to make some sort of move, felt his focus narrow to a single prick of white and black that lay stark against the lush green grass.

But then he woke.

Again.

He resisted the childish urge to howl in frustration.

***

"A babysitter?" Arthur said dubiously from his quilt on the living room floor. Those fantastic little woolly sheep were dangling above his head, suspended on a yellow plastic frame patterned with dragons. He loved those sheep – they were so entertaining. He tore his attention away to attempt to raise an eyebrow askance.

"You forget, your majesty," his father said kindly, "you can't even sit up on your own yet."

Arthur, who couldn't exactly prove the statement wrong, said grudgingly, "Okay. I guess. Enjoy your night out, Dad, Mum."

"Thanks, darling," his mother said, and smiled. It was one of those real smiles, one of the ones where she realized that maybe everything was going to be okay and that her life hadn't turned out all strange and terrifying. She was smiling like that more often, lately, and Arthur was proud of himself to be part of why that kind of smile was ending up there.

Then the doorbell rang. His mother went to answer and his father gave him the thumbs up. Arthur tried to roll his eyes. Then he tried not to think about what they might be doing out alone tonight. And *then* he tried not to think about what it would be like to have a sibling.

The young girl came in ahead of his mum, blonde and probably about fourteen or so. Arthur wasn't so good at estimating people's ages any more – back in his first life, this girl would have been a woman already, preparing to marry or perhaps with children of her own. In this life, kids this age seemed stuck in a strange limbo between childhood and adulthood, irresponsible and yet filled with a coltish sexuality and raging libido that had no direction, and instead exploded all over the media.

There was something different about this one, though. Something in her that Arthur had never seen in the hundreds that were splashed all over the television that he watched with his father while cuddled on his tummy, or that his mother read about from the tabloids to help Arthur get sleepy enough for his naps. Her eyes looked old. Her bearing was comfortable, as if she completely inhabited her skin, was used to being in there.

It wasn't until his mum had kissed him on the cheek and reminded him quietly that normal babies didn't speak in fully articulate sentences, his parents had left, and the girl had come to sit on the floor beside him and tweaked his toes that Arthur finally clicked.

"*Merlin?*" Arthur squawked.

The girl scowled, a little wrinkle forming between her eyebrows that Arthur knew quite well. "What the hell do you think, your majesty?" she said. Though her voice was high and sweet, the old sorcerer's tone hadn't changed at all in the few thousand years since the king had last been chastised by Merlin. It very clearly said: *you are my king and I respect you and love you in a brotherly way, but by all the dragons that once roamed Albion, are you a frigging idiot.* "It's not as if I planned this. The universe and Albion chose, not me. Besides," she said, and took a moment to pop her hideously pink bubble gum with an obnoxious snap, "You should see *Lancelot.*"

"Ugly?"

"Very."

"Awesome," Arthur said, trying out one of the new words that the people around here seemed to like so much. "I hope his vanity is wounded. About time." Arthur, understandably, had little love for a man who poached other people's queens.

Merlin snorted indelicately.

"Well," Arthur conceded, waving his chubby toes in her direction, then put them in his mouth because, well, he could. Around his toes he added: "I guess I don't feel so cheated after all."

Merlin looked at her wristwatch, snapped her gum again, and said, "The football final is on. Mind if we watch?"

"Football?" Arthur asked. "I don't know football. Is it a sport?"

Merlin snorted again, that mannish sound that was so wrong coming from lips slick with gloss. "It's a religion. This is a nation obsessed, your majesty. Even you won't resist for long."

Merlin propped Arthur up on her lap and Arthur leaned back into the warmth of her stomach and the reassuring patter of her heart. He watched with interest as Merlin explained the rules, and the work and passion the various nations of the world invested in the FIFA tournament.

It wasn't until partway through the second half that Arthur realized that while he had never watched football before, he *recognized* the pitch and the stadium. And when the game was over and the blokes in orange were declared the tourney winners, Arthur immediately recognized the golden cup being hoisted aloft.

"The saviour of Albion, indeed," he murmured.

Merlin just snapped her gum.

Zmeu

The crying echoed and tripped along the roof of the cavern like a light-footed dancer. Zmeu winced and pulled his wings over his head, hoping to muffle the sound by encasing himself in a leather cocoon. It was childish, he knew, but he couldn't *think*.

He hated the sound of women crying. Of all the sounds he hated most, women-crying-because-of-him was #1. Maybe #1. If not, it was a close second to the-sound-of-the-door-being-slammed-open-by-another-stupid-Prince-Charming. Under the cocoon he tried to have a good think, but he couldn't hear himself having the think over the sound of the crying in question.

Exasperated, Zmeu dropped his wings into his lap and sat back against the arm of his sofa. The young woman flinched but didn't stop the horrendous noise.

"Look," Zmeu said. The woman wailed louder. "I'm *sorry*!"

For the first time, the woman looked directly at him. Her sobs stuttered to a halt.

"You're *sorry?*" she snarled, dropping her hands, arms, and accompanying tear-soaked hoodie sleeves into her lap. "You *kidnap me* on the eve of my wedding and you're *sorry?*"

"Well… yes?" Zmeu ventured. He scrunched down in his corner of the sofa and tried not to look miserable. "It was an accident."

"An accident?" It wasn't a question so much as a double-dog-dare.

"It's an instincts thing," Zmeu said lamely. In this form he had arms, legs, and a torso, so he folded his legs up under him and put his chin on his knees. He tried to look pathetic and adorable, despite the wings, red skin, horns curling back from his temples, and the tail he had coiled around his ankles to keep it from twitching. "Hear a crying woman--"

"Snatch her out of her bed. I totally get it." The young woman scoffed. "I fight that instinct every day."

Zmeu had no answer. The woman took a moment to suck in a great breath, to steady her nerves. Scraping her hair back from her face, she wiped the tears from her cheeks.

"You're going to take me home now."

"So… " Zmeu said. "You don't want to… marry me?"

The woman blinked at him. Once. Twice. Three times. She took a breath. She opened her mouth. She clicked her teeth together, licked her lips, puffed out a sigh, and said, "That'd be a no."

"Oh."

Another silence filled with not-speaking, blinking, shifting, and for variety, nose-scratching. "Are you… disappointed?"

Zmeu turned his gaze to the room's only door and tried to formulate an answer that didn't sound petulant. "Yes," he decided on.

"Because I won't marry you."

"Yes."

"You *did* kidnap me."

"It's what I am," Zmeu insisted again.

"Someone who kidnaps and marries people."

"Only women."

"Ri-ight," the woman said, uncurling from her end of the sofa, shifting so that she was seated more comfortably but also so she'd have the leverage she needed to kick him in the nuts. Zmeu wanted to get up, sit somewhere else, but there was purposely only a sofa: not as suggestive as a bed, not as formal as wingback chairs, and not as scary as bare rock and a light bulb. And he didn't want to stand either, that would make him loom. He'd had a lot of practice with first impressions.

"Just out of curiosity, do you marry a lot of women?" she asked.

"Never. Listen, this is dumb, but what's your name?"

The woman considered him for a moment before answering. "Tanara."

"I'm Zmeu."

"That I knew," she said.

"Your grandmother's stories?"

"The Internet," Tanara corrected. "I read a wiki page about Romanian fairy tales when I agreed to marry Frumos. He's Romanian."

Zmeu snorted. A curl of smoke drifted out of one nostril. Tanara watched it wreathe the room, eyes wide in fearful awe.

"Wh-what do you do to the women who won't marry you?" Tanara asked. Her whole body trembled again and Zmeu politely offered her the blanket draped across the back of the sofa. "Are you're going to eat me?"

Zmeu's scales clicked as they ruffled and puffed. "What do you take me for?" he bawled."A *monster*?"

Tanara sniffled. "You don't eat plump young maidens?" Her lower lip trembled, but she bit down on the flesh. Zmeu looked away before it gave him the kind of ideas that he couldn't entertain until Tanara had given him the go-ahead.

"Mostly I eat frozen dinners," Zmeu said.

"How?"

"Online grocery delivery."

"You have an address?"

"Have to have an address to get electricity. And the Internet."

Tanara looked around the room, clearly trying to reconcile this room with what he'd said.

"This room isn't much," Zmeu said. "I tried to keep it… free of distractions."

"I have no idea how to deal with this," Tanara finally said. "I thought you were supposed to be… lustful and masculine and overpowering … just, crude and evil and things."

Zmeu shrugged. *Now* he got up, keeping his wings folded tight against his back, hiding the sweep of his tail. He curled the leather pinions over his groin for modesty. Not that he much cared, he mostly walked around starkers, but he hadn't wanted to leave Tanara alone to grab clothing while she was still upset. "History is written by the victors. Many of my past loves would be shamed into saying that I raped them, rather than admit that I was a better lover, a better *person* than the Prince Charming who took them from me."

Tanara quirked an eyebrow at him. "So you've never been married, but some of the women became your loves?"

Zmeu offered his most charming grin. "You did just say that I was the epitome of Slavic masculinity."

Tanara startled them both with a sweet, high laugh of incredulity.

Encouraged, Zmeu was about to ask if she wanted a drink when his actual #1 least-loved sound crashed throughout the cavern. The door slammed back and scraped against the rock.

"Hey," Zmeu snapped, scales flaring in annoyance. "I just refinished that door. Be *careful*, you rube!"

"Babe!" the Prince Charming at the door grunted.

Zmeu, talons and teeth bared in preparation to snarl, nearly swallowed his tongue instead. The "prince" may have had a handsome face once, but it was now lost under lanks of greasy hair, and a scraggly beard that vanished into the popped collar of a stained shirt. He smelled like a gym sock.

Zmeu looked at their shared damsel.

"Really?" he asked, hitching the thumb of his wing at the bulk in the door. "That?"

Tanara scowled. "Why do you think I was crying?"

Zmeu, conceded the point. "Arranged?"

"Nobody does arranged marriages anymore," the prince boasted, slouching against the doorframe in way that seemed to make his bounty of rolls… rollier. "I'm rich."

"And you're desperate?" Zmeu asked Tanara.

She scowled. "My father is a drunk. And a gambler."

Zmeu's appendages drooped. "Sorry."

"Thanks."

"Naw, babe," the prince said. "We're getting' married cause I love yer tits. They're great tits."

Zmeu sucked in air so hard that he coughed."Did he really just say…? And you *let him?"*

Tanara raised two fingers and rubbed them together.

"For god's sake," Zmeu huffed. He reached up for the jewel embedded in his forehead. When he got upset, his scales puffed and the emerald never sat *quite* right in the indent, so it was easy to pry loose. "Here," he said, holding it out. "That oughta pay all the debts *and* for your mother's divorce."

Tanara reached out, and then stopped, tucking her hands under her armpits instead. "Is this a trick?"

"No!"

"I won't have to marry you?"

"It's a *gift*, okay?" Zmeu said. "I'm not even going to demand a kiss or an hour to just talk or anything! Gifts that come with strings aren't *gifts*. They're the mark of a man who—"

"Knows how to get what he wants out of a chick!" the prince guffawed.

"Shut up, Fat Frumos," Tanara snapped.

He sniggered and raised his palms, mock afraid. "Touchy babe, touchy." He dropped his hands, scratching his balls through the pocket of his saggy jeans. "Rescuing is hard work. When we get back, can you make me a sandwich?"

Zmeu raised another eyebrow in Tanara's direction.

"You're not much better!" Tanara bawled, scrambling to defend her… fiancé. "*Kidnapping* people!"

"It's an *arrangement*," Zmeu howled back. "There was a Princess—"

"Isn't there always?" Fat Frumos snorted.

"*Shut up!*" Tanara and Zmeu barked in perfect stereophonic tandem. They took a microsecond to blink at one another, startled by their accidental synchronicity. Then Tanara asked:

"An arrangement?"

"She didn't want to get married."

"And you wanted a young bride to ravish," Tanara snorted.

"I did not. Ravish means rape, and I don't do that sort of thing."

Fat Frumos was laughing. Tanara was not.

She rolled her lips inwards, considering. "You don't? Ever?"

"Why would I?" Zmeu threw both hands and wings heavenward. "Would *you* want to marry your rapist?"

"No!" Tanara said.

Zmeu cupped his left wing toward her to say, *See? There you go.* He went on: "Her father had picked a horrible Prince from a neighboring dukedom. He was fat, stupid and *old.*" They both looked at Fat Frumos and wisely said nothing. "The Princess... she... er..." he stuttered, red skin flushing positively indigo. "She hadn't had her first blood yet, see? She was... ermm..."

"A virgin," Tanara said, because – incredulously- it seemed the big virile man-dragon *couldn't.* "Which, by the way, is a social construct designed to steal a girl's ownership of her own body and sexuality."

"Yes," Zmeu said. "That's what I told her!"

"That's what you *told her?*" Tanara asked, incredulous.

"Well, in old-y time-y words. It *was* six centuries ago. Or so."

"Or so," Tanara echoed. She sounded winded. Perhaps slightly impressed? Zmeu could only hope.

"That was my first attempt," Zmeu said. "I realized I was lonely. So I kept at it."

"At what?"

"Finding a bride," Zmeu said. "The Princess and I had an arrangement. I got her from the tower like I promised, but her stupid fat prince sent a knight and kidnapped her back. I heard she eloped with him. Good for her, but bad for me."

"No young bride to deflower?"

"No need to get glib," Zmeu said. "I already said I don't rape."

"But you kidnap."

"I *rescue*," Zmeu corrected. "I only take away women who don't want to be there. Who are *crying*. And then we… have a chat."

"I was crying." A light bulb seemed to have come on for Tanara.

Again, they both glanced at Fat Frumos. Again, no words passed their lips.

"And if they want to go?" Tanara asked.

"I let them." Zmeu scoffed, a pained little frown wrinkling the bridge of his manly nose and a hurt little manly pout sliding across his plush, kissable manly lips. "I already said I'm not a *monster.*"

Tanara took a moment to chew on her thumbnail and ponder what he'd said. Eventually, she spit out a curl of nail and said, "So it's the 21st century. Why not… online date?"

"Right," Zmeu scoffed. He spread both wings and arms in demonstration, and felt his stomach clench in breathless pleasure as Tanara's gaze dripped down to his manly manliness. "And what would I say? *Mythological dragon-man seeks young woman who wants to tie him down and use him to explore the power of her own sexuality. Must be willing to live in a cave far away from her family*. And failing that, I'd be a hit in the bar scene."

"You'd be a hit in the Furry scene," Tanara corrected. Then she blinked, as if she'd just finished processing what he'd said about himself. "Tie down?"

Zmeu shuffled, trying not to look as embarrassed. "Yes?" he said. "I mean, yes. I'm big you know? I don't want to… hurt anyone. Makes it hard for me to enjoy myself if I know that if I let go I'm going to…"

"Squash her?"

He cleared his throat.

Tanara looked at the emerald. It was about the size of a chicken egg, and it had been worn smooth on the underside by Zmeu's scales. It was still warm, retaining draconic body heat. Slowly, carefully, she accepted the gem and put it in the kangaroo pocket of her hoodie.

"Okay," Tanara said. "Why not?"

It took Zmeu a second to process her words. "Really?"

"Has no one ever said yes?"

"No!"

"Yes to what?" Fat Frumos asked.

"Yes to you *leaving*," Zmeu crowed. He shoved the prince back through the door.

Tanara sprang up from the sofa and slammed the door for Zmeu.

"But *babes!*" Fat Frumos whined through the wood.

"Don't babes me, dumbass!" Tanara yelled back. "I know you're banging Bogat!"

"*Babes.*"

"Shut up!" Zmeu and Tanara snarled at the same time.

There was a scuffling sound from the other side of the door, the distant slam of the cavern's front gate, and then Zmeu and Tanara were alone. Sighing in pleasure, Zmeu grinned down at his… fiancé.

"You know," he ventured slowly, folding his hands politely behind his back to keep from reaching out and running his hands through her hair without invitation. "You don't have to marry me just to get away from him."

"I know," Tanara said. Then she licked her lips. "But you're not exactly the typical dragon-man, and I'm not exactly the typical damsel, either."

"Oh?"

Tanara spread her fingers and pressed her whole hand against his chest. "You said something about tying down?"

"Uh... " Zmeu swallowed hard. His whole brain turned fizzy.

"Yes," Tanara breathed. Her lips parted, and then she blinked, intrigued. Daring. "Well."

"Well," Zmeu agreed. "Not a virgin, then?"

"Definitely not."

He bent his neck, pursed his lips and ran face-first into her palm.

"What happens now?" Tanara asked. "If I kiss you, will you turn into a handsome human prince?"

Zmeu flinched like he'd been slapped. "Do you... want me to?"

Tanara's gaze slithered all the way down and then all the way back up. "No."

Relief splashed up Zmeu's spine. Followed very quickly by something else. "Good. Besides, that's ridiculous. Kisses transforming people into things they're not. Marriage makes people more of who they are already, not less. I'm a dragon-man," Zmeu snorted. "I'm not *magic.*"

The Moral of the Story

Her fingers brush the soft skin, the small smooth of bone under thin flesh behind my left ear, brushing back through wiry hair to where I've got it pulled back in preparation for hard work. Lake water, brackish here where it mingles with the St. Lawrence, slides down the side of my neck, summoning goose pimples in its wake. The slick, cool brush of membrane kisses the lobe of my ear and I feel my eyes slide closed involuntarily, as natural as the slight gasp that parts my lips, inflates my lungs, brushes the taste of water and breeze and sunlight across my tongue.

"You came," the woman in the water says. Her voice is sibilant and filled with nearly inaudible clicks and hard-palate burrs, an accent never before heard in the lower plains of Quebec.

Never heard before the Melt caused all the water levels to rise. Never heard before the Great Dark came and killed all the technology. Never before the Daniel-Johnson dam stopped working, the regulating of the Manicouagan became too much and the river broke through its cement prison. Never before Baie-Comeau was overborne and drowned.

Possibly, perhaps - and maybe I flatter myself a little - never before in the whole of human history. But then, how could we have stories of things like her, if I'm the first to converse with one?

Arrogance is a sin. It's one of the sins that brought the Great Dark.

"I came," I say, opening my eyes. Sunlight on water dazzles like diamonds. I squint. It's a comfortable gesture. The lines beside my eyes folding into place is familiar, nearly soothing. "How could I stay away?"

"But did you come for *me?*" she teases, dipping her chin into the water in a gesture I've learned is meant to be coy, flirtatious. Dark hair slips and pools along the surface, shifting and curling like squid ink.

I sit back in the boat, take up my nets, and fling them over the side that she doesn't occupy. She whistles and clicks, face in the water, summoning fish. This is our deal. She fills my nets, I fill her mind, and we neither of us attempts to harm the other. Actively.

***

I had more hungry mouths to feed than fear of rumours, and that is what initially drove me out onto the unnatural lake. The stories said that there was something in the water that feeds on man-flesh. But I am no man, and we needed the fish.

For the first few weeks, it was subtle. An elongated shadow too far down to see clearly, too solid to be a school, but too large to be any breed of fish I had ever caught before. Sometimes, it was a splash on the surface of the otherwise calm lake. Once, my little rowboat lurched under my feet, against current, violent, *wrong*.

I was being hunted, I realized. Even as I harvested fish, something else sought to harvest me. The rumours were not *just* stories.

I stayed away for three days. On the fourth my youngest brother patted his stomach morosely and cried, unable to understand why he hungered so. Defeated by his tiny misery, I fetched my father's harpoon from the hunting shed, and made the short walk back to the rocky shoreline.

My little boat was tied up where I had left it, undisturbed. But, no, see — there were four long scratches in the wood of the stern, naked against the dark stain of tar sealant, brackish water, and age. I bent down, breath caught in the hollow of my throat, and splayed my palm against the slashes. They were finger-width apart from each other, come from a humanish hand.

There was a Creature in the lake. And it was mad at me.

Mad because I dared to fish? Or mad because I did not come back?

I nearly turned away then, abandoned the boat, and the lake, and went to find another way to contribute to the supper table. I am old enough to go to the steam-driven factories, now, but then who would care for the littles?

I could spare a few hours each day to go onto the lake, but I cannot leave them for eight or more hours each day to work, and then shop. My parents would be furious. And I cannot hunt, I have no skill with a bow and arrow, we have no gun and ammunition is too expensive, and the Mayor Creature has not given us express permission. That is courting disaster.

No choice. I had to go back onto the lake.

I hesitated, but I could still hear the little ones' frustrated wails ringing in my ears. So I gathered up and solidified my courage. Die of hunger, or die on the water.

Those were my only choices.

***

I have been longing to lay my hands again on rangy muscles and endless lucent skin. To clap eyes on the soft bob of white breasts, half hidden by the sun sparkling on rippling water. It looks as if someone had thrown a thousand, million little dimes into the water, and that they are flipping and flirting with the sky every time a breeze sends a playful ripple along the skin of water. I have dreamt of her, and I don't know what that means beyond that I have, perhaps, become irrevocably ensnared. Knowing such will not loosen the bonds.

I lean further into her touch, rest against the side of the boat so that my head and shoulders over the water, dip my fingers into the golden gilt. I expect it to be warm, but the lake water is cold. Always cold. Warm enough for swimming in summer, if one were to dare it, but frigid enough come autumn to cause someone unlucky enough to take a dip to freeze to death even if they made it back to dry land.

"Come swim," she says, coy and enticing. It is the top of summer now, and the lake is as comfortable for a human as it is ever going to be.

I was sure, the first time I finally see more than just a shadow under the water, that I was as good as dead. That scaled arms would reach into my boat and capsize me. That maybe there are tentacles with which I'll be throttled before I could drown. That maybe I would die bubble-screaming at the teeth of a she-shark, rather than with a lungful of water.

What I cannot have anticipated was the way a wet book flopped up onto my deck. It flapped open like a gasping fish, splayed on the illustration of a golden-haired princess half-running and the paper weak with the weight of decades of water.

Hans Christian Anderson, the spine read when I had nudged it with the butt of my spear. I'd never heard of such an author. This might have been one of the Forbidden Books, the ones about the Creatures that the Great Dark exposed to the world.

We weren't allowed to read these books; they told lies about Creatures.

The she-thing lifted its head from the water, peered at me with eyes shuttered behind transparent eyelids. Watched me as I watched it, and watched the book. Eventually, when I made no move to speak to it – and I feared how quickly it could retaliate should I heft my harpoon – the horizontal lids peeled back and she regarded me with a startlingly human gaze.

"I have seen humans telling stories from these," the she-monster said, and those were her first words to me. "Teach me to tell the stories."

I lifted my harpoon then, swung the tip towards her, steady and slow and cautious. Ready to throw at the least sign of malice. She did not move, was not intimidated.

"Teach me your language, as you set it down," she said. "Teach me."

It was bad form to deny a Creature anything it requested. Moreover, it was illegal for a base human to deny a direct order. Magic, and those beings borne of it, rule. The Great Dark was theirs, and thus the world and all the crawling animals that live upon the world and in that Dark. Including us.

And yet, how can I obey if I it means that I must put down my harpoon? I would be eaten, without a doubt, and my father would have no eldest child to watch and feed and care for the littles while he worked in the steam-factory.

More than that, it asked me to read a Forbidden Book. If I disobeyed, my life was forfeit. If I obeyed and another Creature found out, it would take my eyes and tongue.

I hesitated too long. A low slap of impatient flesh against water, and in the corner of my eye, a sinuous tail retreated below the surface – indigo and emerald, slick, slim, eel-like.

She whistled under the water and suddenly a mackerel, big enough to fill both the stew pot and our bellies for the next three days leapt the gunwale of my little boat and bashed its head against the deck, dead instantly. I was badly startled and jerked backward, heel tripping on the edge of the seat. I tumbled down against the sacking I'd left in the stern to haul home my catch. I had enough sense, yet, to cling to my harpoon. I would not be without a weapon.

My heart leapt into my mouth, beating against my tongue. My skin tightened and prickled in horror. Now, surely *now* the thing would tip me over and swallow me down.

Yet. Silence. Nothing happened. I levered upright, ready to defend myself. But there was no answering aggression. She was waiting, watching. Patient. Predatory.

"This is my bargain," she said, and too terrified that I was staring my end in the face, I only licked my lips and nodded.

Desperation made rebels of even the most obedient.

***

"No," I say, and she tickles the back of my neck with her claws, pricking lightly, teasing and warning all at once. "It's too cold."

She's been pushing for a week now. Every day is an invitation into the water.

"You say always that it is too cold," she whines, and her pout is coral and slick. "And now the weather will turn, and the water will freeze, and you will never swim. Come. *Come.*"

I want very much to say yes. But my nets are filling and I don't dare disturb the fish. A fission of warning radiates out from where her claws rest against my scalp. A thread of unease.

"I've brought a book," I say instead.

***

There is a woman in the lake, and I am teaching her how to read. The library was never emptied, you see. Books. Posters.

People.

All still there, because they had no warning. There was no way to send a message down to the city before the water arrived, save a messenger on foot. And he was lost in the flood, they say – the wave caught up to him.

When the Great Dark fell, there was no more electricity. That meant there was no way to regulate and run the dam. The doors froze shut. And the flow of the water was having none of that, of course. Concrete cracked. Walls were overborne. And so, *pouf*, where once there was a valley, and a town, now there was a lake.

They say the bodies floated downstream by the hundreds. All washed up on the shore of the Rideau. They say that after the town was scoured, they had to dive underwater using only wetsuits and snorkels to cut away the church spire. It was the tallest thing in the town, you see, and it poked out of the water like an obscene tomb marker. They say it was horrific to see.

So they cut it away. My father was one of the divers. That way the shallow punts and fur-trader canoes could traverse the new water way without fear of being beached on the world that could no longer be. That no longer was.

They say that if you paddle to the exact centre of the lake and wait for the noontime shift in the tide, you can hear the church bells ringing. The clapper is set to motion by the underwater currents,

That is a rumour, I am both proud and ashamed to admit honestly, that is entirely, eerily true.

When I had first asked the woman in the water what brought her to the drowned town, she smiled, shark teeth sparking white in the sunlight reflecting off the ripples of the surface, and said: "Meat. There was lots of it in the water those days."

"Didn't they—" I choked on the question at first, horrified by my own disrespect. Then curiosity displaced propriety, and I asked anyway. "Didn't it go putrid?"

"There is enough salt in the water. It lasted weeks." She licked her lips.

Scavengers and fisherwomen the both of us. And I couldn't hate her for it, any more than she could hate me for filling the bellies of my brothers and sisters with fish-flesh. We all do what was necessary to survive.

In the Great Dark, meat was meat.

***

I reach behind me and retrieve the book. I'd wrapped it in oilskin to keep it dry. It is one of the machine-printed ones, from before the Dark fell, and a prized family heirloom. I hold it up carefully, keeping it above the boat, in case she uses her grip on my neck to scrabble for it.

"What is it?" she asks, loosening her hands enough to indicate her curiosity. "More Fairy Tales?"

"The Bible."

She scoffs. "I don't want to read that. It's all about your father."

"Our father," I correct. "The one who made the world."

"I don't like that Fairy Tale," she says, and lets go of me completely. She ducks back under the water, pouting.

***

Months and months passed. Out of spring and into summer, the world slid. She hovered beside the boat as we spoke, sometimes pulling herself up the gunwale to peer more closely over my arm. My nets filled, and at my request, she brought me children's primers, ABC books, and children's books that are all the same Forbidden. They had strange names like The Little Prince, The Hobbit, and Harry Potter. I tried to forget what I read as soon as I said the words out loud. I tried not to dream about lion kings and magical wardrobes, about Creatures that were monsters and easily slain or Creatures that were protectors of the weak and the innocent.

There were neither such Creatures in reality. They were as varied, as cruel, as selfish and as capricious as humans were before the Great Dark came. They were our masters, and our punishment. God had sent them to be our torment, and the realization of all that we were. They were the dark mirror, twisted.

And then the she-creature began to bring the Fairy Tales, tales of terror and the intimate lives of Creatures, things that I should not be even touching, let alone reading. If the Creature who ruled my village ever knew…

And yet I read at the behest of another Creature. Surely, that would spare my life? And this one cared more for my family than he did. She filled our bellies. And perhaps that was the danger.

Oh, God, the things I read…

And she was getting better, she was. Did she practice on her own, under the rippling waves? And when she spoke, she spoke more and more like me – burrs and clicks still, but her English grew a Quebecois-tinged accent.

One day she brought me a Psalm book.

"I found it in the tall building," she said. "The one to which you anchor?"

"The one with the spire?"

"Yes."

"It is… *was* a Cathedral." When she wrinkled her pearlescent brow I added, "A church? It was a religious meeting place."

She flung her elbows over the gunwale, pillowed her chin on a scaled forearm, watery eyes wide and eager. "What is *religion?*"

"Ah, um, the systemized rituals of belief?"

"Oh!" Lips the intimate pink of the inside of a clamshell pursed. "Belief of what?"

"In *whom*," I corrected. "In God."

"And who is God, exactly? Was he the magister?"

"Who's... God?" I repeated, spluttering, disbelieving. "Are you... don't you... God the creator! God, our Father who dwells in Heaven?"

She flicked the opaque membrane that was the terminal fin of her tail in a vaguely easterly direction. "My father dwells on a cove beyond the Bay that Rises Twice In One Day. What did your father create?"

"He's not really my... it's a term of endearment. He was the progenitor of us all."

"Of all the humans?"

"Of the world!"

"Whose?"

"Ours. This one."

She laughed and it was a tinkle of silver bells and the soft rush of waves on a deserted beach. "No! No one creates worlds. Worlds create worlds."

"This world didn't just *come into being.*" Dear God, I was having a metaphysical debate with a Creature of myth. One who ate people. Could eat me.

"Of course they do. Slowly. Generation after generation. Water erodes stone, plants grow, Creatures spawn, and change, and spawn again."

"Evolution. You're talking about evolution," I said, voice low with horrified awe. Evolution was Forbidden too, but I know about it. We all sort of know about it – there are heathens that had kept the science text books in the hopes of bringing back the old ways, but electricity simply does not work anymore. There was no way to harness it. This was our punishment and they sought to circumvent it. Blasphemous.

Among those text books saved from the Creatures there were also biology books, and this was where Evolution is written. But nobody believed in Evolution, not really. The

Bible had nothing of Evolution in it, so it's fiction. Pointless. Forbidden.

"I'm talking about the beginning of all things," I said, trying to steer the topic away from what was Forbidden to me. "The start. Where do your people think the world comes from?"

"What do you mean?"

"Where do you come from? Your creators?"

"My mother and father. She created me, he bore me."

"Like seahorses?" I blurted before I realized I had.

"Yes."

"Okay. Um. Well, where did they come from?"

"Their mothers and fathers. And so forth, why do you ask?

"Well, where did the first of your people come from?"

"Our tales say a human and a dolphin swam together back when the seas still boiled."

"And who made that human and that dolphin?" I asked, feeling my eyes glittering as I honed in on my point. I wondered vaguely if they looked like onyx in the sunlight, the way that hers looked like watery pearls.

Instead of answering, she furrowed her brow again and readjusted her grip on the edge of my little boat and said: "Why do you ask such useless questions?"

"Don't you want to *know*?" I countered.

"Will knowing make you happy?"

"Yes! Maybe," I admitted. "I don't know. It's supposed to." The wind blew, the current shifted, and the clapper of the church bell banged against the dome. A dull, drowned clang filled the silence between us, vibrated right into the core of me, where my faith lived, and shook it just that little bit looser.

"Does religion make you happy? Is that why your people do it?"

I let that question linger as well. "I don't know," I confessed with a deep, damp sigh. "Sometimes. But it also makes people unhappy, or feel guilty, or causes wars. Sometimes it makes people kill other people."

"Barbaric," she dismisses "Useless."

"...maybe."

She tilted her head, black hair sliding along her shoulders, dry and slightly frizzy at the top from being out of the water too long. She was an endearingly imperfect picture, an angel with a fly-away halo, painted in shades of night. Shark teeth pressed worryingly into her bottom lip.

"You're sad again," she said.

"Some people say that God punished us. He promised no more cleansings, but that technology angered Him. So he just took it away. He made it stop working."

"Why do they say He did that?"

"So we'd rediscover awe and wonder. The Bible is filled with magic, and angels, and miracles, and wonders, but we had stopped believing in then. We stared at screens instead of skies. The priests say that after the Great Dark fell upon the world, all the electricity falling away and all the things breaking, that The Swelling came, and all the magic leaked back into the world. Angels and demons and Creatures of all manners."

"Your God took away the screens so you'd look to him instead of at them?"

"So they say. There *is* magic in the world. I mean—" I gestured to her, a wide arc taking in her face, her ends of her hair floating on the surface of the lake, the flash of silver-blue below it, the membranes between her fingers. "I'm talking to you, aren't I? But we forgot."

"Foolish," she scoffed. "Childish."

"How do you mean?"

"A parent should teach with love, not punishment. Your God, The Father who dwells in the heavens and creates — he sounds more like a petulant child who breaks his favourite toy when it does something he does not like; who hits a pet for daring to grow up."

***

"Don't do that," I plead, patting the surface of the water with my palm. "We'll read the Bible another time."

"You always bring that book, and I like it not," she mutters when she breaks the surface.

"Many of the books you bring are Forbidden to me," I counter.

She quirks a saucy eyebrow at me. I don't know where she learned that expression, I don't remember making it at her. Perhaps it is one of the universal ones. Blind people still smile, without ever having seen a smile. She-creatures flirt, maybe, without ever having seen a human woman do it.

"But entertaining," she says softly.

I set the Bible down, and she takes this as invitation to explore my hair again. She pulls out the tie. My bun springs free, puffing up like dandelion fluff in the summer breeze. She burbles, her version of laughter and sinks both clawed hands into the mass. It brings my face closer to the water than I'm comfortable with, but I wait, patient, as she explores.

My face is even with her collarbones, the soft bob of her breasts, and I squeeze my eyes shut and bite my tongue to keep the soft moan of appreciation behind my teeth.

She hears it anyway, and slides her hands around to cup my cheeks, raise my gaze to her own.

"Open your eyes," she says. When I obey, she is blinking with both sets of lids. The day is bright – perhaps too bright for her in the open air.

I don't know what she's looking for in my expression, but she seems to find it. She makes a satisfied clicking sound with the gills that flutter along the sides of her neck, and then, unexpectedly, lake-cool lips press against mine.

***

"Teach me this word," she said, pointing a finger frosted with silver scale and translucent membrane linking it to its neighbour at a word on a sodden page. Lust, the word read.

"Oh." It's a dumb response. I sat back a little and she frowned at me, pursing her lips.

"No," she said. "There's an 'l' and a 't'. But I know not how it sounds in the middle."

"Lust," I say, and just using that word out loud, with her sprawled over one of the boat's benches, her hip on the edge and tail sliding over the side and into the water, the tip of her tail holding the opposite oar-lock for balance, *naked* under the sunlight, it made my face warm.

"And what is lust?"

A man and a woman, God made them, and he made them for each other. Not for… no. I look away and ignore the curl of warmth that echoes the flush in my face, but lower, sort of back a bit. I know what lust is. But I had no way to describe it to her, not without giving myself away.

It seemed that I wouldn't have to. Something in my expression betrayed me, it must have, because she smiled then, wide and sweet, and arched her back to thrust her breasts up toward the sun, and undulated in a way that was sinuous and terrifying, and oh, how I wanted to *touch*.

Dangerous. This was very dangerous water I was sailing into.

"I see," she said, and licked her lips, and then with a flick and a lurch, she had disappeared over the side of the boat, barely making a sound as she needled into the water.

I waited, hand straying to the harpoon I had hidden underneath the sacking since we'd first made our bargain, but she didn't come back. Was she insulted? Angry? I had no idea.

I waited on the water until the sun set, but she didn't return.

So I hauled in my catch, rowed to shore, and left.

I didn't return for a week, and when I came back, she was waiting, and behaved as if nothing at all had happened.

***

I try to scramble back, startled and terrified. She's going to eat my face!

"No!" I whimper, but then something slick and cool slides between my teeth, into my mouth and I… it is a *kiss*.

I gasp. That just gives her more room to invade my mouth. She pulls away then, presses puckered lips against the corners of my own, my jaw, down my neck, and I groan, dig my fingernails into the side of the boat, praying that the pain will be enough to punish my body, keep the ardour from rising.

I must not... I must *not*…

"Why?" I ask her hair, and realize I've turned my nose into it, wuffling in great lung-fulls. She doesn't smell of fish at all, but brine and sunlight and vegetation.

"Because you are delicious," she says. "Come swim with me."

Her tail slides up the back of my calf, the dextrous membrane somehow finding my belt, wriggling up under the hem of my shirt, splays like a lover's caress against my bare back. It must be arching over the starboard of the boat, for I am leaning out over the water on the port side.

She tugs on the collar of my shirt. Her mouth is back on mine, her tail dipping under and around, sliding along my stomach and down to... unf!

"Come swim," she breathes into my mouth. I raise my hands to her neck, and her gills flutter against my palms, unfamiliar and slightly sickening, but oh, so wrong in such a right way.

"Yes," I consent, defeated at last. And then she *pulls.*

***

The truth of it is, once all electronic technology was gone, once the Dark had happened, there was the Great Swell. And every previously unknown well of magic overflowed, as if to make up for the lack of technology's blue glow. Mankind became terrified of the night once more, and the Creatures that used to bump in it spoke up and said: "We were always real. You just forgot us. But, look. Look. Here we are. We're here. We're here. And you will not forget us again."

***

She is wrapped around me. Long tail, and long arms, long tongue. My hair becomes even more like coral in the water, tight curls relaxing and spreading out and tangling with her seaweed locks.

Her claws prick where they hold my shoulders, and she is breathing into the kiss, water into her gills, oxygen into my mouth. Her tail squeezes and writhes, slides between my legs and then pinches them together at the ankle, and the sensation of her spiny scales is enough to... to… *ah!*

Stated and sleepy eyed, I try to extricate myself, turn my head to the surface. We break into open air, but she does not let go.

"Now me," she says.

"How do I …?" I ask, wriggling a little to dislodge the grip of her tail. Instead of loosening, she tightens it. "You have to let me go so I can—" I stop, because it is not a smile she is directing at me. It is her teeth. "No," I say.

"Now me," she says again and then bites, *hard*, on my neck. I feel her teeth slice into flesh and I am so stunned with the pain of it that I cannot scream. I gasp at air as she laps at blood.

"Please! Are you quite sure what you mean to do?" I beg. I yelp. "I kept my side of the bargain! Please!"

"And I mine," she hisses, the words frothing red where her bottom lip dips into the lake. "But now it is over."

"The stories we read said sirens only hunted men," I gasp with my last breath, words bubbling in the water that I can't seem to keep out of my mouth. I am sinking. Oh, God, forgive me I was weak and this is your punishment, and I am *sinking.*

"Men, women," she says with a shrug, claws digging harder into my arms. Blood stains the world, like tea from a tea bag dropped into a cup, swirling, falling. In the dark below us, where the streets still shoot straight and true through the town, shadows stir. Tempted. Hungry. Oh, God.

She leans in and whispers wetly against the shell of my ear: "Meat is still meat. And now I can read bedtime stories to my children. They are hatching. They are hungry."

Oh *God.*

My lungs fill with water – burning cold, wet and terrible and *oh, oh, I see. How foolish I have been,* I think, mind slowing as I drown, distending each last moment like maple syrup on fresh snow. Strings and gobs of final thoughts, tugging and stretched thin. *I have been reading Fairy Tales for months and never realized that they were filled with lessons.* My limbs become sluggish, I cannot thrash, and when I look up at the sky, the world is gilt with sunlight and diamonds, opal skin and coral lips, inky hair and sharp, ivory teeth.

And here is the moral of the tale: *Never make bargains with monsters.*

♫𝄞♪ The Twenty Seven Club

Liquid shivers at the end of the needle. It's clear, vaguely blackish in the way that the curve of the drop reflects in the low light of the dimmed pot lights, and enticing. I have no idea what it is, but I do know that it's deadly.

Terry wouldn't be offering it if it wasn't.

"No," I say. "I've...I've changed my mind." I move to get up off the edge of the tub, but Terry's hand is on my shoulder. She doesn't push, she just presses her nails lightly against my bare skin. A thrill rushes up my spine, chiming inside my brain, filling my ears with the addictive hum of songs that have yet to be written down.

Terry laughs. It's like a hundred strings being plucked together. Sometimes it's heavenly when she laughs, orgasmic joy in the *pizzicato* ripple of a sound wave, perfect, delicate harmony. Today it sounds like a toddler mashing a piano keyboard.

"You can't change your mind," she says.

"But I have. I have!"

She sighs, put-upon and patronizing and even that makes my fingers itch for a pencil and some staff paper. "Okay, fine. You can change your mind. But that won't change your fate. You signed the contract. We have a deal."

She waves the syringe at me, and the droplet splashes onto the pristine tile. The movement of her arm is a *glissando* against the air. Her toes tap beside the poisonous splatter, a barefoot drumming in perfect four-four. I spare a thought for the poor hotel maid who is going to find me. I suppose that thought should be one of charitable pity. Mostly, it's fury that some poor hotel maid is going to find me *at all*, and I can't stop it.

"I kept my end of it," Terry says. "Your turn."

"But I don't want to. Can't I just...can't you just take it back?"

"You think you're the first one to try to bargain on the precipice?" Terry snarls, anger flooding her classic features briefly before melting away, leaving her face statuary blank. "You think Kurt didn't whine? You think Dickie, and Leslie, and Alexandre didn't suddenly decide that they'd rather be has-beens?" She purses her pouting lower lip, tapping the syringe thoughtfully against her flesh, a small white indent against shiny strawberry-flavoured gloss. I want to kiss her so bad. I want to *everything* her so bad, so bad it hurts in ways that no one else can ever understand. Well, no one who hasn't had a contract with Terry would understand. No one who hasn't had her skin burn their palms. "Jimi, though. Jimi went with his pride intact, head high. Good man, that Jimi. Kept his promises."

"I was a kid!" I try. "What was ten years of fame to a teenager? I didn't realize that I'd want the rest of it, too."

"Greedy," Terry admonishes. She leans down to lick the side of my ear. Whole albums of melodies pour out of her sigh. "You've lived more in a decade than most people do in a lifetime, and you want more? More cars, more vacations, more booze, more concerts, more groupies to fuck? More designer denim and designer drugs?"

"But there'd be more for you too. wouldn't there? A hundred more--"

"Ringtones and compilation records and parody songs? No. I've sucked all the art out of you, my darling. You've got nothing left to give."

"But I do!" I should be ashamed that I'm crying. Thick, wet sobs, mucousy, desperate and disgusting, no accord between my choking coughs and the clench of my fists in the fabric of her trousers. But I've never had shame in front of Terry. She stripped it all away, all the confusion, all the self-loathing, all the awkwardness. She made me *swagger*. I gave her everything in return. All of it. Anything she asked for. *Everything* she asked for.

Except this.

"You don't have any more. You're a husk."

"I can hear it. When you touch me."

"Those aren't for you."

"You goddamned *tease*." I try to push her away, to shove past her, but Terry isn't the kind of person that you can just shove away. She is the earworm that nibbles at your brain until you go mad with it, mad for *her*. Mad for her breath against your neck, her legs around your waist, her hair, the pluck of her fingertips as she plays your spine. "Why show it to me if I can't *have* it?"

"You can have this." She holds up the needle.

"No!"

She sighs again, *adagissimo*, petulant. "Really, my darling, this tantrum is getting ugly. You made the deal. It's even signed in *blood*, you theatrical little thing, you. I've used you up."

"So just go away and *leave me alone.*"

Terry laughs like a chorus of silver bells, a rolling *roulade* against the empty glass and cold ceramic that embraces us. "Oh, no. If you live, then everything else you've done up until now becomes *meaningless*. You do understand that, don't you? That's been the whole point of our little living arrangement. For your work to *feed* me it has to be respected, treasured, rare. There can't be any more. No slow slide into ignominy. No gigs at has-been clubs for lusting cougars. No embarrassing reunion tours. It all has to be gone. Completely. And in an instant. And for that to happen, you *have to be dead*."

I've been arrested for assault before, but I've never hit Terry. That's why it surprises her when I ball up my fist and crack her across the jaw. *Con Bravura.* Even the most loyal of dogs fight for their lives when they're backed into a corner. Shock gives me the opening I need to dart past her. I am out of the bathroom and slamming down the hotel corridor. I expect to hear an enraged scream, or a *crescendo* of laugher echoing after me.

All I hear is some stupid gaggle of tourists gasping. "That's--! Omigod, I can't believe it, that's really--! Did you see!?" their voices screech, *allegretto vivace*. They raise their camera phones, sway forward, catch themselves, suspended in their self-surprise for a long heartbeat, then press back against the wall. They are caught in that beautiful magnetic metronome that makes them shy away from celebrity and yet grasp for it at the same time. The three-four waltz of attraction.

I used to love that dance. The seduction, the slow smile, the gesture--plucking one of them out of the safety of their numbers for a night, making that one special among his or her peers, just by laying my hand on theirs. Transferred divinity.

I'll never do that dance again.

The slam of the fire door against the concrete wall of the staircase rattles in my ears. Blood rushes to underscore the sound of my feet as I run down the stairs, a harsh counterpoint in the arching suck of air whooshing in and out of my lungs. Music in everything I do, even as I flee.

I swerve when I hit the lobby, take the back way out, past the paparazzi parked by the valet stand. I always dive straight towards the cameras, that's my habit, living life *con force.* Breaking habits might save my life. If Terry can't anticipate what I'll do next, maybe I can...

Night air slaps my cheeks. Terry is standing by the side of the service road. Waiting. Smiling. Arms open, hands empty. No syringe. My heart splutters into a *caesura*, silent indefinitely, until it ratchets back up, pattering in cut time.

As if I could ever outrun her. Silly me.

I slow to a jog, then stop beside her. "Terry," I plead. "Please."

"If you didn't intend to keep your end of it, you should have never signed the contract."

"I was a kid. It was my first gig. You fucked me in the coatroom. How could I say no?"

"Human weakness is not my sphere of influence," Terry says with a shrug. Unfeeling bitch. "It's time, my darling."

She takes my hand, and I can't fight the automatic muscle memory that makes me curl my fingers around hers.

"Please."

"It's less tragic, but this will do," Terry says. She sounds regretful. "I did so want something a bit nobler for you. You could have gone out like Jimi."

She pulls me forward, right to the edge of the sidewalk. Around us, the streetlamps spark and crack, plunging this section of the roadway into dangerous darkness. I am wearing black. I never wear anything else. Appearances are everything in this business. And no one but me can see Terry.

She cranes her head to the left. The lights of a lone delivery van bobble along the road.

"No!" I dig my heels into the edge of the kerb, struggling against the *coda*. "They O.D.ed! All of them! All the rest! That's how it's supposed to go! Not like this, Terry. Please!"

"Don't be silly," Terry breathes, her breasts hot against my arm. "Don't you use Wikipedia? If it isn't drugs or booze, it's usually an auto accident." And then she shoves.

The pain is so fleeting that I don't bother to catalogue it. The crunch is loud. I don't know if it's coming from inside my own body or if it's the sound of a windshield fracturing. Hitting the tarmac drives the air out of my lungs. It takes an inordinate amount of time to drag more back in.

Legato, dolce, a quiet slow hiss in the rest between movements.

The horn blares, the driver shouts. It's some poor stupid roadie who is probably going to sue my estate for millions for the emotional trauma. That's fine. I don't need my millions any more. I don't need anything.

Except, maybe... Yes. I think I am allowed to want *that*. One last time. It's the least she can do.

"Terry." I turn the ruin of my wrist, pulp of a hand palm up, fingers cupped, like she taught me. I reach towards her as a supplicant. Praying.

Terry smiles softly, colourless eyes sparkling. She crouches. She takes my hand.

Nothing. *Silenzio.*

The music is gone.

"No." I think I say it. Something burbles in my chest, wet and red. It might come out sounding like the word. I bet Terry understands, anyway, so I try again. "Not fair!"

Something is wrong. It's not working! For the first time in ten years, the brush of her otherworldly skin against mine makes no sound at all.

That hurts far more than getting run over ever could.

I scream.

"Happy birthday to you, happy birthday to you..." Terry warbles into my ear. *Al niente.*

The Dark Lord and the Seamstress

Once upon a time, oh yes,
So very long ago,
There was of course a lovely girl,
Who came to learn to sew.

Deft hand at knots and ties,
Fingers nimble on a seam,
Her fame spread far and even wide,
O'er every hill and stream.

And as it goes, fair listener,
She learned to sew so well
That even the Dark Lord himself
Heard of her talent, down in Hell.

Now the Dark Lord was a kindly fellow,
Not like he's drawn in books,
But He was old, and his style was too,
And he longed to change his looks.

He sent a fiery imp up
For to ask the girl
If she would care to join Him,
Down where the sulfur curls.

He promised needles made of gold,
And threads of finest silk,
And devils to attend on her,
And pour her morning milk.

The lovely girl was wary,
But her family was quite poor,
And if she came, the Dark Lord said,
Fortune would find their door.

So she kissed her Mom and Father,
And packed herself a sack,
Followed the imp down the road to Hell,
And never once looked back.

Now, they said her special talent
Could not be outdone,
But of her stunning beauty,
The Dark Lord had heard none.

So when she came into His Hall,
That dark and brimstone cove,
With mind so bright and skin so smooth,
The Dark Lord fell in Love.

Hell was filled with much despair,
And sinners all lament.
Life and purity like hers
Had time in Hell ne'er spent.

He bowed and then she curtseyed,
And He rose to kiss her hand,
And vowed to himself right then
She'd be Queen of his queer land.

They sat and dined together,
And they talked an awful lot,
About the colours he should wear;
Of trousers, shirts, and frocks.

It was very close to cock's crow
When He saw her to her room,
And left alone His bride-to-be
To cut patterns in the gloom.

Now, our little seamstress was not slow,
Nor was she blind or laze,
And it was obvious to her blue eyes
That the Dark Lord was quite crazed.

He seemed to think Magenta Pink
Would suit His skin of red.
He also seemed to think that she
Ought join him in a marriage bed.

So the lovely girl sat and sewed
And pondered as she went:
How to turn down Hell itself
When its Master's will was bent?

Then just before she fell asleep
Somewhere around noon-time,
She struck upon an answer
That seemed to suit just fine.

And when she woke at sunset
To find the Dark Lord at her door,
She went with Him to dinner,
And they spoke just as before.

He asked after her parents,
And wondered what they were like,
Asked her if she was married,
With a husband and a tyke.

When the lovely girl did answer,
It was with a heartfelt sigh.
She wrung her hands and bowed her head,
and gasped, "How alone am I!"

The handsome Dark Lord, quite confused,
Asked her what was wrong.
She pursed her lips and took a breath,
And sang this little song:

"A maiden with a talent,"
She sang with voice so sweet,
"Cannot be wed to any man
Who her talent cannot meet.

If she happens to be a baker,
He must make cakes, too.
If she is good at writing books,
Then he an author through-and-through

Thus has it been for ages,"
The lovely girl did lie,
"So unless my groom makes a wedding gown,
I'll never be a bride."

The Dark Lord thought a moment,
Then excused Himself and left,
And pondered on His course of action
Lest of a bride He was bereft.

She waited 'till He parted,
Then began to laugh out loud.
She had invented that whole song,
A feat that made her proud.

For it was notorious,
That although the Dark Lord did well
At snatching souls and cursing Gods,
He couldn't sew worth Hell.

He'd try, she knew, to woo her,
With cloth, and snaps, and thread,
But his gown would be quite dreadful,
And she, out of the red.

So she returned unto her chambers,
To finish up her task,
But heard a dreadful howling sound
In another room she passed.

She peeked into an open door,
And there was struck quite dumb,
To see the Dark Lord on His rear,
Sucking on His thumb!

Around Him sat the finest cloth,
All dyed a spotless white,
And needles scattered all about,
But something wasn't right.

The lovely girl's pride vanished,
As she glided to his side,
The Dark Lord, He was crying,
As He looked up at his bride.

He began to try to speak to her,
And when He parted lips,
Blood slipped down His pointed chin
In three heart-wrenching drips.

The Dark Lord, He'd been sewing
With all his mien and might,
To make the dress just perfect,
Trying to make it right.

But the needle had gone and gotten stuck,
Tho' He pulled, and yanked, and tried,
And the needle pierced His thumb quite deep,
And the pain had made Him cry.

The lovely girl took pity,
And bandaged up his hand,
And began to finish up the gown,
The most brilliant in the land.

The Dark Lord, he did protest.
It was against the rules,
For her to help Him sew the dress,
That He'd been made a fool.

But the girl, she'd had a change of heart,
When she spied him sitting there,
and she no longer hated Him,
Had nothing left to fear.

For she had seen, in that moment,
When His blood had fallen out,
That it was red, just like hers,
And now she did not doubt,

That although her groom-to-be
Had a pretty nasty job,
He really was a sweetheart,
And a fairly decent sod.

So when the dress was ready,
The two of them were wed.
And above her heart, on her gown,
Were three tiny drops of red.

The Dark Lord and his wifey,
Were happy from there on,
And both were always sharply dressed,
In Green, and Blue, and Fawn.

But hold yet, gentle reader,
There's one moral left to find,
Before we leave the proud Dark Lord
And His blushing bride behind.

The seamstress is the reason,
When buried in the ground,
That everyone is always wrapped
In a lovely winding shroud.

When they meet the seamstress,
Whether Up or Down,
She makes for them a replica
Of her lovely wedding gown.

And thus are all radiant angels clad
In robes made with pure love,
And if you look quite closely,
You'll note the little drops of blood.

The living, when they see them,
Think they represent Holy Christ,
But we, down here, know full well
The reason they're so bright.

For the Devil is a person too,
Just like all those above.
And He's not such an awful guy...
After all, He fell in Love.

In, Two, Three, Four, Five

The first clue that something big is going down is the *basso profundo* clatter-growl that tickles our ears, just on the human-side of hearing. It shakes the pastry case's glass shelves. The pies shiver and the lamps overhead swing ever so slightly in a slow, unnatural circle. Dust from the crown molding falls like grey snow.

Everyone in the café goes quiet, tense; prey, suddenly realizing that nearby there is a danger, a predator in the shadows and unseen places of their small world. They wait for a sign, for the next clue, for an indication in which direction they should run, or where they should burrow, or, if it comes to it, who they should push out for the danger to pick off. They wait to see where death will come from. And hope that said clue, when it arrives, does not do so in the form of an unstoppable streak of teeth and blood – too quick, too fierce, too late.

Another heavy boom. The café shivers again, a distinct ca-chunk lurch for all that it is subtle.

Heads turn to the window.

Whatever is making our small world shake isn't close enough to spy on this street. But perhaps, judging by the sound of things, it might be *tall* enough, *big* enough to see around other buildings. To see how close the danger has stalked.

If it is, indeed, some creature or mechanical in motion. And not, say, a series of explosions getting closer.

Hands tense on the arms of their chairs. The patrons ready to press up into a run. Heads swivel and thigh muscles tense.

I put the coffee carafe down on the polished countertop and slowly, deliberately, inhale to a count of five, exhale to ten.

He had said that it would help with the anxiety attacks, the panic, the... worry.

Because, of course, if there are creatures, or mechanicals, or explosions, then that's where he will be. *Has* to be. Right in the middle of it. Always.

I asked him, once, a few months ago, as the sweat cooled in the dips of our spines, the hollows of our throats, in the intimate pink shells of our ears, why it had to be him. Why he didn't hang up the tights, the cape, the gauntlets. Why he didn't put away the gadgets and the goggles, and let someone else do it.

"Who else?" he'd asked. He had gotten out of bed to fetch us a refreshment, and been pouring red wine. He didn't stop to look up. He just kept on, as if he already knew what my expression would reveal: my concern for him. Certain. "There is no one else. No one half so powerful."

"Surely there's... other professionals."

"Not anybody who can do what I do. And civilians... they'd get killed on the first punch."

He finished pouring, set the bottle on his bedside table, and crawled back between the sheets. We toasted. We didn't talk about it again.

Several months later, on the day he gave me a copy of his apartment key, he came home to find me clutching one of his sofa cushions and staring, goggle-eyed, at the television. I was doing my best to stiffen my chin, to keep it from wobbling. I thought if I didn't blink, then I wouldn't cry. His sudden appearance at the door – soot-stained, smelling of burnt leather and plastic, singed hair, costume covered only haphazardly by a pea jacket – startled the tears out of me.

"I–! I thought–!" I'd sobbed, sudden and embarrassed, as I shot to my feet. My cheeks burned with relieved shame at my overwhelming emotional breakdown, and were cooled by my tears. But they also burned with anger. I was so damned furious that he had nearly died, right in front of my eyes, live on national television. "I saw–!"

He'd tried, at first, to shrug it off. He was smirking in that lopsided, superior little way that first caught my eye across the café where I waited tables. But when he saw how genuine my distress was he came over, sat on the sofa, and folded me against the embossed emblem on his chest. He petted my hair until all the embarrassment, all the relief, all the anger had been sobbed out.

"I was careful," he had whispered into my ear. Tugged lightly on my little earring with his teeth. "I'm fine."

"You didn't look fine," I had said.

"Take a deep breath. In through your nose. One, two, three, four, five. Good, and out for one, two, three, four, five, six, seven, eight, nine, ten. Good, again, sweetheart. Very good. Just like that. Do you feel calmer?"

"A little."

"It's a good trick."

"Do you use it?"

"All the time."

I inhale and exhale again, and the café rumbles me back into the present. A woman with a stroller is strapping her child into a carrier on her chest, getting ready to abandon the contraption and hoof it if need be. An older man is carefully counting out change to leave on the table. I wonder if he thinks that if we all run, I'll stay behind to bus the tables and collect my tips from the candy dish by the front door. The boom is louder, closer, and this time I can hear the stacks of plates and chipped, coffee-stained cups rattle against one another.

A couple slips out the door without paying, but I don't care. I go to the window, not at all concerned that I'm blocking the view of others, and press my hands against the morning-cool plate glass. Look up. Look around. Crane my head, press each cheek in turn to the glass, straining, searching...

There!

Across the street, on the other side of the brownstones, just tall enough that I can see it through the chimney stacks. A flash of deep blue plated armor, steam rising from turrets.

Oh, that's definitely a mechanical he's never shown me before. I wonder briefly if it's new, or if it's so old that it was crammed in the back of the workshop where I wouldn't have been able to see it through the other detritus, the piles of scrapped vehicles and junked parts.

There is a great squealing shriek of tires on pavement, a crinkling crunch not dissimilar to the sound of a candy wrapper being opened, and then suddenly an armored van is smashing into the asphalt directly in front of me.

The whole café jumps: me, the people around me, the tables and the chairs and the very foundations of the building. A laugh burbles and bubbles up my throat, but it is nervous and tinged with hysteria. The woman with the baby swings around the counter, tears through the kitchen, and I can hear the fire alarm wail and snarl as she forces open the emergency exit. A stream of patrons follow her out like lemmings, like fish in a school.

I should go. I should go with them. I should run.

I could be hurt. The glass of the window that I'm pressed up against could shatter, shards flying into my eyes, my mouth. The armored van could explode. The café could come down on my head or the foundation crumble under my feet. But I stand, motionless, waiting. Because he is here, dressed as his alter ego, and I trust him to save me.

Witless. Naïve. Possibly even stupid.

But I trust him to save me if I need it. And until that time, I want to *see*. I want to watch him in action, brave and fearless. I want to see that inner beauty of his shine out of his face, light up the underside of his cloak, spark along his gauntlets.

I want to see him dazzling in the sunlight, bright and wonderful, and *heroic.*

In, two, three, four, five. Out, two, three, four, five, six, seven, eight, nine, ten.

See, even the driver of the armored van has gathered his wits enough to scramble out of the window of the cab. He draws his gun, turns back towards the brownstones he was thrown over, and I can't help my snicker. A gun. A very small gun. Against powered people. Ridiculous.

The night-blue vehicle climbs over the brownstones, drops onto the street right beside the van, and I can see that it is accented in brass. It is dented, and worn, and parts of it are smoking that probably shouldn't be, and parts of it are sparking that definitely *shouldn't* be, but it is...

It is the product of *his* imagination, *his* blueprints and hard work, and so, for all that the mechanical is crab-like and squat, it is *gorgeous.*

A pincer waves at me, and though I cannot see his familiar smirk though the viewscreen, I know his mouth well enough that I can tell that he is smiling, just like that, for me. I wave back, though the glass, excited.

And then the pinchers jerk up. A roundel that I mistook for a crab eye on a swaying stalk orients itself on something high above it, and then the crab jerks and leaps. It's gone from my sight in an instant, and the security guard looks around, looks up, bewildered and white-knuckled. He raises his gun and fires – one, two, three, four shots. Nothing falls from the sky.

The whole café lurches under my feet.

Ah, he landed on our roof!

More dust and this time ceiling plaster rains down on me. Right. Now is probably a good time to leave. I take the street exit, scrambling up to the back of the armored van. The guard sees me, waves me over into the lee of the chassis, head still raised to the sky and one hand still tight around his gun.

"What's going on?" I ask.

"Incrediman, and Skye High..." he starts, and then swallows. "I don't know what Vertego wants, no one told me what was in my truck, but he sure as hell ain't gettin' it!"

The roar of a flamethrower above us drags my attention upwards. The flame coming from the pincher is so hot that it warps the fire escape and singes my eyebrows. The guard curses and ducks into the safe, cool shadow of his cab. I keep watching as the mechanical crab vomits fire.

The battle is hypnotic, a ballet in the air before me of ducking bodies and close misses and I cannot look away. A small, cold fear grows in me that if I look away, if I stop murmuring endearments and half-articulated prayers for his safety, then his luck will change and he will lose. He will *die*. And so I watch, my fingers balled tight, painful in my apron. The fabric twists and tears under the strain of my anxiety.

In, two, three, four, five. Out, two, three, four, five, six, seven, eight, nine, ten. Be safe. Be careful. Oh! No, behind you! In, two, three, four, five. Out, two, three, four, five, six, seven, eight, nine, ten. Be faster. Be better. Come home to me. In, two, three, four, five. Out, two, three, four, five, six, seven, eight, nine, ten. Come home to me. Come home to me alive.

As the fight weaves back and forth across the rooftops, lurching, drunken, the security guard turns away. The motion catches my attention and I watch as he jams his gun back into his holster and uses both hands to wrench at the twisted lever of the back door. He manages to lift a panel, and fumbles for the oversized, elaborate key handcuffed to his wrist.

His hands are shaking so badly that the key slips between his fingers, dangling, impotent, no less than four times. He gives a snarl of frustration.

"Let me help," I say, go over, lift the key, slot it into place. It is big, unwieldy, and takes both of us to turn it.

I look down. He hasn't snapped the strap back over his gun, so when he throws open the heavy door and overextends his step to hoist his bulk into the back of the truck, his gun slips down his leg and clatters against the pavement. It's a quiet sound, barely audible above the wailing sirens that are creeping closer, the crush and crashes above us, the roar of the crab's flamethrower. But we both hear it, tense. Wait.

The gun doesn't go off.

I bend down to scoop it up.

"Careful," the guard says as I extend it towards him.

"You really don't know what's in your truck?" I ask.

"No, only that mine's the real one. It's not one of the decoys. Gimmie the gun, help me get this out of here. Vertego can't get at it. We'll hide it."

"Good idea," I say.

Then I flip the gun around and shoot him in the foot.

The guard screams and falls back into the far corner of the box, swearing and grunting. The air smells of warm copper and gunpowder. I can't believe I just did that. I never thought I'd be able to do something like that.

But then, he always said that I could. That he believed in me.

In, two, three, four, five. Out, two, three, four, five, six, seven, eight, nine, ten.

He believed in me, and I did it.

I did it!

I pick up the briefcase. It's light. It feels empty. Is it empty?

The guard's face is white with agony, and I hope, for his sake, that he passes out soon. I turn back, jump out, toss the gun into the café. The air is still and silent. I breathe in, deep, two, three, four, parse the scents of grit, dust, fire, fear, and the great swelling sense of pride and wonder. Alone in a city, the buildings empty, the windows drawn, or dark.

Glorious.

The crab mechanical swings down to street level and then, with a pneumatic hiss, the spindly legs fold under it, lowering the carapace to the asphalt. The mechanical's mouth opens.

I look up, around, but he is alone. No one is waiting to drop down on us. No ambush in wait. The world is silent, waiting, waiting.

He steps onto the gangplank and I hold up the case, waggling it at him, overjoyed.

"Come and get it, if you want it!" I tease.

He laughs. I try out his smirk.

He rushes at me, sweeps me up, and then his mouth is on mine, hot, wonderful, wet.

"God, you're perfect. Absolutely perfect, sweetheart," he says, his breath puffing straight into my lips. When he puts me back onto my feet, I offer him the case. He pulls it open easily, snapping the locks with the strength of his fingers, and digs in. As he's fishing around, I reach up, tug his goggles away, smooth back sweat and mechanical-oil-slicked hair.

"Thanks sweetheart," he says and gifts me with one of those lovely lopsided smirks. "Whew, that was close, eh? Nearly squashed the café! Wouldn't want to destroy such important memories, eh?"

"Yes, then where will I work?" I ask, laughter in each syllable, too joyful, to relieved, too flush on his kisses and his successes and my love, pure and deep and ridiculous, for the spandex-clad man pressed against me.

"Work? Oh, sweetheart, you're never going to have to work again."

"Oh?"

Then he holds it up. It's a diamond.

The diamond that I read about in the paper that morning. The one cut by one of the most powerful magical mystics the powered community has seen in the last three hundred years. The diamond that is said to have been cut so perfectly that any focused beam of light through its prisms emerges as a laser powerful enough to burn through any material, and whose refracted rainbows are said to grant any that they fall upon an immeasurable increase to their own powers, whatever they may be. The diamond that was supposed to be travelling via an unknown route in armoured transport, while a dozen other decoys travelled with it along all sorts of strange side streets from the airport to the museum where the it was meant to go on display.

That diamond.

Oh, my man is so clever.

Already, he looks quicker, happier, fresher. Under the concrete dust and the blood, his skin glows with returned youth. And I, I feel marvelous. The repetitive strain in my wrist is draining away as the rainbows thrown up from the jewel skitter across my face, my headache pulsing away to nothingness, the soreness of my feet after the non-stop work of the morning shift nearly gone.

"Sweetheart," he murmurs again, and then he turns us back to his machine. "Wanna go for a ride?"

"Sounds fun."

"Hop up."

I cast around for a seatbelt and he just laughs. "It's safe, believe me, it's safe."

Safe. Such a liminal word. He sees the worry flit through my eyes. "Hey, I have an idea," he says, and that smirk licks back up into his mouth, curling, sensual, into the dimple there. "How would you like to never have to worry about me ever again?"

"I'd like that a lot."

"Great, sweetheart. Then I have a gift for you. Under the seat."

I curve low, reach, and retrieve a case. On my knees – unlatched—oh. *Oh.* "It's a ... gun?"

"Sort of."

"What am I supposed to do with it?"

The smirk stretches across, catlike, to take up the other corner of his lip. "I left Incrediman in the bottom of a crater. He's probably still alive."

"What about Skye High?"

The smirk flickers and flirts. Delicious.

"Really?" I ask.

"Really – she's as dead as a body can be. And if Incrediman still lives, then you can do the honours with that, sweetheart."

Oh!

Now that *is* a gift. Never having to worry about his capture, his death, his whole life rotting in jail, or his turn on the electric chair. Never having to worry about him being abused on the inside, or intimidated, never having to worry about him being hurt in street brawls or defeated in battle ever again.

He will be safe. Safe. Safe.

"Let's go!" I say, and clutch the gun tightly, anticipation crawling like a delicious shiver down my spine, spreading out to the tips of each tingling digit. I peel off my apron and toss it out the window, followed quickly by my name badge. That's not who I am anymore.

Now I am his. And he is mine.

Oh, to have him safe. And free. And powerful. Young. Hale. Whole.

And mine. With me. Always.

This is going to be good.

Oh!

How lucky I am that he smirked at me across the cafe. I am so excited, so excited, that I need to breathe. *In, two, three, four, five. Out, two, three, four, five, six, seven, eight, nine, ten. In, two, three, four, five. Out, two, three, four, five, six, seven, eight, nine, ten. In, two, three, four, five. Out, two, three, four, five, six, seven, eight, nine, ten...*

Another Four Letter Word

Funerals, Jennet decides, both literally and metaphorically *suck*.

Metaphorically in all the ways they talk about in entitled poems, and empty hymns, and useless novels about vast open spaces and disillusioned young men with something to prove. Literally, because when they lower her father's coffin into the cold, damp earth, it feels like she's about to be pulled down on top of it.

It had only ever been the two of them. Jen and David against the world. Happiest pair that ever was. Strong. Defying all the stereotypes of men who can't care, can't nurture, can't *mother*. Father and daughter, powerful together.

And now separated forever.

Jennet clutches a slim ash tree, leans close to it and does her best to breathe wet, chill, cemetery air; to remain upright; to not pitch nose-first into her Da's grave. She has no mother, no uncle, no brothers or sisters to hold her upright, help her stand firm. Only Mrs. MacDonald, the cook and housekeeper, hovers beside her elbow but does not touch. They don't have a close enough relationship for that, but if Jen was pressed, she'd have said that the woman was the closest thing to a female role model she'd grown up with. Her father hadn't believed in governesses. Too Victorian, he'd thought.

When she's invited to speak about the deceased, Jen just shakes her head, fingers digging into the bark. Mr. Coldwell, the only other servant and the man who was chauffer, mechanic, valet and friend to her father, steps up instead. He pulls a folded card from his breast pocket, clearly anticipating that Jen's grief would make her mute and the task would fall to him. That is the nice thing about Mr. Coldwell: he is so good at anticipating when he would be needed.

Jennet listens with half an ear, the rain on the leaf mold and the canopy above them too much of a hindrance to her sorrow-soaked brain to catch all Mr. Coldwell's words. When he's done, he presses the card between Jen's fingers. Mrs. MacDonald takes it, tucks it into her small black purse, and Jen is absurdly grateful that it will be kept safe. She wants to read it, but she can't worry about keeping track of it just now.

Then the priest is calling her forward, and she goes on shaking legs, the heels of her pumps sinking into the wet grass. He presses a clump of soil into her hands and she steps to the edge of the wound in the world and opens her fingers. It lands with a wet plop right about where her father's face would be.

She stumbles back, horrified with the visual, and covers her own face with her soil-streaked hands. The rain is freezing, sharp fingers against the back of her neck. Mrs. MacDonald touches her shoulder, and that's it, that's all Jen can take. Enough.

She turns and flees back to the house, leaving mud and rainwater in her wake like fairy-story breadcrumbs. She shuts herself up in the close, quietness of her Da's en suite shower stall. The pouf still smells of his cologne body wash, fills her nose with the scent of warm, gripping hugs she will never have again, and she crumples against the tiles and weeps, and weeps, and weeps.

***

Despite the large house and the land surrounding it, Carterhaugh Estate isn't wealthy. Nor is it really an estate. Jennet and her Da were not part of the peerage, never mind that the people of the nearby Selkirk call them "Lord" and "Lady" out of respect, and Jennet herself draws only a modest stipend from the family trust.

The house itself is two stories above ground and one below that comprises the pantry and kitchens with big dug-out windows. She and her father had apartments in the upper part of the house at the front, and there are two guest rooms and a study at the back. The ground floor is home to the formal dining room, the informal breakfast room, a sitting room that her father had filled with cleverly hidden electronics like a television and a sound system, two servant's quarters occupied by Mrs. MacDonald and Mr. Coldwell when they aren't in the mood to head back to their homes in Selkirk, and their shared bathroom. The house was old enough and well cared for enough to qualify for heritage status with the government, but that would mean needing to put in some cash for the restorations, and frankly they just don't have the money.

As the only surviving blood kin to the Lord of Carterhaugh, Jennet is entailed the manor, the grounds, and a hundred acres of farmland which has been rented by the same family for the last three generations. Jennet inherits very little beyond the trust, the interest on which pays the salaries of Mr. Coldwell and Mrs. Macdonald, and for their consumables. The money from the farming tenants goes towards the upkeep of the house, and Jennet's admittedly modest lifestyle. Jen doesn't work, per se, but she does sit on the board of several of the local charities, arts centres, and business associations.

Included in the manor's grounds is a triangular plain crisscrossed with famous, so-called fairy circles, and just enough forest to get lost in. The forest borders both the Yarrow and the Ettrick, inhabits the fork where the two tributaries come together and head off as one to the far away North Sea.

From the window seat of her apartment, Jennet can see a doe with her fawn grazing along the edge of the lawn, sticking close to the trees. Her father's grave is on the other side of the house, hidden behind the crumbling family chapel, and she is absurdly thankful that it isn't visible from her sitting room.

She's fled here after a day full of long, painful discussion and even more heart-breaking choices. She watches the deer and clutches a cup of tea and does her best to empty her mind. But even mother nature, it seems, is determined to not let her hide away from the thought of children.

The truth of it is this: Jennet can afford to remain at Carterhaugh, could probably live on the trust and the entail indefinitely, but the question has become – who will get it after? Who will Jennet name as her heir?

***

A few decades ago, Carterhaugh was open to tourists, like the grand houses of the Historical Trust used to do in the old days. There once were parts of the house that were staged, but so few people came out to the manor that they had repurposed the spare rooms as Jennet's nursery and her Da's study when she'd been small. With no wee ones in house and the building aging at a rate that is beginning to outpace the living's ability to keep up the repairs, perhaps it is time, Mr. Coldwell floats as the three of them huddle over a pot of tea on the rough scullion's table in the kitchen, to revisit the idea of turning the east wing into a bed and breakfast?

They could hire a part-time maid from the village to take care of the bedrooms, Mrs. MacDonald could do the cooking, Mr. Coldwell could pick up visitors from the train station in the old Model T that he has meticulously restored, and Jennet could play hostess? The only down side is, of course, that Jennet isn't sure she could smile that much around strangers. She wouldn't mind it so much if she could just avoid that part of the house, but of course part of the draw is going to be getting to interact with the Lady Carterhaugh herself. To take brandy in the sitting room, tour the ornamental and kitchen gardens, perhaps go for a horseback ride around the boundaries of the forest.

"And," Mr. Coldwell says gently, "We'd have to rent out your father's apartments."

Jen's fingers go tight on her teacup and she bites her lip hard to keep in the instinctual *No!*

"It would make a lovely honeymoon suite," Mrs. MacDonald agrees, voice low and deferential. It's a conversation that has to be had, Jennet knows. But that doesn't mean any of them like having it. "If we made it a bit less…"

"Like Da's," Jennet finishes.

Mrs. MacDonald quaffs her tea in a single, wincing gulp. "Yes." She pours more for everyone, warming up what's left in their cups, and they drink in silence for a moment. "Fresh coat of paint? Something lighter. Get the pipe smoke smell out, and some nice landscapes on the walls. Maybe leave up the family portraits?"

"No," Jennet says. "I mean, the rest, I… okay. But the portraits, I want them moved to my sitting room."

"I'll arrange for—" Mr. Coldwell begins, but Jennet shakes her head.

"I'll do it." She lets go of her teacup and balls her fists against her eyes, pushing hard to keep the tears at bay. She's so damn sick of crying. "It's *my* family. I don't want some workman I don't know to touch… no, I w-want to do it."

"Okay, dear," Mrs. MacDonald says, a gentle, dry hand cupping the back of Jennet's head. "Okay. We'll help you."

***

Over the course of the weekend, they remove all the paintings from the wall that surrounds Jennet's sitting room fireplace. They patch and paint it with a fresh coat of butter-cream colour that will offset the gilt frames of the portraits nicely. It's the longest wall in her apartments, the only one not interrupted by windows or doors. The sitting room itself is divided by décor into a library and study corner, the comfy visiting area around the fireplace, and a small private breakfast nook. The main entrance to the apartment is beside the stuffed bookshelves with the squashy reading chair, two tall windows to the right, the fireplace and its wingbacks to the left, the small mahogany dining set ahead, and beyond that the door into Jennet's bedroom and en suite.

Jen lines the portraits up in order of age against the wall, trying to determine the best hanging arrangement. The first is an oil painting of a wide, barrel-shaped man with startlingly ginger hair. He is swathed in Selkirk plaid, an almost eye-bleedingly tight pattern of blue and red. He stands behind a solid looking lady-wife, and a dour daughter of about twelve who looks remarkably like Jennet at that age. It's a large painting of the Laird, Master of Carterhaugh, and family, and it is easily as tall as Jennet. Next to it is a painting in which the young woman, Margaret, all grown. Jennet turns her attention to Margaret's husband, a puckish young man painted with vividly green eyes and a bit of a cheeky grin. He wears no plaid, only the trousers and jacket of a well-off young man in the late 15th century.

He has one arm wrapped tight around Margaret's shoulders, possessive and nearly inappropriate for a formal portrait of the Lady, but Margaret is leaning into his touch, clearly enamored. A small baby boy grins out of the canvas from a froth of white fabric and lace in her lap, and his father's hand cradles his head lovingly. There was another child in the painting at one point, Jennet knows, but then he was painted out. Her Da had told her it was a common practice of the day when a child died. She can see the darkish smear by the husband's hip, the place where two different shades of black don't quite match. Nobody knows what happened to the little boy, which means that he probably died young. She brushes her fingertips over the blotch where the boy's chubby cheeks would be in apology for his short life, the grief of her father's passing welling momentarily against the hollow of her throat, and swallows hard.

Clearly this was a family that adored one another, and it breaks her heart a little more that the boy-child is missing. The surviving boy's name was Thomas, Jennet knows that, but the father's name she doesn't recall ever having learned. A quick peek at the back of the canvas is no help – it's been papered over by the framers.

The next painting is Thomas with his own children, a brace of four boys and a young girl cuddling a strangled looking spaniel. The children are dressed as adults, as they did in the day, down to the little powdered wigs. The second eldest boy features in another portrait, in a much more portable size than the family ones, with a young man they say was a great favourite of his among the townspeople. Here they are both about twenty, hands around each other's waists in a congenial manner, and smiling conspiratorially. Whether the young man was a friend or a lover, no one can be sure, but Jen's Da had always liked the idea of the two men finding contentment together.

He would have, considering.

After that is another two family portraits, one more with a child painted out, and then they give way to muted, black-and-white tin-types, silvery daguerreotypes, sepia-faded photographs, and finally the colour-muted family photo portraits from the twentieth century. There are photographs here of every generation of Carterhaughs for as long as the medium has existed.

The appalling legacy of children dying in their first decade marches on, and without realizing it, Jen finds her hand splayed over her own, slightly paunchy stomach by the time she reaches the end of the row. She has no siblings, but her father had a sister once. The very young woman is grinning out of a photo taken at some pleasure chalet or other. She looks so very much like Margaret Selkirk that they could be the same person. And Jennet, she's been told, strongly favours her late aunt Jane.

***

It takes four months of good, hard scrubbing, painting, and furniture rearranging, a visit to Edinburgh to meet with a website designer, several long days filling out paperwork and standing in government queues, but eventually the Carterhaugh Manor Bed and Breakfast is open for business. Everyone in Selkirk takes a tromp thought the house, shakes the hand of Lady Carterhaugh and takes a cup of coffee in the dining room the first Saturday, just for curiosity's sake. When her neighbours ask why Jen decided to follow through with the plans, she says "It's something to do," instead of "I don't know if the living would last." The latter is the truth, but it's too honest for polite company.

Their first customers, three days later, are an American couple come over for a research trip, delighted to be able to stay right where the fairy stories they're writing about originated. Within an hour Jennet is sick to death of talking about an imagined history and what it all might *mean*, a headache forming at the crest of their brash, broad voices. She begs out of the conversation by making up a phone call to a friend she's meant to be making.

Once she's ensconced in her apartments, curled in her squashy reading chair, she does indeed call one of her friends in Selkirk.

"Jennie!" Karen says. "I haven't heard from you since… well, never you mind that. What's up? Just want a chat?"

"Yes. And sorry."

"Never you mind. You needed your time. But oh, what you've missed." Jennet spends an hour hearing all about the toddler's favorite new words ("bloody bugger piss!") and the teenager's sky-high mobile phone bills. It feels normal, boring, and it helps Jen find her centre again.

"Can't believe you have a teenager," Jen sighs as Karen winds down.

"I can't believe it either. Wasn't it just last week when *we* were teenagers?" Karen says, and somewhere in the background something makes a smashing sound. "Oh, for god's sake!" Karen bawls. "Matthew, that's it! I'm selling you to your auntie Jennet!"

Jen laughs. "I don't want him," she says when Karen comes back on the line.

"Need an heir yet, don't you?" Karen asks, and the question is casual, but the real concern is there.

"I don't want to talk about that," Jen says, softly.

"Okay. Okay, Jen, I know… but it's been five months since your Da, and you not being… well, with it all…"

"That's over, it's done," Jen says. "I don't want to talk about *that.* I just… it's too soon, I can't think about that, okay? And now I've got this damned bed and breakfast, all this work, the paperwork, the house is always noisy and I just feel like I can't get any *rest.*"

"Okay, Jennie, okay," Karen says. "Never you mind then. Hey, come down to ours for dinner this week?"

"I'd like that," Jen says.

"Good, good, I'll text you when later." Another smash in the background. "*Heaven preserve you Matthew Simmons Junior!*"

She yells. "I need to ring off. Sure you don't want to buy him? Even a trade? I'll take that handsome new gardener of yours, the one I saw wandering down by the woods? Never you mind, gotta go. *Mattie—!*"

Karen hangs up before Jen can tell her that she hasn't hired a new gardener.

***

Jennet waves off the Americans as Mr. Coldwell drives them into Selkirk for their dinner reservations, then puts on her wellies and her good thick pea coat. It's early in autumn yet, but it rained that morning and the forest is always damp and chill after a storm. And a pallid frost has been laddering up her spine since the phone call, a sense of apprehension that she just can't to shake out of her vertebrae.

She tours the grounds first, and doesn't see anything out of sorts with the ornamental garden, or the kitchen patch. Mrs. MacDonald, when asked, suggests that the young man Karen saw lurking around the grounds might be the new maid Brandy's boyfriend, a young musician named Alex. Brandy says Alex hates nature, would never go wandering in the woods if he could help it, and has only ever been up to Carterhaugh to pick her up from work.

Jen remembers the sound of his motorbike, the voices by the back entrance, the glimpse of riding leather and dark hair sticking out of a helmet. No, he didn't seem the type to just take a walk through someone else's property to pass the time.

Crossing the plain, Jennet avoids stepping on the milk-white scars in the earth that her predecessors had named fairy-circles. Not because she fears them, or even really believes in them, but because it was just respectful. Habit. Her Da had always walked around them, so Jennet does too.

So too would her heirs if she ever... *goddamn it.*

Stepping into Carterhaugh woods is like stepping through a mirror. Or, at least, it is what Jennet thinks Alice must have experienced, how she had imagined it when she'd read *Through the Looking Glass*. The air is suddenly chillier; the colours are a bit more muted, a bit bluer; the world is lined with silver and diamonds where a good, hearty Scottish mist clings to the ground brush, and dew and moisture sparkle on the flat leaves.

Her breath plumes between her lips, and a frisson of something *else* slides across her skin, tries to get up under her cuffs and collar. Her Da had told her so many nursery stories about this place, about what had happened under its canopy in generations gone by, that Jennet genuinely doesn't know if the feeling of walking through a wall of magic is her own imagination, fed by the tales, or just the change in the microclimate.

She stops where she always stops, where her father had always stopped – three steps in, on a small mound left by a rotting log, beside an oak tree that has to be at least as old as the Carterhaugh manor house. Perhaps its brothers hold up the beams of the roof above Jennet's head as she sleeps.

She lays her right hand on the bark, in the same place that a dozen generations of Carterhaugh residents have done, and that one palm-shaped patch is as smooth and shiny as a well-oiled banister. She closes her eyes, leans against the tree, and tries not to think about how this is the first time she's been here since her Da was put in the ground.

That the last person to touch this spot had been David Carter.

Without thinking too much about it, without giving herself time and space to feel foolish, Jen presses her forehead against the rough bark above the handprint. She kisses the smooth place in the bark, between her own fingers.

It smells of damp and wood, of skin and salt, of her lavender hand cream and the bacon sarnie she'd had for lunch, of the rich tapestry of forest and the father she'll never hear fairy stories from again.

"That's new," a voice with a thick burr rumbles somewhere far ahead of her. If the forest could have a voice, then this is what it would sound like. Old, and Scottish almost to the point of being a stereotype, thick and dark. Male. Curious. Complex and fizzy, like raw ginger on the tongue.

Jen lingers on the tree for a moment more, refusing to have this moment cut short, refusing to allow her observer make her feel foolish. Then she leans back and stands up straight, and peers into the mists.

When she has found the blotch of shadow that is different from the rest, she rests a hip against the oak tree. The pose mirrors the speaker's own cocky posture, a deliberate call-out. Jennet smiles calmly, thinly. "You must be my new gardener, then." She folds her hands across her chest, waiting.

"Must I?" the voice is rich and amused.

"That's what they're saying in Selkirk, I hear. Funny thing, I don't recall hiring you."

"Nor would you," the voice agrees.

"So what are you doing in my forest?"

A light laugh, like air through branches. "*Your* forest?"

"My father left it to me," Jennet says. "Carterhaugh is mine."

"Oh, the echoes of time," the voice says, and his burr is blurry and wistful.

"Right, whoever you are, I have a mobile with me. Come out, or I call 999."

A repressed snort of laughter. "But *that* is different."

"Seriously, now," Jennet says, fishes the mobile phone from her coat pocket and lifts it demonstratively. The blue glow cuts through the gloom and lights on the figure, just a few paces away. It is thin, slumped, hands shoved in the kangaroo pocket of a hoodie, and when it looks up from under the hood, green eyes glitter in the light.

"Oh, Maggie, how bold you've grown."

"It's Jennet. Who the hell are you?"

The figure sweeps a deep and ironic bow. "Liam. Ma'am."

"Miss," Jennet corrects with knee-jerk reflex. "And that's still no answer to why you're skulking around in my woods."

Liam stands to his full height, pulls back his hood, removes his hands from his pockets, and steps into a slanting shaft of late afternoon sunlight. Motes and pollen dance in the air between them, and his hair sparks gold and straw. Jennet lowers her mobile as he spreads his arms, palm up.

"Do you know who I am?" he asks.

"No," Jennet says.

He grins. "Good."

Jennet presses the 9 button twice. The electronic beep is harsh and flat in the small, mist-battened clearing.

Liam No-Last-Name laughs. "I'm no threat to you, Mistress Carterhaugh. Nor to your guests. I come for you, only."

"*Come* for me?" Jennet repeats, both eyebrows caterpillering towards her hairline. "And you think that *doesn't* sound threatening?"

"I live down the way," he says, gesturing vaguely behind him. "I walk the woods often. More now that I've clapped eyes on you. I saw you, at the funeral."

Jennet sucks in a breath, hands suddenly shaking. "Right, now you're sounding like a creeper. Just so you're aware."

"I came upon it by accident, I swear," Liam says, hands now towards her, placating. "And you looked so sad."

"I was burying my father!" Jen snarls.

"Of course," Liam allows. He looks younger when his smile dissolves, his face relaxing into pity, the lines falling away. Far too young for a man who is now suddenly holding her free hand, a thumb running along the back, soothing and very obviously attempting to be seductive. Succeeding, if she's honest.

Right, Jennet reminds herself, *this is how missing persons reports begin.* But there's something so *entrancing* about his touch, the look in his green, green eyes. Something... *irresistible.*

His breath is sweet and cool against the back of her hand when he lifts it to his cheek, eyes closed as if the texture of her skin is the most exquisite silk. "And in your bedroom window, such *sorrow* upon your face when you look to the woods."

Right, no. Never mind. The spell is frayed with a sharp slap of worried disgust.

"You're a stalker," Jen says, and it's meant to be an accusation but it comes out far more weak, like there's is something... different in his touch. Something calming. Something nearly magical, only there is no such thing as magic.

She reaches for the self-righteous fire she throws at all the men who think a woman of Jen's age and marital status are easy prey, but finds it banked into a small coal of absent-minded worry. She has nothing to throw. That's... wrong.

"A stalker, no. I am an *admirer,* and you must admit, I am a polite one," Liam purrs. "No obnoxious boom boxes, or pebbles thrown at your window. Put away your mobile, Jennet."

She swallows hard and pushes her mobile into the back pocket of her jeans, unthinkingly. Then she wonders why she did it. She reaches for it again, perturbed that she did as she was asked so quickly, so neatly, but is distracted when Liam's grip on her hand shifts. He slides them so that they are palm to palm, fingers folded over the backs of each other's knuckles, and he pumps her hand in a slow shake.

"Pleased to make your acquaintance, Lady Carterhaugh," he whispers. His eyes are gravity wells. As deep and as appealing as Da's grave.

"Pleased to make yours, Liam," she replies, enchanted far too easily by his smooth manners.

He raises her hand to his mouth, brushes a dry kiss across the back of it. Then, from somewhere behind him, he produces a flower. It is one of the late-blooming wild roses, two blossoms fully blown on a single stem.

Jennet can't help it. The spell is broken. She throws back her head and guffaws.

He stands there, roses upheld, looking equal parts surprised and hurt.

"Oh, your face!" Jennet howls. "Did you think that would *work?*"

"It always has," he pouts. "Do ladies no longer like roses? Have they fallen out of fashion?"

"Do you *hear* yourself?" Jennet laughs. "You sound like a period drama!"

Liam drops her hand and turns away, obviously upset, and rubs his free palm on the thighs of his dark jeans.

"Oh, come on," Jennet says, calming down. "Don't get your feathers in a ruffle. It's a very nice rose. And your manners are lovely. And I do appreciate you not throwing rocks at my windows."

He turns back to face her, face twisted in a strange rictus of amusement and horror. "Ladies are not at all what they used to be," he says, definitive.

"Nope," Jennet agrees. "And thank the Lord for that."

Liam runs a frustrated hand through his hair, and gold fluffs up like dandelion down. "You're not making this easy, Jennet," he huffs.

"What's meant to be easy?" Jen counters. "Me?"

"Oh, no," he says, eyes immediately round and apologetic. "I didn't mean it like that."

"Tell me how you meant it, then, and choose your words carefully." She pats her back pocket expressively.

"How is a man enchanted with a woman meant to behave, if not like this?"His arms spread in askance. The heads of the roses bob, as if to agree with his frustration.

"Well, threatening the safety of a woman by behaving like a horrible creeper is right out of fashion, now-a-days," Jen says, and she can't help the lilt of tease that slips into her voice at the end.

"And what then?" Liam asks, receptive to her smile. His frustration is ebbing, replaced with interest in her explanation.

"Most guys chat up women in the grocery store, or in a bar," Jennet says. "Somewhere *public*, you know? Sometimes they even *call* a girl. Or message them on the internet. Send them cards, or knock on their doors. Anything but skulk around, alone in the forest with roses and cheesy lines."

Liam grins puckishly and dips another theatrical bow. "But it worked, didn't it?"

Jennet snorts. "Only because I decided to listen to you instead of brain you with a branch. Which I may yet regret."

"Oh, no you won't, Jennet," Liam vows, his eyebrows and the tilt of his chin serious. "I'll do nothing to make you regret giving me this chance."

Jennet snorts again. "Who says I'm giving you any chance? Cocky."

He holds out the roses. "Please?"

Jennet reaches out and plucks the flowers from his hand. A thorn bites into her thumb and it feels good, feels *real*, so she lets it stay. She buries her nose in the topmost blossom, breathes in the fresh air, good sunlight, clean soil, crisp water. Life.

His smile doubles, not in size but in brightness. "Will you allow me to escort you home, Miss Carter?" He crooks his elbow.

"No," she says. "You're still a strange man who's been staring in my bedroom windows. I should report you to the police."

"But you won't," he hazards, more hope in his voice than she thinks he knows.

"I should."

"But you *won't*."

Jennet twists her mouth into a moue of disapproval. "You're a forceful fellow, and too young for me. Go home, Liam, and forget your stupid crush. And I'll forget to report a trespasser on my property."

Liam bites his bottom lip enticingly. "Or you could meet me here again tomorrow and we could talk again."

"That's not happening," Jennet says, grinning as she waves the rose at him, "But good try. If I see you in these woods again, I *will* be calling the police. Good day, Liam."

"Good day, Miss Carter," he replies, and turns back into the shadows, and vanishes.

***

"How much time do we have?" Liam asks as he pops out from around a fir tree.

"*Jesus!*" Jennet yelps, hand pulled close to her breast like a Victorian heroine. Liam laughs and bows a little hello and waits with hands folded behind his back for her to swallow her heart. "Time until *what*, you *lunatic?*"

"Until the police arrive," Liam says, as if this is the most obvious answer in the world. "You said you'd call them, and you must have seen me out by the forks, or you wouldn't have come down to the woods. So, how long until they arrive?"

"Why do you want to know?"

"So I know how much time to woo you I have left," Liam replies. His mouth, his plush bottom lip, is serious; but his emerald eyes spark with mischief. "If it isn't long, I shall have to forgo the longer poem for a sonnet. They're not as good, but they're quick."

"Oh, shut up," Jennet says, pulling her shawl around her shoulders. She hadn't thought to put on her pea coat this time, too peeved at having caught a glimpse of Liam from her library chair as she was going over the accounts for the first week of the B&B. She had just stormed out, intent on slicing into him with the sharp edge of her tongue. "I haven't called them."

"Oh, Miss Carter, you do care!" he crows.

"I don't. I just don't think it's fair for an obviously bright young man to get nicked for something that is – and I am really giving you the benefit of the doubt, here – a harmless misunderstanding. Now don't get it into your head that I condone stalking, because pestering and street harassment are very real crimes. But you seem to be under the illusion that this is allowable, and it's absolutely, one hundred percent *not*. So. You've been told. I've made it perfectly clear. *Do not* wander around my woods alone, staring through my windows again. Shove off."

"I don't mean to be making you uncomfortable, Jennet," he says, and his regret does seem genuine. "I'm not *stalking*. I just like looking at you."

Jennet throws up her hands and sighs loud and long. "Which is the *exact* definition of stalking. So, here it is, my last mercy." She reaches out and flicks his forehead hard with her fingertip, leaving behind a small red mark. "Are you listening? Next time I *will* call the police."

***

Next time she *does* call the police, but they never find Liam. Not even any footprints, they say, none that are recent enough to have been imprinted on the ground less than an hour prior.

The fourth time, he walks up to her in the supermarket, while she's trying to decide between two brands of butter, and slips a bottle of red wine into her hand-cart.

"There now," he says softly, a dark purr beside her ear, "Is this a more appropriate way to chat up a woman?"

"Much," Jennet says, but doesn't give him the satisfaction of turning to face him. She continues to contemplate her butter.

Silence. Liam rocks on his heels and Jen reads labels.

"Well, what happens next?" Liam asks, and his voice held a note of a petulant whine.

"Oh, you really are bad at this," Jennet says, and puts one of the tubs back onto the chilled shelf. She places the butter in her basket, pats his shoulder consolingly, and wanders down the aisle. "Thanks for the wine. Good choice."

She leaves him standing there, mouth hanging open.

"Jennet!" he calls, scrambling across the slick tiles after her. "Really. Please. What do I have to do to catch your attention?"

"You could *ask* for it," Jennet suggests, now deeply engrossed in picking a brand of yogurt.

"I... you..." Liam gawps for a few minutes, and Jennet is happy to realize it is the first time she has giggled since her father died. The realization dampens the glee immediately, but she forces the smile to remain. "Jen... Jennet Carter!"

She can't be miserable forever, and despite the rocky, slightly illegal start, Liam *is* endearing. Cute, perhaps too young, but earnest and right now, Jen needs to feel beautiful. Feel *wanted.* And it is very easy to call the police if he continues to overstep.

"Yes Liam?" she asks, choosing a low-fat Greek yogurt and popping it in beside the red wine.

"Would you like to go on a date with me?" he mutters.

"Yes, Liam," she says. *Now* Jennet turns her full attention to him, and graces him with one of her warmest smiles. He seems to grow taller, to unfurl under her gaze, his own puckish grin sliding back across his mouth. "I think I would like that. Let me pay for these, and then why don't we go to the café down the main road?"

"I would like that very much, Miss Carter," Liam replies with another endearingly formal head-tip, and this time when he holds out a crooked elbow, Jen takes it.

***

Months pass. Nearly a year since her father died, and Jennet wouldn't have thought this time last year that she would be smiling by now. Laughing. Flirting.

Happy.

And Liam does make her happy.

The thing is, Jennet knows this is all silly, and doesn't much mind. She tells Karen that she's been seeing someone, and that he is far more serious about it than her, and her friend yells "finally!" and pours them both another glass of wine and turns off the telly and adds, "So, details!"

"None really," Jennet says. They are taking it slow, oh so slow, because Jennet still hurts behind the smiles. Because she feels guilty for finding joy when her Da is dead and in the ground.

But Liam is kind, and clever, and quick. He moves like a ballet dancer and smiles like the sun, and he is everything that grief-damp and sorrow-grey Jennet has feared she would never feel again. She is a full decade his senior, and yet he makes her giggle and blush.

And on their third meeting, when he brushes a sweet kiss across her cheek and asks her to meet him in the woods tomorrow for a walk, she turns positively crimson and agrees.

So here she is, being honest to goodness *wooed* as she walks the woods.

"I like it when you visit me here," Liam says, guiding her over a split rock in the path. "It feels like our secret."

"Not much of a secret," Jennet says. "My family's been meeting lovers in the woods for centuries." She realizes what she's just said, what she's just insinuated, and covers her face with her hands, positive her blush is phosphorescent.

Liam laughs at her discomfort and pretends he didn't hear it in a gentlemanly manner. "Oh, how those robust, virile Carterhaugh men loved their women. So many children they had, so many little heirs running about, but the families got smaller and smaller. The men loved their women just the same, though."

"True," Jennet allows, still mortified, but unwilling to let her male ancestors have all the bragging rights. "And the women their men."

"Look, here," Liam says, leading them to a gentle stop beside a lump of weed and bracken about twice wide as his own shoulders. "Do you know what this is?"

"... dead ivy?" Jennet answers.

Liam grins and crouches down, yanking on the dead vines until a small circle of grey stone is revealed.

"Oh, a well," Jen says, kneeling on the moist leaf-mold to peer down it, hands braced on the ground rather than the rim, in case it's unstable.

"The well from which Tam Lin was reborn."

Jennet laughs. "Oh, no, you know the song, too?"

Liam laughs with her. "And the tales. But it's not a tale, Jennet. It's true. 'Twas your own ancestor Margaret clung to Tam Lin as the Faery Queen transformed him into a lion, and an adder, and a rod of red-hot iron. She flung her lover into the well and he became a man again, reborn in the waters of a woman. They cleaved to one another their whole lives after."

Jennet rolls her eyes. "Which is, you have to admit, the prettiest way to talk about what was probably a road-side tryst. A length of red-hot iron? The waters of a woman? Sounds a lot like shagging to me."

"Why Jennet," Liam says, voice pitched to mimic a particularly offended maiden aunt, and slides down to sit beside her, one of his thighs pressed along her hip. "Your mind is positively in the gutter today. Was there something you wanted to proposition?"

"*My* mind is in the gutter?"

"We could take a roll here, like the heroes of the great

tales. Make love in nature. Declare ourselves under the stars, all that romantic nonsense."

She is tempted. *God* she is tempted. It's been two years since her last serious boyfriend, and there is only so much batteries and fingers could do, but she has no condom and Liam is already dangerously infatuated. What would a twenty year old man allowed to have sex with an older woman think?

She lets him put his hand on her thigh, fingernails scratching the denim puckering around her knees. Here is the moment of truth. Does she say yes, or no? Or later?

"What is a hero, really?" Jen muses, instead of answering herself. The coward's way out, but she needs to think. Not *if* she's sleep with Liam, she'd decided she will weeks back. But if she will sleep with Liam *right now*. Right here.

And if she does, will she tell him about *that* before, or after, or not at all?

"How do you mean?" he asks, palm sliding towards her inseam. She doesn't stop it.

Jen smiles and leans into his arm, parting her legs a little further, inviting him to wander northward. Nothing wrong with some harmless flirting. "Was Margaret the hero, because she rescued Tam Lin? She held on, and was granted marriage with Tam for her courage? Even though he told her how to do it all? How to win?"

"That's how the other stories go," Liam allows, accepting the invitation of her spread thighs. "Rapunzel tells the prince how to defeat the witch, the princess on the glass hill rolls apples down to the farmer boy; the captive chooses their rescuer and eventual husband, and tells them how to win. It's less the challenge for the valiant knight that makes him the hero than it is the woman consciously choosing her mate."

"So what, their heroism is empty because the princess has already decided? 'Oh, that one looks humble, and kind. He's make a good king and he won't beat me. I'll pick him to marry me, but I have to make him think he's winning of his own cunning and strength?' Some sort of centuries old mind-games that the Grimms and Perrault never caught on to?"

Liam grins. "Tell me how it is any different now? Men ask to wed a woman after dating them, after spending months or years proving their worth as a husband, as a father, and the woman is the one with the veto power. She says yes, or no."

Jen can't help but echo his grin. "You make it sound like a meat market. That's *not* what it's like. Besides, sometimes the woman asks the man. Sometimes there is no woman, or no man. Sometimes like my Dad, they don't want to get married."

"I am generalizing," Liam allows. "But you know what I mean. One person does valiant things to prove their worth, even if those valiant things are just taking out the trash and doing the dishes, and the other one decides they get to keep them or not."

"You're still missing the point," Jen says. "It's a marriage, not a property contract. People choose to stay together not because one person wants and the other one consents to being wanted; they stay together because they *like* each other. They want to stay in each other's company, make the other one happy, make them smile, comfort them when they're hurt and take care of them when they're sad and sick. The other person increases their happiness when they're around, when the other person does something nice for them, when they do something nice for their partner. They *both* want and they *both* consent."

Liam leans forward. "Well said, Jennet of Carterhaugh." His face is so close to hers, his breath a warm puff against her lips that tastes of mint and the bottle of cider they've been passing back and forth along the walk. "Will you let me make you happy?"

"Sure," Jen allows. A single kiss can't hurt.

He leans forward just far enough that their mouths touch. Then he giggles, lips vibrating against hers in a thrilling, delicious sensation that makes heat slide down her spine. "See?" he asks, flesh to flesh, the words smeared against her skin. "One asks, one consents."

Before she can answer, he pushes that clever tongue between her lips, and Jen opens for him. Opens her arms, her mouth, allows herself to feel good, to feel for herself, for the first time since her father had passed. Liam kisses the scar on her stomach over, and over, and over again and produces a condom from the kangaroo pocket of his hoodie.

"I consent," Jen murmurs amid the late autumn roses.

And Jennet allows herself to remember that she is a human being who deserves good things, and Liam is more than happy to help her get there.

***

Jennet is more relaxed than she's been in probably a decade. She's just had about three spectacular orgasms on the forest floor, a hot bubble bath in her en suite, and there are no people staying over at the B&B so she was able to have dinner alone. Now she's reading in her squashy chair, a fire crackling in the grate and really, all is well with the world.

Somewhere out there, her *lover* is at home, probably doing the same.

He could be doing it here, but he hadn't asked. He'd just wiped his chin and handed her a bouquet of late-blooming roses fresh picked from the bush beside them, smiled his cheeky, twinkly smile, and sauntered back towards the little house he'd told her about. He's never invited her back, either, but Jen likes to imagine it as an enchanted cottage, small and wood and covered with a carpet of ivy so thick that it would be invisible to all but those who know where and how to look. Romantic nonsense.

She is just turning a page when a flash of blonde hair and green eyes catches her attention. At first she thinks Liam has come to visit, snuck in to the house somehow to continue what they started, and she turns with a smile and a tingle on both sets of lips. But when she looks at him, she realizes that it's not Liam at all. It's just the painting of Margaret and her husband. She's still not used to having the portraits in her room.

She smiles at Maggie and her man, and is about to resume reading when something about the portrait arrests her attention. Now that she's really *considering* him, she can see that Margaret's husband looks an awful lot like Liam. She sets aside her book and goes over to the painting, tracing the curve of his weskit with her fingers. The man was painted nearly life-sized, and up close, the detail is as remarkable as the resemblance. Well, it's a small county, and people have been intermarrying for years. It's entirely possible that Margaret's husband might resemble Jennet's new lover.

She closes her eyes and compares Liam to the late Mr. Selkirk, or whatever his actual family name was, and is amazed to understand that they are not only similar, but to her memory they are damn near identical. Creepy.

A shiver crawls over her shoulders and Jen turns to fetch her shawl from the warming rack by the fire. As she swirls it over her shoulders, another flash of emerald catches in the corner of her eye. She turns to the small, hand-sized picture of the two men, the ones her Da called lovers. There, again, is a young man who looks so very much like Liam that he could have sat for the portrait.

No. No, no, this is silly. This is just family resemblance. Like Margaret Selkirk and auntie Jane Carter, and Jennet. Jen clutches the shawl close around her arms, fingernails digging into the scratchy wool, and takes a step back. Then another. All the way to the wall between the windows, and narrows her gaze, lets it slide across the wall of family, really *looking* for the first time. There, in the first photograph, a twenty-something young man in a full formal dining suit, light hair and eyes and a cheeky smile. He is slightly apart from the family, perhaps an uncle or a brother-in-law, but one of the daughters is looking at him out the corner of her eye, and she is just the right age to be besotted. There, again, in a mid-century Polaroid, maybe the sixties judging by the hair styles, here is the green-eyed blond man holding up a stubby brown bottle of beer and grinning out at the antics happening on the loch. Under his face it says 'Cousin Lin' in someone's blue, feminine penmanship. There, in a somber black suit among the military uniforms of the brothers Carter as they take one last family shot before half of them are sacrificed to the First World War; there, whispering with a young man in the back of a ballroom; and there again, in the early nineties, auntie Jane sitting on his knee, face half-obscured by the glass of wine in her hand.

And all of them, every single face, is Liam.

***

Liam has no mobile phone. He's always just shown up, or met Jen at an agreed upon time and place. It is the middle of the night, there's no way he'll be in the woods, but Jen puts on her boots and a turtleneck and her pea coat anyway, clutches close a torch, and plunges into the woods.

"Liam!" she calls. "Liam!" She turns in circles, doing her best to follow the path back to the well. She'd know it in daylight, have no problems at all. She was bloody near born in these woods, played in them all her childhood, but now they are close and cold and creepy. Her torch light cuts harsh streaks across the gloom, startling deer and foxes and ravens from their rest. The birds protest loudly. "Liam!"

"Here, sweeting," a voice like black honey says, and Jennet turns into an embrace that is suddenly right where she needs it to be. Which is terrifying in its own way. "What's the fuss?"

"The paintings!" she pants. "Oh, god, the *pictures*."

"Ah," is all Liam says, and the way he says it means that he understands the rest.

Jennet jerks back, trying to peer up at his expression in the dark, but unless she wants to blind him with her flashlight, she can't make it out.

A scream is building behind her larynx, confusion and terror behind her eyes. But Jennet is Lady of Carterhaugh and master of her own body. She swallows heavily. "Come back to the house," is all Jennet says. It is rather more order than request. "We need to talk."

Liam takes her shoulders in his hands and bends down so their faces are a breath apart. "Be very certain, Jennet of Carterhaugh, that inviting me in to your home is what you really mean to do."

"I'm not scared of you," Jen says.

He searches her gaze, her face, eyes on her mouth, the lopsided dimple that only appears on her left side, as if testing the mettle of her resolve.

He nods slowly, meaningfully, just once. "Then lead the way.

***

When they reach Jen's apartments, she heads straight for the en suite, plugs the tub, and opens the taps. Liam is filthy and shivering. He hasn't washed since their tumble by the well and he stinks of rot and stale sex. They make love again in the bath. In the bubbles it is slow, and desperate, each clinging to the other, reaffirming that they are real, human, here.

Then she swaddles them both in thick terrycloth robes fetched from the B&B linen cupboard, and presses a snifter of brandy from her Da's private collection into his hand. She swirls her own, admiring the heady scent as Liam stands silent and solemn before the wall of Carterhaughs. Jen stands behind his shoulder, studying his face. Their hair leaves small wet spots on the carpet.

"Tell me I'm crazy," she says.

Liam turns to face her. "I can't."

"They're all you."

"Yes."

"You're *fucking with me.*"

He sets the snifter down on the mantle-place and cups her face in his hands. "My dearest Jennet, why would I lie to you? About this, the most important secret the Carterhaughs hold? I am the gift that one generation leaves to another."

"And did you sleep with all of them?" she spat, her confusion twisting into hurt and fury. "I mean, I thought... I thought I was *special.*"

"You are. You are mine now, and now you are special to me."

"But these others. Her, and her! And Him, and aunt Jane? Did you love them?"

Liam smiles sadly, then pries the brandy from her hands and sets it beside his own. "Are you jealous, my sweeting? I love you, now."

"But this is impossible," Jennet protests. "*What are you?*"

"Yours." He kisses the tip of her nose sweetly and she tries to fight off the way it makes heat pool low in her belly, desire crackle along her flesh. "And all the children of Carterhaugh. However few of you there may be. I begged your father to take a wife."

"My dad was gay," Jen says.

"And yet, there is you," her lover replies, a grin splitting his face.

"He was gay, not a dead fish," Jen counters. "He wanted to be a father, he could. It *is* the twenty first century."

"That it is," Liam agrees, his words amiable, his tone light, but something in his eyes grew dull and the sparkle ebbs for a moment. "Do you have another father, then?"

"Dad had a lover—" Jen began, but then stops herself. "I never met him. They were together before me, and after…" she trails off and shrugs. "They'd meet up now and again, out this way, but I never knew him."

"Eventually David's desire to be a father overrode all other loves," Liam says gravely. "I pushed too hard."

Jen snaps her gaze up to his face. "How did you know my father's name?"

"The Lord of Carterhaugh?" he mocks. "Everyone knew him. Or *of* him, at least."

Jen groans. "That old acorn? Really?"

"So you *do* know the gossip?" The glimmer returns to Liam's eyes.

Jen rolls her own.

Liam presses her close against his chest, his green gaze intent as he studies her face, sweeping down to take in the roses in her cheeks, the red blush on her chest. "The song, the fairy tale, it's famous. Everyone knows how my story began. But the rest of it?"

"What the old ditties in town say? About father being the last heir of Margaret and Tam Lin?"

"Well, that would actually make *you* the last heir now, wouldn't it?" Liam says.

Jen pauses, startled by the realization that he is correct. She's never thought of it like that before. The superstitious old folks always talk of boys when they make mention of fae lovers in the woods, of traditions and cutting the corners off houses to leave room for fairy paths, of bowls of milk and honey-soaked bread left out for the kind folk. Or at least to bribe them to remain kind.

"I suppose," Jen allows.

"It is the twenty first century after all," Liam mocks.

Jen scowls. "Not that it matters. They're just *stories*."

"Ah, but stories hold a truth. And what about you, my darling Jennet? Am I the only man in your life? In your bed?"

Jen jerks out of his grip. "How can you ask that? I've been dating you, only you!"

Liam smiles. "I have not asked you for monogamy. It is the twenty first century."

"Well, I'm not poly," Jen says.

"So then it is up to me," Liam replies darkly and reaches for her again, burying his nose in the damp strands of her hair. "I'm sure I can get you with child."

"I'm sure you can't," Jen says, grabbing the small tender hairs at the back of his neck and tugging hard, forcing him to meet her eyes. "And I think you need to slow the hell down. We've just established that you're *not fucking human*. That you're what, a fairy?"

"Fae-touched, please," he corrects with a moue of distaste. "I was not born so cruel."

"*Fae-touched*, whatever that means, so I think you can hold the hell up on the kids talk."

Liam grinds his hips forward, and Jen wouldn't be human if she didn't admit it got her a little hot under the collar.

"Why? You want me, and it's very easy to do. Your father managed an heir. Surely you could."

"It's not that easy," Jennet deflects. She presses her lips to his neck, tasting sweat and bath soap and well water.

"Sure it is," Liam says with a grin. "Just lie back and think of Carterhaugh."

"Shut up, Liam," Jen says and reaches down to tug on the belt of his robe, spreading the halves and pressing into the warmth between them. "Just can the kids talk. It's not erotic."

Liam inhales heavily through his nose, animalistic, strong, *so damn hot*, but then he ruins it by biting her lobe and saying, "But don't you want my children, Jennet? I will fill you with my seed, I will fuck a baby into you and our son will be *beautiful.*"

Jennet shoves him back so hard, so full of disgust, that he actually ricochets off of one of the wingback chairs. It falls over, whacking the wall, and one of the brandy snifters topples, smashing on the hearth and spilling alcohol into the fire. It flares and crackles, spitting indignantly as Jen shoves her hands into her robe pockets to keep from putting Liam's stupid, insensitive head through the goddamn *wall.*

"Jen, what have I—"

"Don't you *dare* try to override my desires with your own! Don't you *dare* try to change my mind when I have already told you what I do and do not want. You don't know better than me!"

"Jennet I—"

"I'm not a *child* you can just talk around to it!"

"Please, Jennet," Liam says, scrambling to get upright, wincing as he jostles his hard-on when he gets his rump back under him. "I didn't mean it like that. Only that I want—"

"I can't have kids!" Jennet fumes, refusing to allow him to continue. "I'm all messed up inside, okay? Happy now, Mister Sticks-his-nose-where-it-doesn't-belong? *Bloody hell!*"

Liam goes a new and interesting shade of pale and pulls himself to his feet. They aren't steady and he grips the mantle-place, avoiding the broken glass and gulping down the remains of the brandy from the second snifter.

"Sorry," Jen whispers after he manages to get a hold of himself. "We kept it pretty quiet but… there will be no heir of Carterhaugh."

"None?" Liam asks, and his voice is rough, and raw, and small. "None at all?"

"Not of my blood," Jennet says. "I could adopt. Maybe I should adopt. Such a big house, I'm sure there's a child in care who would love it. Carterhaugh does need an heir.

"But the heir of Carterhaugh *must* be of your lineage!" Liam blurts, spinning around to face her. He reels, knocks the second snifter and it smashes next to its brethren, small shards of glass flying up and scoring Liam's shins. He doesn't seem to notice. His face is suddenly flushing, even though his lips remain ghost-white. "Or else the—" He catches himself and bites down hard on the inside of his own cheek.

Jennet laughs. "Don't tell me you actually *believe* all that fairy tale nonsense."

Liam says nothing. He stares down into the fire, eyes distant and dim, and for a while Jennet lets him.

"What's wrong?" he finally asks.

Jen hates this conversation. She's had it over, and over, and over with well-meaning busy bodies who *do not understand* what it means to have to choose between a hypothetical future and a devastating present. She's not in the mood to have it again, so she flops down into the remaining wingback chair and crosses her arms petulantly. "Nothing, now."

"But if nothing's wrong, then why can't you have children?" Liam thunders.

Jen scoffs in the face of his rage, unaffected by his display of man-child rage. "Leaving aside the fact that you're making one *hell* of an assumption about whether I even *want* children, and a second bloody huge assumption about how a woman is *broken* or *wrong* or *useless* because the mechanism in her body has malfunctioned, it was either my uterus or my life, okay? *Jesus*."

Liam turns large, wet eyes to her. "You nearly died?"

"Yes," Jen bites out. "Complications from Polycystic Ovarian Syndrome."

"What does that mean?" He crouches down, lays his hands on her knees as if to console her, but it is patronizing and she *hates it* when someone tries to make her feel like a small child who just needs to have things explained to her better and then she'd understand, then she'd *care* Only she doesn't care, and she doesn't need to have it explained better, and she sure as *fuck* doesn't need anyone to make her feel guilty about saving her own life, so she sneers and says:

"They took out all of it. Everything."

"*Everything?*" Liam asks, horrified.

"Don't judge me," she spits. "This isn't your choice to make, you know. It's *my* body. I decide what is and is not injected into it, how it's cut up, what's taken out or what's put in. God, you're just like the doctors! All those old white guys, telling me they know what's best for me, making choices about my reproductive organs as if I was just a baby machine that has broken down and not a human being who has consciously and contentiously chosen *not to have children.*"

Liam cries so prettily, Jennet has to give him that. "But did they have to remove everything?"

"No," Jen says, "But I told them to anyway. To keep it from coming back."

"So you *made* them *cut out your*—"

"Not that it's any of your business, but yes!"

"I didn't know. David never—"

"Why would my father tell *you?*" Jen kicks his stomach gently, getting him to back up, and he stands. She regards Liam carefully, through the lens of this new information.

Liam shifts uncomfortably under her gaze, then stills himself and meets it. "It doesn't matter, now," Liam whispers.

They are silent again for a long time, neither of them willing to break their staring contest first.

"You can't honestly tell me it bothers you," Jen finally says.

"That you can't have children? It does."

"Why?" Jen spits. "It was *my* uterus. It has nothing to do with *you.*"

"It has *everything* to do with me!" Liam roars. And then he is gone, the door to her sitting room crashing against the wall, making the books in her shelf shiver with the force. He is a shadow streaking through the night, when she rushes to the window, swallowed by the trees, lost to the darkness and the woods.

Jennet sits on her little window seat and shakes, one hand pressed hard against her mouth, the other cupping the wide, grinning scar that smiles on her stomach.

***

Jennet doesn't see Liam for a week, and that makes her viciously pleased. When Karen and her husband and kids come over for dinner, Jen steadfastly does not allow herself to look at little Mattie and wonder. When Karen asks what happened to her beau, Jen tells an extremely edited version of the truth, and the three adults drink to being rid of douchebags.

It is Thanksgiving in the new world, and the elder Mathew Simmons is both Canadian and vegan. They celebrate with tofurkey and cranberry sauce, which Jen thinks is over-sweet and vile and ruins the flavor of the tofu, green bean casserole made with almond milk, and an utterly delicious agave pumpkin pie. When the meal is done, the Simmons go home, and the manor is devoid of servants and guests, and Jen feels horrifically, suddenly *alone*.

A bottle of wine and then some sloshing around her system, Jen puts on her pea coat and shawl and grabs a candle. A torch feels too *harsh*. When she is outside she walks to the plain, lights the candle and sticks it into the grass by her knee, and sits in the middle of a fairy ring. She's not surprised in the least when Liam sits down across from her after a few moments, clad once more in a green hoodie and black skinny jeans, even though Jen knows for a fact that he left them on her bathroom floor.

"*How* does it affect you?" she asks with no preamble.

"I missed you." He reaches for her hand and she pulls it back, hides the pair of them in her pockets.

"How?"

"Do you know the worst part about the stories?" Liam asks. "It's the magic. The *things* that the fae can do. They're not sweet. They don't laugh like bells, or have delicate dragonfly wings, or any of that. They are dark. They are *cruel.* Eyes of wood and a heart of stone," Liam says, touching his own chest. "That's what the Fairy Queen threatened."

He rubs with the heel of his hand against his sternum, as if to make sure that his heart is still there, still warm, still beating. "He was human. He was employed in collecting heather and he fell asleep in a fairy circle. This one."

Jen resist the recoiling urge to stand and jump out of it. But Liam, *Tam Lin*, is here with her, and she accepted his roses. She feels safe, here. When he reaches for her again, places his free hand on her knee, she doesn't push him away.

"He begged her not to, told the queen who had captured him, forced him into her entourage and bed, raped him… he begged her not to take that, too. To blind and murder him. And the queen didn't, because it was the human soul in his eyes that she loved so well, and his human heart that could swell and break that she loved to hold in her hands."

"She hurt him," Jen says, voice an awed hush, loathe to break into Liam's story, to startle him away from it. But she has to ask.

Liam blinked slowly, inner gaze still on that faraway court, still wandering the fairy lands. "The Good People, we call them. The Kind Folk. But it's not a name, it's an invocation. It's a plea. Be good to us, we beg. Because the Fae… they aren't good. They're capricious. What is a joke to them is crippling, maiming, murder to us. What they call lovemaking, we call rape. They forget that we're so very breakable. And they love to see pain. Hurt reflected back in a lover's eyes, a heart beating too fast, adrenaline sweat and cold fear. Wooden eyes can't cry. A stone heart can't bleed."

And now he is starting to panic, breaths becoming gulpy and shallow, desperate, fingers twisting into his hoodie.

"Liam," Jen says softly, reaching out to touch his shoulder.

He jumps, blinking hard, and made a sound like an aborted sob.

"I'm fine," he lies, after he has caught his breath again.

Jen let the falsehood hang heavy in the air. "In the stories, Margaret saved Tam Lin."

"That she did," Liam agrees. "And she loved him well. But they realized after a time… *we* realized, that Maggie was aging and I …was not. The Faery Queen had accepted that Tam Lin would not be her tithe that year, and released me to wed my rescuer. But she did not let me go."

"I don't understand."

"There was a child, in that painting," Liam whispers, his voice crackling over the grief.

"The art historian said so," Jennet agreed. "A little boy."

"Rab," Liam says. "He was seven years old. He died on All Hallows Eve."

Understanding struck swift and cold. "Dear God."

"Yes. I thought that was the Fae's revenge for having humiliated their queen. To take my firstborn son. But then our third child, a girl, the queen took her too, in her seventh year. So Margaret bore no more children. Thomas grew up and I did not grow older. So on the next tithing I threw myself on the mercy of the queen, begged her to take me instead of him, for he was twenty one then, with a wife and a babe of his own. And she laughed and took my grandson instead. And she said to me, *Tam Lin, I will take all your children for all of time, or I will take the world. I will stop the tithe and Hell will be upon this earth. Which would you prefer?* And so I… what else could I do, Jennet? What else could I *do?* My blood, my children, for as long as there are children, or me and then *everyone else?*"

"What do you mean, your children?" Jennet asks. "It's been centuries. Surely she can't still be after… us. Me?"

Liam takes her hands and kisses each of the palms.

"The closer to my blood, the better," Tam Lin explains. "When it grows too thin, I rejoin the family. I am a new lover, a husband, a cousin come a-courting. All Hallows Eve is next week, Jennet. You see my desperation."

"You fuck your own descendants and get them pregnant on *purpose*?" Jen asks, aghast. She tries to pull her hands back and he doesn't let go. The candle sputters.

"They enjoyed it, every one," Liam says with a shrug. "You've had no complaints."

Fury makes her suddenly strong. Jen wrenches a hand free and slaps him hard across the face.

Liam just grins as his lip splits and dribbles blood. "Ah, there's my Maggie."

Jen stands, stalks out of the circle and around it, too furious to leave, too upset to sit still. "And then what, you just let them die?"

"The Faerie Queen demands her tithes. Every seven years they must send a soul to hell, and about a third of the time she remembers that I owe her mine. The time between tithes is getting longer. It was nearly fifty years this time. Maybe one day she'll forget."

"And meantime, you give her your sons!"

"Sometimes the daughters," Liam says, light and unconcerned, perhaps slightly confused by her fury.

"You *vile, disgusting*, unbelievable *monster*!" Jen snarls.

"They all volunteered! They consented!" Liam protests. "Each and every one of them! Out of love! If not for me, then for their family!"

"Love!" Jen screeches. "What does a *seven year old* know of love and sacrifice! That is not *informed consent*."

"They knew the songs, the stories, they knew that one day they would—"

"Oh my god," Jen hisses, and her knees dump her onto the edge of the circle with such force that she hears a crack. She falls onto her side, to desolate to sit up. "Oh my god, *Da*."

There is a long silence, and then Liam crawls across the grass and buries his fingers tenderly in Jen's hair, massaging gently across her scalp. "He did it for love of you, Jennet Carter. He wanted to save the world from hell and he consented. He saved me," Liam finally chokes. *Tam Lin*. "He took my place."

"It was a heart attack," Jen protests.

"He was a tithe. He was a hero."

"It's not heroism," Jen protests. "It's suicide!" Jennet wrenches away from his touch, sitting up, turning around and shoving his shoulders hard enough that he slams back on the ground. His green eyes are wide and, for the first time, filled with fear.

"It could have been you. It *should have been you*, you revolting *coward*."

Fire snaps in that emerald gaze, burning away the surprise, and he kneels up and shoves her back. "And then who, Jennet Carter of Carterhaugh? After the Faery Queen has had her *Tam Lin*, then who would she come after? My descendants? There's only you left, and then who? Seven years after that? Who would she pick? The nearest human? Perhaps your Karen? She does so love her walks in the woods."

Jen claps her hands over her ears. "Stop."

"Or little Mattie?"

"Shut up!"

"Or perhaps some of your tourists, or your Mrs. MacDonald."

"*Shut up!*"

"I will not!" Liam roars. "Because *you will understand me*, Jennet Carter!"

"No!"

He grabs her wrists and yanks her hands down, trapping them in one hand. The other he digs into the hair behind her ear and holds her head still, so she can't look away, can't break his gaze.

"When my Maggie saved me from the tithing the Faery Queen vowed her revenge, and she is old, and she is dark, and she *has not forgotten.* The Faery Queen will *never give hell* one of her Fae, she will empty the world of humanity before she gives up her kin, and because I cannot *bear* to see the world destroyed I rip out my own heart and give it in their place. I give her children of my blood, yes, because they are raised to know what I will ask of them, and because I can *hold them here.*" He flings away her hands, thumps a fist into his own chest so hard it echoes through the night.

And does that make him a villain, or a hero, Jennet wonders, dazed.

Silence jams her ears, loud. Sizzling. It is broken only by wrenching, horrid sobs. Liam is curled on the grass, face against the dirt, shuddering, shivering, wracked. "I am a monster," he moans. "I hate myself and I hate her and it's not *fair.* I did no wrong, Jennet. I only fell asleep in a fairy circle. I didn't mean to. How was to know that the Fae love children so much? The Erokling…"

A frozen horror stabs into Jen's joints. Ghastly disgust and understand pull at her guts, and she swallows hard on the urge to vomit.

"What do they do to the children they take?"

Liam only sobs harder. "Ask me not, oh, ask me not," he weeps.

Jen stands outside of the circle they currently occupy. She watches the candle burn low, the stars wheel overhead. Slowly Liam's sobs go quiet, then still. He is limp with exhaustion, cradling his head, moaning and shivering in the damp of the grass and the chill of the night.

As he's been weeping, atoning for his sins, Jennet has been thinking. She is the daughter of Margaret, who stole Tam Lin once. It can be done again.

So when the candle is nothing more than a puddle of wax and a tenuous flame, she reaches out and pulls Liam's head onto her lap. She threads her fingers through his golden hair, dries the tears from his freckled cheeks, and asks: "How do you summon a Fae Queen?"

"Jennet, no!" he says, jerking upright.

"Tell me, or I'll find a way to do it myself, and I'm certain I'll do something wrong. So. Tam Lin of legend, tell me how to summon a Fae Queen."

"You need merely ask," a deep and melodious voice says, from somewhere just outside of the circle. It is accompanied by an uncomfortably chill breeze and the scent of nightshade. Her voice is devoid of all accent, flat and unnatural, and all warmth as well.

Liam buries his head in Jennet's lap and moans in fear.

"Ah, my Tam-a-Line," the Queen croons.

"*My* Tam-a-Line," Jennet corrects, straining to meet the Queen's gaze against the dark of the night, but her skin is obsidian and her eyes are white fire, and though Jennet raises her chin in defiance, she cannot meet the Queen square.

"I have heard that from one like you before. I shall assume that my wee man means to attempt to escape me in the arms of a mortal woman again."

"No," Jennet says. "This time it's I who defies you. And, I think, this means I'm the one to bargain with you."

The Queen laughs, and Liam scrambles into Jennet's embrace, holding her tight, pressing the bridge of his nose under her ear and whimpering, "No, don't do it, don't, don't, my sweeting, say nothing."

Jennet pets the back of his head, cleaves to him, clings, and whispers back, "This princess has chosen her husband. Now let her lay the path for rescue. Hush." She looks up at the Queen. "I understand your preoccupation with him, your majesty," Jennet says aloud, infusing her voice with as much coolness as she is able. "He's so beautiful when he weeps. His skin pinks so prettily." Liam whimpers and Jennet forces an indulgent laugh at the sounds. "He is a kitten. I will trade you for him."

"What can you have that I would want?" the Fae Queen asks.

"My children," Jennet offers, voice low and as emotionless as she can make it. She bites the inside of her cheek hard, to keep it from quivering. To maintain her bluff. "And my children's children."

"If they are of Carterhaugh blood, they are already mine," the Queen sneers.

"Ah, but only on the tithing. I offer you this: all the children of my womb. As soon as they are born, they are yours. Changelings for your court."

The white fire in the Queen's face burns brighter. "You would give me this? *All* your children?"

"I offer you all the children born of my womb as soon as they are free of it," Jennet agrees. "In return for Tam Lin's mortality. I want him human again, and free of your geis. He will begin to age again, slowly, naturally, and you will have no claim to him, nor any resident or visitor to Carterhaugh, for your tithing again."

"Done!" the Fae Queen cries. "Take your husband, human woman, and I will see you nine months for the first of my prizes!"

The breeze flutters again, the snuffling puddle of candle goes out, and slowly, all around them, the birds and the insects of the night resume their careful, cautious humming.

Liam looks up from his lap and stares at Jennet in awe.

"You…" he begins, but Jennet kisses him quiet.

"Not in the circle," she says, and they help each other stand, legs numb from the dew and the cold. As the sun rises, bloody and cold, they pick their way back to Carterhaugh manor. They share a bubble bath and when he combs the long strands of his hair out of his eyes, quiet and numb, Liam gives a cry and scrabbles at his head.

"What is it?" Jennet asks.

"A grey hair!" He turns in the tub, looking up into her face, and holds her tight, water-slick skin flush against hers. "Jen! Grey I'm free! Oh, my hero! My lover! Marry me!" he crows. "Take your prize, you've saved your damsel!"

"On two conditions," Jennet says, kissing his giggles into her own mouth. "First, tell me you love me for me. Not what is or isn't inside of me."

"Jennet, my Jennet," he whispers and smears kisses and promises against her neck. "You saved me, you saved me, and I am yours, forever. I love you, I love *you.*"

Jennet grins, a smile curling on her face to match the stretch of scar on her stomach. "And the second: do think your Fae Queen knows what a hysterectomy is?"

"No," Liam, *Tam Lin* says. "So let's go to bed and get a start on making that first child for her. Earnest effort will have to go into the endeavour."

"It's a deal," Jennet says, and takes him by the hand and leads him out of the waters of the bath, and into life; glorious, wonderful, messy *life.*

The Maddening Science

Bullets fired into a crowd. Children screaming. Women crying. Men crying, too, not that any of them would admit it. The scent of gun powder, rotting garbage, stale motor oil, vomit, and misery. Police sirens in the distance, coming closer, making me cringe against old memories. Making me skulk into the shadows, hunch down in my hoodie, a beaten puppy.

This guy isn't a supervillain. He isn't even a villain, really. He is just an idiot. A child with a gun. And a grudge. Or maybe a god complex. Or a revenge scheme. Who the hell cares what he thought he had?

In the end, it amounts to the same.

The last place I want to be is in the centre of the police's attention, *again*, so I sink back into the fabric, shying from the broad helicopter searchlights that sweep in through the narrow windows of the parking garage.

If this had been before, I might have leapt into action with one of my trusty gizmos. Or, failing that, at least with a witty verbal assault that would have left the moron boy too brain-befuddled to resist when I punched him in the oesophagus.

But this isn't before.

I keep my eyes on the sky, instead of on the gun. If the Brilliant Bitch arrives, I want to *see*.

No one else is looking up. It has been a long, long time since one of...us...has donned sparkling spandex and crusaded out into the night to roust the criminal element from their lairs, or to enact a plot against the establishment, to bite a glove-covered thumb at 'the man.' A long time since one of us has done much more than pretend to *not* be one of us.

The age of the superhero petered out surprisingly quickly. The villains learnt our lessons; the heroes became obsolete.

A whizzing pop beside my left ear. I duck behind the back wheel of a sleek penis-replacement-on-wheels. The owner will be very upset when he sees the bullet gouges littering the bright red altar to his own virility.

I've never been shot before. I've been electrocuted, eye-lasered, punched by someone with the proportional strength of a spotted gecko and, memorably, tossed into the air by a breath-tornado created by a hero whose Italian lunch my schemes had clearly just interrupted.

Being shot seems fearfully mundane after all that.

A normal, boring death scares me more than any other kind—especially if it's due to a random, pointless, unpredictable accident of time and place intersecting with a stupid poser with the combination to daddy's gun drawer and the key to mommy's liquor cabinet. I had been on the way to the bargain grocery store for soymilk. It doesn't look like I'm going to get any now.

Because only the extraordinary die in extraordinary ways. And I am extraordinary no longer.

I look skyward. Still no Crimson Cunt.

Someone screams. Someone else cries. I sit back against the wheel and refrain from whistling to pass the time. If I was on the other side of the parking garage, I could access the secret tunnel I built into the lower levels back when the concrete was poured thirty years ago. But the boy and his bullets are between us. I've nothing to do but wait.

The boy is using a 9mm Berretta, military issue, so probably from daddy's day job in security at the air force base. He has used up seven bullets. The standard Barrette caries a magazine of fifteen. Eight remain, unless one had already been prepared in the chamber, which I highly doubt as no military man would be unintelligent or undisciplined enough to carry about a loaded gun aimed at his own foot. The boy is firing them at an average rate of one every ninety-three seconds—punctuated by unintelligible screaming—and so by my estimation I will be pinned by his unfriendly fire for another seven hundred and forty-four seconds, or twelve point four minutes.

However, the constabulary generally arrive on the scene between six and twenty-three minutes after an emergency call. As this garage is five and a half blocks from the 2nd Precinct, I estimate the stupid boy has another eight point seven minutes left to live before a SWAT team puts cold lead between his ribs.

Better him than me.

Except, probability states that he will kill another three bystanders before that time. I scrunch down further, determined not to be a statistic today. This brings me directly into eye-line with a corpse.

There is blood all around her left shoulder. If she didn't die of shock upon impact, then surely she died of blood loss. Her green eyes are wide and wet.

I wonder who she used to be.

I wonder if she is leaving behind anyone who will weep and rail and attend the police inquest and accuse the system of being too slow, too corrupt, too over-burdened. I wonder if they will blame the boy's parents or his teachers. Will they only blame themselves? Or her?

And then, miraculously, she blinks.

Well, that certainly is a surprise. Perhaps the trauma is not as extensive as I estimated. To be fair, I cannot see most of her. She has fallen awkwardly, the momentum of her tumble half-concealing her under the chassis of the ludicrously large Hummer beside my penis-car.

I am so fascinated by the staggering of her torso as she tries to suck in a breath, the staccato rhythm of her blinks, the bloody slick of teeth behind her lips, that it's all over before I am aware of it.

This must be what people mean by time flying.

I'm not certain I've ever felt that strange loss of seconds ever before. I am so very used to being able to track everything. It's disconcerting. I don't like it.

And yet the boy is downed, the police are here, paramedics crawling over the dead and dying like swarming ants. I wait for them to find my prize, to pull her free of the SUV's shadow and whisk her away to die under ghastly fluorescent lights, too pumped full of morphine to know she is slipping away.

I wait in the shadow of the wheel and hope that they miss me.

They do.

Only, in missing me, they miss her, as well. She is blinking, gritty and desperate, and now the police are leaving, and the paramedics are shunting their human meat into the sterile white cubes, and they have not found her, my fascinating, panting young lady.

Oh dear. This is a dilemma.

I am reformed. I am no longer a villain. But I am also no hero and I like my freedom far too much to want to risk it by bringing her to the attention of the officials. What to do? Save her and risk my freedom, or let her die, and walk free but burdened with the knowledge of yet another life that I might have been able to save, and didn't?

I dither too long. They are gone. Only the media are left, and I certainly don't want *them* to catch me in their unblinking grey lenses. The woman blinks, sad and slow. She knows that she is dead. It's coming. Her fingers twitch towards me—reaching.

A responsible, honest citizen would not let her die. So I slink out of my shadow and gather her up, the butterfly struggle of her pulse in her throat against my arm, and slip away through my secret tunnel.

I steal her away to save her life.

***

It occurs to me, when I lean back and away from the operating table, my hands splashed with gore, that I've kidnapped this woman. She has seen my face. Others will see the neat way I've made my nanobots stitch the flesh and bone of her shoulder back together. They will recognize the traces of the serum that I've infused her with in order to speed up her healing, because I once replaced the totality of my blood with the same to keep myself disease free, young looking, and essentially indestructible. The forensics agents will know this handiwork for mine.

And then they will know that at least one of my medical laboratories escaped their detection and their torches. They will fear that. No matter that I gave my word to that frowning judge that I had been reformed, no matter that the prison therapist holds papers signed to that effect, no matter that I've personally endeavoured to become and remain honest, forthright, and supportive; one look at my lair will remind them of what I used to be, what they fear I might still be, and that will be enough. That will be the end. I will go back to the human zoo.

And I cannot have that. I've worked too hard to be forgotten to allow them to remember.

I take off the bloody gloves and apron and put them in my incinerator, where they join my clothing from earlier tonight. I take a shower and dress—jeans, a tee-shirt, another nondescript wash-greyed hoodie: the uniform of the youth I appear to number among. Then I sit in a dusty, plush chair beside the cot in the recovery room and I wait for her to wake. The only choice that seems left to me is the very one I had been trying to avoid from the start of this whole mess—the choice to go bad, again. I've saved her life, but in doing so, I've condemned us both.

Fool. Better to have let her died in that garage. Only, her eyes had been so green, and so *sad*...

I hate myself. I hate that the Power Pussy might have been right: that the only place for me is jail; that the world would be better off without me; that it's a shame I survived her last, powerful assault.

***

When she wakes, the first thing the young woman says is, "You're Proffes—"

I don't let her finish. "*Please* don't say that name. I don't like it."

Her sentence stutters to a halt, unsaid words tumbling from between her teeth to crash into her lap. She looks down at them, wringing them into the light cotton sheets, and nods.

"Olly," I say.

Her face wrinkles up. "Olly?"

"Oliver."

The confusion clears, clouds parting, and she flashes a quirky little gap between her two front teeth at me. "Really? Seriously? *Oliver?*"

I resist the urge to bare my own teeth at her. "Yes."

"Okay. Olly. I'm Rachel." Then she peers under the sheet. She cannot possibly see the tight, neat little rows of sutures through the scrubs (or perhaps she can, who knows what powers people are being born into nowadays?), but she nods as if she approves and says, "Thank you."

"I couldn't let you die."

"The Prof would have."

"I'm Olly."

She nods. "Okay."

"Are you thirsty?" I point to a bottle of water on the bedside table.

She makes a point of checking the cap before she drinks, but I cannot blame her. Of course, she also does not know that I've ways of poisoning water through plastic, but I won't tell her that. Besides, I haven't done so.

"So," she says. "Thank you."

I snort, I can't help it. It's a horribly ungentlemanly sound, but my disbelief is too profound.

"Don't laugh. I mean it," she says.

"I'm laughing *because* you mean it. Rachel." I ask, "How old are you?"

She blushes, a crimson flag flapping across a freckled nose, and I curse myself this weakness, this fascination with the human animal that has never managed to ebb, even after all that time in solitary confinement.

"Twenty-three," she says. She is lying—her eyes shift to the left slightly, she wets her lips, her breathing increases fractionally. I see it plain as a road sign on a highway. I also saw her ID when I cleaned out her backpack. She is twenty-seven.

"Twenty-three," I allow. "I was put into prison when you were eight years old. I did fifteen years of a life sentence and was released early on parole for good behaviour and a genuine desire to reform. The year prior to my sentencing I languished in a city cell, and the two before that I spent mostly tucked away completing my very last weapon. Therefore, the last memory you can possibly have of the 'Prof,' as you so glibly call him, was from when you were six." I sit forward. "Rachel, my dear, can you really say that at six years old you understood what it meant to have an honest to goodness supervillain terrorizing your home?"

She shakes her head, the blush draining away and leaving those same freckles to stand out against her glowing pale skin like ink splattered on vellum.

"*That* is why I laughed. It amuses me that I've lived so long that someone like you is saying *thank you* to me. Ah, and I see another question there. Yes?"

"You don't look old enough," she says softly.

I smile and flex a fist. "I age very, very slowly."

"Well, I know that. I just meant, is that part of the...you know, how you were born?"

"No," I say. "I did it to myself."

"Do you regret it?"

I flop back in my chair, blinking. No one has ever asked me that before. I've never asked myself. "I don't know," I admit. "Would you?"

She shrugs, and then winces, pressing one palm against her shoulder. "Maybe," she admits. "I always thought that part of the stories was a bit sad. That the Prof has to live forever with what he's done."

"No, not forever," I demur. "Just a very long time. May I ask, what stories?"

"Um! Oh, you know, social science—recent history. I had to do a course on the Superhero Age, in school. I was thinking of specializing in Vigilantism."

"A law student, then."

"Yes."

"How urbane."

"Yes, it sort of is, isn't it?" She smiles faintly. "What is it about superheroes that attracts us mousy sorts?"

"I could say something uncharitable about ass-hugging spandex and cock cups, but I don't think that would apply to you."

"Cape Bunnies?" she asks, with a grin. "No, definitely not my style."

"Cape Bunn—actually, I absolutely have no desire to know." I stand. I feel weary in a way that has nothing to do with my age. "If you are feeling up to it, Rachel, may I interest you in some lunch?"

"Actually, I should go," she says. "I feel fantastic! I mean, this is incredible. What you did. I thought I was a goner."

"You nearly were," I say.

"And *thank you*, again. But my mom must be freaking out. I should go to a hospital or something. At least call her."

"Oh, Rachel," I say softly. "You've studied supervillains. You know what my answer to that has to be."

She is quiet for a moment, and then those beautiful green eyes go wide. "No," she says.

"I am sorry. I didn't mean to trade my freedom for yours. I thought I was doing good. For *once*."

"But...but," she stutters.

"I can't."

She blinks and then curses. "Stupid, I'm not talking about that! I mean, they can't really think that about you, can they? You saved my *life*. This...this isn't a bad thing!"

I laugh again. "Are you defending me? Are you sure that's wise?"

"Don't condescend to me!" she snaps. "That's not *fair*. You've done your time. You saved me. Isn't that enough for them?"

"Oh, Rachel. You certainly do have a pleasant view of the world."

"Don't call me naive!" The way she spits it makes me think that she says this quite often.

"I'm not," I say. "Only optimistic." I gesture through the door. "The kitchen is there. I will leave the door unlocked. I've a closet through there—take whatever you'd like. I'm afraid your clothing was too bloody."

"Fine," she snarls.

I nod once and make my way into the kitchen, closing the door behind me to leave her to rage and weep in privacy. I know from personal experience how embarrassing it is to realize that your freedom has been forcefully taken from you, in public.

***

I built this particular laboratory-cum-bolthole in the 1950s, back when the world feared nuclear strikes. I was a different man then, though no less technologically apt, and so it has been outfitted with all manner of tunnels and closets, storage chambers, libraries, and bedrooms. The fridge keeps food fresh indefinitely, so the loaf of bread, basket of tomatoes and head of lettuce I left here in1964 are still fit makings for sandwiches. I also open a can of soup for us to share.

She comes out of the recovery room nine thousand and sixty-six seconds—fifteen point eleven minutes—after; a whole three minutes longer than I had estimated she would take. There is stubbornness in her that I had not anticipated, but for which I should have been prepared. She did not die in that garage, and it takes great courage and tenacity to beat off the Grim Reaper.

"I'm sorry, Oliver," she says, and sits in the plastic chair. I suppose the look is called "retro" now, but this kitchen was once the height of taste.

"Why are you apologizing to *me?*" I set a bowl in front of her. She doesn't even shoot me a suspicious look; I suppose she's decided to take the farce of believing me a good person to its conclusion.

"It sucks that you're so sure people are going to hate you."

"Aren't they?"

She pouts miserably and sips her soup. It's better than the rage I had been expecting, or an escape attempt. I wasn't looking forward to having to chase her down and wrangle her into a straitjacket, or drug her into acquiescence. I would hate to have to dim that keen gaze of hers.

I sit down opposite her and point to her textbook, propped up on my toaster oven for me to read as I stirred the soup. It had been in the bloody backpack I stripped from her, and seemed sanitary enough to save. Her cell phone, I destroyed.

"This is advanced, Rachel," I say. "Are you enjoying it?"

She flicks her eyes to the book. "You've read it."

"Nearly finished. I read fast."

"You didn't flip to the end?"

"Should I?"

"No," she blurts. "No. Go at your own pace. I just...I mean, I do like it," she said. "Especially the stuff about supervillain reformation."

I sigh and set down my spoon. "Oh, Rachel."

"I'm serious, Oliver! Just let me make a phone call. I promise, no one will arrest you. I won't even tell them I met you."

"You won't have to."

She slams her fists into the tabletop, the perfect picture of childish frustration. "You can't keep me here forever."

"I can," I say. "It is physically possible. What you mean to say is, 'You don't *want* to keep me here forever.'"

She goes still. "Do you want to?"

I can. I know I can. I can be like one of those men who kidnaps a young lady and locks her in his basement for twenty years, forcing her to become dependent on him, forcing her to love him. But I don't want to. I've nothing but distaste for men who can't *earn* love, and feel the need to steal it. Cowards.

"No," I say.

"Then why are you hesitating? Let me go."

"Not until you're fully healed, at least," I bargain. I'm not used to bargaining. Giving demands, yes. But begging, never. "When no trace of what I've done remains. Is that acceptable?

But in return, you must not try to escape. You could hurt yourself worse, and frankly I don't want to employ the kind of force that would be required to keep you. That is my deal."

"You promise?"

I sneer. "I don't break promises."

"I know," she says. "I read about that, too. Okay. It's a deal."

***

I spend the night working on schematics for a memory machine. I've never tampered with the mind of another before—I respect intellect far too much to go mucking about in someone's grey matter like a child in a tide pool—but I have no other choice. Rachel cannot remember our time together.

Rachel sleeps in one of the spare bedrooms. She enjoyed watching old movies all afternoon, and I confess I enjoyed sitting beside her on the sofa. We had frozen pizza for dinner, and her gaze had spent almost as much time on the screen as on my face.

In the morning, my blueprints are ready and my chemicals begin to simmer on Bunsen burners. I leave the lab and find her at the kitchen table, drinking coffee and flipping through my scrapbook. It's filled with newspaper articles and photos, wanted posters and DVDs of news broadcasts. I've never thought to keep it in a safe or to put it away somewhere because, besides Miss Rachel, no one has ever been to this bolthole but me.

"You found the soymilk, I see," I say. She nods and doesn't look up from her intense perusal of a favourite article of mine, the only one where the reporter *got it*. "And my book."

"It's like a shrine," she says. "I thought you'd hate all these superheroes, but there's just as much in here about them as you."

"I've great respect for anyone who wants to better the world." I touch the side of the coffeepot —still warm. I pour myself a cup and sit across from her.

"See... that's what's freaking me out, a bit," she says. "You're such a..."

"What?"

"You seem like such a sweet guy."

I laugh again.

"What?"

"Don't mistake my youth for sweetness."

"I'm not, but...I don't know, you're not a supervillain."

"I'm not a superhero, either."

"You can be something in the middle. You can just be a nice guy."

"I've never been just a 'nice guy,' Rachel. Not even before."

"I think you're being one now." She leans across the table and kisses me. I don't close my eyes, or move my mouth. This is a surprise too, but an acceptable one.

When she sits back, I ask, "Is this why you were studying my face so intently last night while you pretended to watch movies?"

She blushes again, and it's fascinating. "Shut up," she mumbles.

I smile. "Are you a Cape Bunny after all, Miss Rachel?"

"A Labcoat Bunny, maybe," she says. "I've always gone for brain over brawn."

"Who are you lashing out against," I ask calmly, my tone probably just this side of too cool, "that you think kissing the man who has kidnapped you is a good idea?"

Rachel drops back down into her seat. "Way to ruin the moment, Romeo."

"That is not an answer."

"No one!"

"And, *that*, dear Rachel, is a lie."

She throws up her hands. "I don't know, okay! My mother! The school! The courts! The whole stupid system! A big stupid world that says the man who saved my life has to go to *jail* for it!"

"I am part of the revenge scheme, then," I say. "If you come out of your captivity loving your captor, then they cannot possibly think I am evil. You have it all planned out, my personal redemption. Or perhaps this is a way to earn a seat in that big-ticket law school?"

She stares at me, slack jawed, a storm brewing behind those beautiful green eyes. "You're a bit of a dick, you know that?"

"That is what the Crimson Cunt used to—"

"Don't call her that."

"Why not? The Super Slut won't hear me say it. Not under all this concrete."

"Shut up!"

"Why?" I sneer. "Protecting a heroine you've never met?"

"She deserves better, even from you!"

"Oh, have I ruined your image of me, Rachel? Am I not sweet and misunderstood anymore?"

"You still shouldn't—"

"What, hate her? She put me in jail!" I copy her and slam my fists on the tabletop. My mug topples, hot liquid splashing out between us. "I think I've a right to be bitter about that."

"But it was for the good! It made you *better*."

"No, it made me cowed. I've lost all my ambition, dear

Rachel. And that is why I am just a normal citizen. I am too *tired.*"

"But Divine—"

"*Don't* say her name, either!"

Rachel stands and pounds her fists on the table again, shaking my fallen mug, and I stand as well, too furious to want to be shorter than her.

"Asshole!" she snarls.

"And she was a ball-breaker on a power trip. She was no better for the city than I! The only difference was that she didn't have the gumption, the ambition, the *foresight* to do what had to be done! I was the only one who saw! *Me.* She towed the line. She kept the status quo. I was trying to change the world! She was just a stupid blonde bimbo with huge tits and a small brain—"

"Don't talk about my mother that way!"

Oh.

I drop back down into my seat, knees giving way without my say-so. "Well, this is a turn," I admit.

"Everyone knows!" she spits. "It's hard to miss. Same eyes, same cheekbones."

"I've never seen your mother's eyes and cheekbones."

"What, were you living under a rock when she unmasked?"

I smile, and it's thin and bitter. "I was in solitary confinement for five years. By the time I got out, it must have been old news. And I had no stomach to look up my old nemesis."

Rachel looks away, and her eyes are bright with tears that don't skitter down her cheeks. I wonder if they are for her mother, or for herself, or because I've said such terrible things and her opinion of me has diminished. They are certainly not because she pities me.

Nobody pities me. I got, as I am quite often reminded, exactly what I deserved.

"What does your mother do now?" I ask, after the silence has become unbearable. There is nothing to count or calculate in the silence, besides the precise, quiet click of the second hand ticking ever onward, ever onward, while I am left behind.

"Socialite," Rachel says. "Cars. Money. Married a real estate developer."

"Is he your father?"

She swings her gaze back to me, sharp. "Why would you ask that?"

"Why does the notion that he might not be offend you?"

Her lips pucker, and with that scowl, I can see it: the pissy frown, the stubborn thrust of her chin. There is the Fantastic Floozy, hating me through her daughter.

"It doesn't," she lies. She twists her hands in front of her again. "Fine, it does. I don't know, okay? I don't think she knows. She wants it to be him."

"So do you," I press. "Because that would make you normal."

She looks up brusquely.

"Please, Rachel," I say. "I am quite clever. Don't insult us both by forgetting. The way you do your hair, your clothes, the law school ambitions, it all screams 'I don't want to be like my mother.' Which, if your mother is a superheroine, probably means that you are also desperate to not be one of...us."

"I'm not," she whispers.

"I dare say that if you have no desire to, then you won't be," I agree. I lean forward to impart my great secret. She's the first I've told and I don't know why I'm sharing it.

Only, perhaps, that it will make her less miserable. "Here is something they never tell anyone: if you don't use your powers, if you don't flex that extra little muscle in your grey, squishy brain, it will not develop. It will atrophy and die. Why do you think there are so few of us now? Nobody *wants* to be a hero."

"Really?" she whispers, awed, hatred draining from her face.

"Really," I say. "Especially after the sort of example your mother set."

Rachel rocks back again, the furious line between her eyebrows returning, and yes, I recognize that, too, have seen that above a red domino mask before.

"Why do you *say* things like that?" she asks, hands thrown skyward in exasperation. She winces.

"Don't rip your stitches, my dear," I admonish.

"Don't change the subject! You wouldn't talk about the Kamelion Kid that way, or Wild West, or...any of them! You'd have respect! What about The Tesla? You respect him. I've seen the pictures on your wall and you—why are you laughing?"

And I am laughing. I am guffawing like the bawdy, brawling youth I resemble. "Because I *am* The Tesla!"

She rocks back on her heels, eyes comically wide and then suspiciously narrow. "But you...Prof killed The Tesla."

"In a sense, he did."

Her eyes jump between me and the door to my lab—the only door locked to Rachel—and back to me. "You were a hero first."

"Yes."

"And it didn't work, did it?"

"...no."

"Because people...people don't want to change. Don't want to *think*."

"Yes. My plans would have been good for society. Would have forced changes for the better. But people just want a hero to keep things the way they already are."

She looks at her law textbook, which rests exactly where I had left it the night before, propped on the toaster oven.

"So you made it look like The Tesla was dead."

"Heroes can save the world. But villains can *change* it, Rachel."

She looks up. "I think I want to hate you, Olly, but I can't figure out if I should."

"It's okay if you hate me," I say. "I won't mind."

"Yes, I think you would," she says. She flattens her right palm over her left shoulder.

We sit like that for a long moment. I forget to count the seconds. Time flies when I am around Rachel, and I find that I am beginning to enjoy it.

***

Rachel sulks in her room for the afternoon, which bothers me not at all, as I've experiments to attend. When I come back out, she is sullenly reading her textbook on the sofa, and she has found the beer. One open bottle is beside her elbow and three empty ones are on the floor.

"It's not wise to drink when you're on antibiotics," I say, wiping my hands on my labcoat. They leave iridescent green smears on the fabric, but it's completely non-toxic or I would not be exposing her to it.

"I'm not *on* antibiotics," she mutters mulishly.

"Yes, you are," I counter. "There is a slow-release tablet under your skin near the wound."

She makes a face and pushes away her textbook. It slaps onto the carpet. "That's just gross."

"But efficient."

She looks up, gaze suddenly tight. "What else did you put in me?"

I walk over and take away her beer. And then, because it would be a waste of booze to dump it down the sink, and I have been on a limited income since I ceased robbing banks, and because I enjoy the perverseness of having my lips on the same bottlemouth as hers after having so recently admonished her for kissing me, I take a drink.

"Not that, if that's what you're implying, my dear Rachel," I say. She blinks hard, my innuendo sinking home.

"What? What, no! I didn't mean..."

"I'm more of gentleman than that."

"I get that!" she splutters. "I just mean...where did you get the replacement blood? What kind of stitches? Am I bionic now?"

"No more than you were before," I say. "Nanobots are actively knitting the torn flesh back together, but they will die in a week and your liver will flush them from your system. The stitches and sutures are biodegradable and will dissolve by then. The rest of the antibiotic tablet will be gone in two or three days, and the very small infusion of my vitality serum only gave your immune system a boost and your regenerative drive a bit of extra gas. You are in all ways, my dear Rachel, utterly and completely unextraordinary. Your greatest fear is unrealized." I finish off the beer with a swig, liking the way her green eyes follow the line of my throat as I swallow, and then go to the kitchen and retrieve two more.

I hand one to her and flop down onto the sofa beside her. She curls into a corner to give me enough room and then, after eyeing the mess on my coat, thrusts impertinent—and freezing!—toes under my thigh. "Dear me, Rachel, stepping up your campaign?"

"You started it," she says. "Re-started it. With the...bottle thingy."

I arch a teasing eyebrow. "Bottle thingy?"

She shakes her head. "I think I'm a little drunk."

"I think you are," I agree.

"Enabler," she says, and we clink beers. She drinks and this time I watch her. Her throat is, in every way, normal. Boring. I cannot stop looking at it. Her toes wiggle. "How can you read me so well?" she asks. "I mean, I didn't even have to say, 'I'm scared of turning into my mom,' but you knew."

I shrug. "I'm a great student of the human creature. We all say so much without saying a thing."

"Do you ever say more than you want to?"

I smile secretively, a flash of teeth that I know will infuriate her with its vagueness. "Rarely, any more. I've had a long time to learn to control my, as poker players would call them, 'tells.'"

"Hmph," she mutters and takes another drink. I swallow some of my beer to distract myself. She wriggles her toes again, and pushes them further. Soon they will brush right against my...but I assume that is the point.

"Careful, Rachel," I warn. "Are you certain this is something you want to do?"

"Yes."

"You are drunk and you want revenge on your mother."

"Maybe. Maybe I want to thank you for saving my life. Maybe I want to reward you for being a good guy."

"What if I don't want your thanks, or your reward?" I ask.

She smiles and her big toe tickles the undercurve of my testes. "Don't you?" she asks, and her expression is salacious. I provided her with no bra, I had none to give, and under my borrowed tee-shirt her nipples are pert.

"I do." I set aside both of our beers and reach for her. She comes into my arms, gladly, little mouth wet and insistent against mine as she wriggles her way onto my lap. Iridescent green smears up her thighs. "But maybe...oh!" I gasp into her mouth as clever little fingers work their way inside my waistband. I return the favour. Intelligence must be rewarded.

"Maybe?" she prompts, pressing down against my hand.

"Maybe I just want revenge on your mother, too."

She jerks back as if I've bitten her. "Oh my god, how can one man be such a *dick?*"

I press upwards so her pelvis comes in contact with the part of my anatomy in discussion. "I am honest, Rachel. There is a difference."

She sits back, arms crossing over the breasts I hadn't yet touched. "An honest supervillain," she scoffs.

I stand, dumping her onto the floor. "I think we're done here."

"Are we, Profess—"

"I've *asked you* not to call me *that!*"

She cowers back from my anger. Then it fuels her. "Fuck you, Olly," she says, standing.

"I thought that was the idea," I agree, "but apparently not."

"You're nothing like I thought you'd be!"

I laugh again. "And how could you have had *any* concept of how I'd be? Did the Dynamic Dyke tell stories? I bet she did. And you felt sorry for me. The poor Professor, beat up by mommy, hated - like you were. An outcast, like you were. Not good enough, like you were. Was I your imaginary friend,

Rachel? Did you write my name in hearts on your binders? Did you *fantasize* about me?"

"Shut up!" she screams.

Her cheeks are red again, her eyes glistening, her mouth bruised, and I want to grab her, kiss her, feel her ass through the borrowed sweatpants. Instead I fold my hands behind my back, because I told the truth before—I am a gentleman. I say nothing.

"You're not supposed to be like this!"

"Be like what?" I ask, again. "Explain, Rachel."

She collapses. It's a slow folding inward, knees and stomach first, face in her hands, physicality followed by emotion as she sobs into the carpet. I stand above her and wait, because she deserves this cry. Crying helps people engage with their emotions, or so I'm told.

When her sobbing slows, precisely one thousand six hundred and seventy-three seconds later—twenty-seven point nine minutes—she unfolds and stands, wiping her nose. I offer her a handkerchief from the pocket of my labcoat, and she takes it and turns her back to me, cleaning up her face.

She picks up the textbook. She opens it to the back, to those useless blank pages that are the fault of how books are bound, and for the first time in a very, very long time, I am shocked.

The back of the book has been collaged with photographs. Of me.

Computer printouts of me when I was the Prof. Newspaper clippings of my trial. Me, walking down the street, hunched into the shadow of my sweater's hood. Me, buying soymilk. Me, through the window of the shitty apartment on which Oliver Munsen can barely afford to pay rent. Me, three days ago, cutting through that same parking garage.

Genuine joy floods my blood. A small shot of adrenaline seethes up into my brain and I can't help the smile, because I missed this, I really did. "Oh, Rachel. Are you my stalker? How novel! I've never had a stalker before."

She snaps the cover shut. "I'm not a stalker."

"Just an admirer?" I ask, struggling to keep the condensation out of my voice. "Or do you want me to teach you how to be a villain? *Really* get back at mommy dearest?" Her expression sours. "Ah. But you already know that you can't be. You knew before I told you that you were born boring. So this is the next best thing." I reach out, grasp her elbows lightly, rub my callused thumbs across the tender flesh on the inside of them. She shivers. "Tell me, how were you going to do it, Rachel? Were you going to accidentally bump into me in that parking garage? Were you going to spill a beer on me in a bar? Buy me a coffee at my favourite cafe? Surely getting shot was not in the plan."

"It's not like that!" she says, but her eyes are closed, her lashes fluttering. Her chest bobs as she tries to catch her breath.

"Then what is it like?"

"I don't know! I just...I just *saw* you one day, okay? I recognized you, from mom's pictures on the wall, and I thought, you know, I should tell her. But I thought I would follow you first, you know, figure out where you live, or something."

"Except that I wasn't being dastardly and villainous."

"You sat in the bookstore and read a whole magazine. And then you *paid* for it."

I smirk. "How shocking."

"For me it was." She tips forward, breasts squishing, hot and soft, against my chest. "The kinds of stories I heard about you as a kid..."

"And you were fascinated."

"And I was fascinated."

"And so you followed me."

"I followed you."

"And then what, my dear Rachel?"

She wraps her arms around my neck and pulls me down for a kiss I don't resist.

"You seemed so lonely," she says, breath puffing into my mouth. "Are you lonely, Olly?"

"Oh, yes." I pick her up and carry her off to her bedroom.

The mattress is new, she is the first person to ever have slept on it, but it still squeaks. After, she drops off, satisfied, mumbling amusing endearments about how wonderful it is to make love to someone who is so studious, makes such a thorough examination of his subjects.

Tonight I decide to sleep. I don't do it very often, but I don't want to be awake anymore. I don't want to think. I close my eyes and force my dreams to stay away.

***

In the morning, I'm troubled. I think I've made a very bad choice, but I'm not sure how to rectify it. I am not even sure how to articulate it.

Rachel was right. I am lonely. I am desperately, painfully lonely. And I will be for the rest of my unnaturally long life. But Rachel is lonely, too. Desperate in her own way, desperate for the approval of a mother I can only assume was distant and busy in Rachel's youth, and then too famous and busy in her adolescence. Rachel wants to be nothing like her mother, wants to hurt her, punish her, and yet...wants to impress her so very badly that she is willing to take the ultimate step, to profess love for a man her mother once hated, to 'fix him,' to 'make him better.' To make him, *me*, good.

Only, Rachel doesn't understand. I don't want to *be* better, or good, or saved. I just want to live my boring, in-extraordinary life in peace and quiet, and then die. I don't want to be her experiment. And yet her fierce little kisses... her wide green eyes...

I look down at the schematics under my elbow and sigh. The scent of burning bacon wafts in through the vents that lead to the kitchen, and the utter domesticity of it plucks at the back of my eyes, heating them. I 'm still a fool, and I'm no less in over my head than I was two days ago.

I abandon the lab and rescue my good iron skillet from the madwoman who has pushed her way into my life. When she turns her face up for a kiss, I give it to her, and everything else she asks for, too.

And I can have this, because I am not a supervillain any more. But I am not a superhero either. If I was, I could turn her away, like I should.

After lunch, I hand her my cell phone. It has been boosted so that the signal can pass through concrete bunker walls, but cannot be tracked back to its location.

"What's that for?" she asks.

"Call your mother," I say. "Tell her you're okay. You're just staying with a friend. The shooting freaked you out."

She frowns. "What if I don't want to?"

"You were arguing that I should let you call."

"Yeah, before."

"Rachel," I admonish. "Do you really want *her* frantically looking for you?"

She pales. I imagine what it must have been like for her when she ran away from home for the first time. "No, guess not," she mumbles and dials a number. "Yeah, hi Mom. No, no, I'm cool. Yeah, decided to stay with a friend instead of coming home from campus this weekend. No, no, it's fine. I'm fine. There's no need for the guilt trip! I said I'm fine! God!...okay. Right. Sorry. Okay. I'll see you next..." she looks at me. "Next Saturday?" I nod. "Next Saturday. Right. Fine. I love you, too." She hangs up and places the phone between us. "There, happy?"

"Yes. I am curious Rachel, how do you intend on springing me on your mother? And how will you keep her from punching my face clear off?"

She picks at her cuticles. "I hadn't really thought that far ahead."

"I gathered." I stand from the table and go to do the dishes. I can't abide a mess.

She comes up behind me and wraps her arms around my waist and presses her cheek against my back, and asks, "What do you want to do this afternoon?"

"Whatever you want," I say. "I'm all yours." I turn in her arms to find her grinning. She believes me, whole-heartedly, and she should. I never lie, and it's the truth. For now.

***

When the week is over, I sit her down on my operating table and carefully poke around the bullet wound. In the x-ray, the bones appear healed without a scar. Her skin is dewy and unmarked. The stitches have dissolved and a scan with a handheld remote shows that the nanobots are all dead and ninety-three percent have been flushed from her system. I anticipate the other seven percent will be gone after her next trip to the toilet.

I do another scan, a bit lower down, but there is nothing there to be concerned about, either. We have not been using prophylactics, but I've been sterile since I used the serum. It was a personal choice. I had no desire to outlive my grandchildren.

Rachel hops from the table, bare feet on the white tile, and grins. "It's Saturday!" she says.

"Yes, it is."

"Time to go!"

"Yes."

She takes my hand. "And you're coming with me, Olly. You're coming with me and then they'll see, they'll all *see*. You're different now. You're a good man."

I smile and close my fingers around hers and, for the first time in many decades, I lie. "Yes, I am, thank you." I use our twined fingers to pull her into the kitchen. "Celebratory drink before we go?"

She grins. "Gonna open that champagne I saw in the back of the fridge?"

I laugh. "Clever Rachel. I can't hide anything from you."

Only I can. I am. When I pop the cork she shrieks in delight. Every ticking second of her happiness stabs at me like a branding iron and dagger all in one.

I thought I would need a whole machine, a gun, a delivery device, but in the end my research and experiments offered up a far more simplistic solution: rohypnol. Except that it is created by me, of course, so it's programmable, intelligent in the way the cheap, pathetic drug available to desperate, stupid children in night clubs is not. My drug knows which memories to take away.

Clever, beautiful, dear Rachel trusts me. I pour our drinks and hand her the glass that is meant for her. I smile and chat with her as she sips, pretending to be oblivious as her eyelids slip downwards, giving her no clue that there is anything amiss.

I catch both her and the glass before they hit the floor. Tonight she will wake in her own bed. She will honestly remember spending the week with a friend she then had a fight with, and no longer speaks to. She will wonder what happened to her backpack, her cell phone, her law textbook. She will not remember the Prof, or The Tesla. Her mother will be annoyed that she will have to tell her the stories over again, stories that Rachel should have internalized during her childhood.

And I will shut down this hidey-hole and go back to my apartment and cash my welfare cheque and watch television. And it will be good. It will be as it should be.

The stupid boy with the gun might have been the bad guy in our little melodrama, but I am the villain.

I am the coward.

Ghosts

Author's Note: *This story is part of the larger world of 'The Accidental Turn Series', about a fictional stereotypical epic fantasy series titled 'The Tales of Kintyre Turn', which follow hero Kintyre and his sidekick and friend Bevel Dom. This story is set after the eighth and final book of that non-existent series, when the author has ceased to write them and the characters - in charge of their own agency for once, but still beholden to the way the Great Writer shaped their characters - are just coming to understand themselves as fully-rounded people.*

The messenger hawk is only odd because it wears a band of Turn-russet around one leg. I'm more used to seeing Carvel-green, or, if Mum can scrape together enough to cover the expense of a hawk and the emergency is dire enough, Dom-amethyst.

It lands first on a branch close to Kintyre's head, overhanging the stream where Kin is grumpily scrubbing our travel pots out with sand. As he always does, Kin ignores the ruddy thing. The hawk chirrups in disdain and hops down to the ground. It bobbles over to me like a grouchy pigeon, sidestepping the still smoking ashes of my morning cookfire. I was in the middle of packing away our leftovers, so I've got some jerky in my hand. I offer it up, and the hawk snips at it daintily, careful of my fingers. The beast is probably the politest of the three of us. Kin and I don't work too hard on our table manners when we're out-of-doors.

"Never know why you lot always go to Kin first," I say, wiping jerky grease on my trousers and then shaking a finger at the hawk. "I'm the one that feeds ya."

As a kind of answer, the hawk fluffs up in the sunlight, resettling its feathers after what has probably been a long flight. I've always liked how sleek the creatures are, how deadly, and at the same time, how much they look like a curious cuddle toy. The hawk lets me scritch along the crest between its eyes, crooning. I smooth back the small plume of white that marks this bird as a messenger, as one of the breed clever enough to recognize different human faces and follow simple verbal commands. Dead useful things, these birds.

Appeased, the hawk lifts its foot and I untie its burden. Covering a yawn—didn't sleep so well last night—I wonder if there's enough heat in the embers of our fire to kick it back up and boil another kettle of tea. It's not like Kin and I have anywhere else to be, and the thought of a long, lazy morning fishing and napping is suddenly delicious. Yeah. Could do lots with a day of nothing.

I'm also missing the warmth of the last lassie we left behind, if I'm honest about it. And that of her father's hayloft as well. But we're one day's walk from Estagonnish, and there's no bloody inns between here and the next sprout of farms. Just sparse forest interspersed with wildflower meadows, and the curving sweep of a balls-cold stream.

Good for catching rabbit and eel. Bad for a good night's rest. And after all the adventures we've been on—and enemies we've made—I'm not too keen on sleeping out in the open. Or, really, anywhere that's lacking a roof and walls, a door that can be boobytrapped, and a window that makes noise when it's broken. Sleeping out under the stars sounds heroic when I write that sort of drivel, but in reality, it fills me with wary paranoia. And it's bloody chilly to boot. 'Cause unless there's a pair of tits between us, Kintyre's not too keen on sharing body heat.

Shame, that.

Of course, this bone-weariness knifing through me doesn't just stem from bad sleep. Not even really from our most recent quest, or from the bloody great sword-fight it took to vanquish the Dark Elf. No. It's from the many, many houses filled with so many grieving people.

I am wrung out from comforting so many husbands and wives, parents, children, and lovers while returning the jars of eyes stolen and collected by the Elf. Their grief is like a greasy smear against my skin. I feel a hundred years old, pulled loose and weak by the weight of it.

Sadness always makes me absolutely *bagged.*

I yawn again and try to cover my mouth, then wince, juggling the hawk's note into my off hand. *Writer's nutsack, that aches.* In my morning haze, I forgot that I wrenched my wrist in the fight. I'm going to have to rewrap it soon. Or maybe I should go shove my arm into the stream for a bit, see if the cold won't do some of its own magic on the swelling.

The bird, freed from duty, pops up onto a nearby branch and preens its wings. It's trained to wait for a return message, if I want to send one. But more likely it's waiting for more jerky. I could send it away, back to Turn Hall, with the hand gesture that means "*go home.*" It would go, empty-pouched and immediately, but . . . nah. Maybe, like me, the damned thing deserves a rest after its long task. Maybe it could use a lazy afternoon on the riverbank, too. I could feed it fish guts, if it wanted them.

Or maybe the hawk might appreciate a mug of reviving tea. That brings up the image of a hawk with its whole head jammed into one of our metal cups and I grin. Then I stand, wiping soot on the thighs of my leather trousers.

"Kin," I chortle. "Post!"

"Who's it from?" Kin asks, standing. He leaves the pots by the shore—hopefully somewhere where they won't wash away again, or I'll put my boot up his arse and make him go for a swim to fetch them back—and saunters his way back to the campsite, in no rush this fine morning. Kin squints at the hawk's leg-band. That wrinkle appears between his eyebrows, the one that I still haven't been able to describe correctly when I write about it. "Not *actually* Turn Hall?"

"Why not Turn Hall?"

"Most likely the Sheriff," Kintyre says, dismissing my question and the assumption that it could be his younger brother all at the same time. "Sneaking Forssy's things again."

"You know, your brother is actually quite generous," I point out. "Never lets us leave Turn Hall without full ration packets and wineskins. 'Course, he'd never admit it."

"He's a pretentious twat."

"I won't argue with that. I'm just saying he's a *generous* pretentious twat. Pointe wouldn't've had to sneak anything, is all I'm saying." I hold out the message, but Kintyre folds his arms and glowers. His stupid rivalry with his brother now apparently includes him not even stooping to open his more-superior-than-thou brother's letters. "Come on," I cajole.

Kintyre's only answer is a huff and rolled eyes.

"Fine," I say, and untie the leather lace keeping the message rolled. "Huh. It really is him."

"It is?"

"It is."

Kin tries not to look interested, but I can tell that he is. He's trying to peer over my shoulder out the side of his eyes. "What's the book-mouse want?"

I suck air in between my teeth, unsure of how to say this without setting Kintyre off. I'm sure as the Writer's calluses not going to actually *read* the message out loud. That's just asking for an hour of pacing and ranting. "You, apparently. We're being summoned."

"He can't summon *me*." Kintyre bristles, and I barely manage to clamp down on my own eyeroll. "*I'm* the eldest."

"But he's the Lordling of Lysse," I remind him. "And he summons us."

Kin grumbles, but asks, "What for?" He leans over my shoulder, taking up all my space, like usual, and sucking all the air out of the world. He peers at the parchment, a tongue of corn-silk hair brushing against the skin just under my ear.

The shiver it causes is entirely involuntary, and I squeeze my eyes closed, and swallow hard.

Bastard. I try very hard not to wonder if he's doing it on purpose. If he *knows*.

Of course he doesn't know.

When I've got myself composed again, I turn my face up to him and grin, ignoring the way his mouth is just *right there* and I could—*auhg*.

Bastard.

"An adventure," I say, and the grin I force across my face has the perfect partner on Kintyre's. Without even looking, Kin smugly waves the hawk back to Turn Hall, message-less.

***

The way to Lysse leads us back through Miliway Chipping, and the road spears through the prairie lands that provide Hain with our staple grains. Farmers don't mind travelers camping on the side of the road, but are understandably wary of grass fires. This means that in the breadbasket of Hain, no traveler is allowed to light a campfire. And that means no nighttime cooking, and no nighttime heat.

It's still spring this far north, and the nights are still just this side of too chilly to sleep without a fire, or alone. I'm now *really* missing that last lassie, and I wonder blithely if it isn't too late to backtrack to Estagonnish and invite her to Turn Hall with us. Of course, what to do with her when we get there is a problem that I don't want to deal with. 'Cause I sure as the Writer's ink-stained fingers don't want to marry that one.

Mum wouldn't approve at all—the lass was all bosoms and no brains. Good for a while, but not good for a wife. And nobody I would trust to leave behind with the resulting sprogs while I go adventuring. She might set the thatch on fire if she tried to cook. Besides, I wouldn't want to Pair up with someone I couldn't take along on the road, anyway, so that excludes pretty much anyone at all.

Except . . .

Aw, ruddy bollocks. Now I'm back to thinking about how Kin and I will have to lay side by side in our bedrolls to stay warm. I scrub my eyes, trying to will the ridiculous domestic fantasy out of my head and pay attention to where I'm walking.

I *must* be getting old, like my brother Dargan teased the last time I was home. He said the older you get, the less willing you become to dither about things that are important. At first I laughed it off, but it's been two months since I last stopped in Bynnebakker and his warning has been eating at me ever since. Prat.

My wrist throbs again, as if agreeing with Dargan's bit of pithy wit. I'm getting old. I'm getting *slow*. I barely blocked that blow from the Dark Elf's sword, and damn near broke my wrist for the trouble. I don't have the protection of an enchanted blade, or the skills taught to a lord's son, like Kintyre. I've just got forge-earned muscles, a good piece of Dwarf-crafted weaponry, and all the wily tricks that come with being the youngest of seven boys. And lately, they're all starting to seem like not quite enough.

I suck on my lips for a moment, thoughtful. Maybe I was hasty in dismissing the idea of a wife. Sitting by the fire, playing with dogs and babies while someone cooks for *me* for once sounds like a kind of paradise right now.

If only it could include my best friend.

Ugh, and there is that damned domestic fantasy crap again. I need a distraction. Fine. I start cataloging what I can remember of our travel stores, and the result makes me groan loudly enough that Kintyre looks back over his shoulder and grunts, questioning.

"We're gonna need to stop before we get to the grasslands."

Kintyre grimaces. "Aw hells, cold rations. I forgot."

"Yeah. For at least three days." I kick at a stone in the path to keep from having to look up at his ridiculous face when

I make the suggestion I'm about to make, knowing he isn't going to like it. "We could rent horses? It would go faster."

Kintyre grunts but otherwise doesn't reply. Kin hasn't been fond of horses since Stormbearer, the horse Kin's father gave him, was slain in the Battle of the Serpent Prince. I hadn't been all that attached to my own horse, a fussy old nag named Hey You who had also felt Stormbearer's death keenly. I'd left Hey You with my older brother Vulej just a little over two years ago.

Vulej's wee ones apparently love the wretch, and whenever I pick up post from my father's forge, there's always shaky pencil smudges on the edges that my sister-in-law assures me are drawings of Hey You giving the twins rides to the Hay Market. I keep them all in a well-oiled leather fold at the bottom of my pack. I have very little in this world aside from Kintyre and my family, so I try to keep both of them as close as possible.

It's sentimental, sure, but a man's gotta have something worth fighting for, something a little more tangible than reputation, and glory, and the fleeting bliss of a lassie's charms.

"Right then, no horses." I sigh, and keep marching. "Arse."

It's just past midday when we reach the first of the farms. Out flung houses surrounded by gleaming acreages of lively, growing green things always mean there's a center of commerce and civilization nearby. If I remember correctly, this particular center had a goodly number of taverns and markets last time we were through.

And good company, too. Blonde, I think she was, but in truth they all sort of blur together in my memory. It's really only Kin that stands out in my . . . *recollections*.

Mind clearly wandering the same paths as mine, Kin finally slows his damnable long-shanks striding and falls back to match pace with me. "Do you think we'll meet someone in town? We've got time for it, right? You can find us one."

My knee-jerk reaction is to stick my tongue out at him like one of my nephews. Or to flick a rude gesture at his back. Or to say: "Aren't I enough for you?" Or sometimes: "If you do, don't involve me. I want nothing to do with it anymore." Or sometimes: "Enough, I'm done with you. I'm going home to work in my Da's forge and forget you." Or sometimes: "I love you."

Writer's bollocks, sometimes I want to say nothing. I want to just grab Kintyre's ears, wrap my fingers behind the tender pink shells and pull him down for a soft, wet, sleepy kiss, full of all the dopey affection I can't seem to rid myself of. Sometimes I want to get my calf in behind Kintyre's knees, give a shove of my hips and sprawl the arrogant prick on his ass, get a fist into the laces of his trousers and slurp down his—

Bastard.

He doesn't even understand all the ways he's killing me. The ways I'm torturing myself, because it's ridiculous. We're Paired, but not like that. And it will *never be* like that, and damn Dargan to all the hells of the Writer's imagination for planting this stupid bloody seed of thought in my chest anyway. I'm going to kick my brother in the nutsack the next time I see him, and damn what his wife has to say about that.

"We've got time," is all I let myself answer from between my clenched teeth.

I shove my hands in my pockets, annoyed by my own cowardice. "We're not to be in Turnshire for a fortnight, and it will only take a few more days to reach Lysse." I heroically don't add that perhaps if this *is* the village with the blonde, we should move on immediately after resupplying. It's entirely possible that either of us may be confronted with the harvest we sowed on our last trip through.

Kintyre doesn't answer, as usual, so I let my mind wander down the path the thought of kids has begun to lay. I always thought there would be children in my life. I actually *want* to be a dad. Being an uncle is wonderful, even though I only see the little pests infrequently. I love the squirts, and it's great to see how much they've grown, all that they've learned, the ways their personalities and preferences develop between each visit. The youngest of the horde seems to think that "poop" is the funniest damned word the Writer ever Wrote.

I want their chubby, sticky fingers locked around my neck, the sweet kisses, the cuddles, the little feet racing through the hallways shouting, "Da's back! Da's here!" There's something *more*, something magic in the way they say that to their fathers, different to the way they shout "Uncle!" when I surprise one of my six brothers at home. Almost like "Da" is a Word, instead of just a word, and one that I want to mean *me*. I would like a home to go back *to*, I think. A place where it's warm, and I can sit by the fire and and be adored by everyone around me because I adore them back.

That had always been the plan, anyway.

Grow up, work with Da in the forge, marry a farmer's daughter, build a croft, raise a brood, and spend the rest of my life shoeing horses and being loved.

But then a handsome lord's son had come along, and that was the end of those dreams. I could have a wife, a home, the children, if I wanted. But that would mean no Kintyre.

A sudden thought drops into my stomach like a fire-warmed stone: *I'm tired*.

This is not the grief-born weariness I was feeling this morning. This is something else, something deeper, something that has soaked into my skin and settled in the dark marrow of my bones. This is something that is etched on the very fiber of my muscles, the pull of my tendons, the lining of my stomach. This is something born of Dargan's careless teasing, yeah, but also the contemplation that his words have caused over the weeks since I was in that tavern with him, both of us a little too far into the keg.

I am tired.

I am tired of walking, tired of traveling, tired of having nowhere to call home, no place to call my own, no pillow and bed waiting at the end of the day, no surety of the next meal. I am tired of following after Kintyre Turn and *wanting*. I am tired of *not having*.

I am tired, and I want to stop.

I could pay for somewhere to call my own, true; I'm not much for banks and moneylenders, but I've squirreled away the reward purses I didn't give over to Mum over the years. I don't need to build a croft now—I've got more than enough clink to buy a cottage, a few acres, some pigs. Probably a calf. Or five. Or ten, really. Right, so there's actually probably enough to buy a title and the estate that goes with it.

Hells, King Carvel has offered me one often enough. Maybe I could just write to him and tardily accept. Though what on the Writer's hairy backside I'd do with the trappings and responsibilities of a lord, I don't know. I wasn't raised to it. I'd have to hire someone to do all the actual work, and the life of an idle gentleperson is not even close to appealing.

The only thing I *am* certain about is this: Kin would never live with me.

Even if Kintyre Turn did finally settle down, turn in his sword for a ledger or a plowshare or a guardsman's cap, it would be with a buxom woman who could gift him with little

Turnlings. More likely, it would be with some nobleman's daughter or simpering princess, and it would be on the coin of a king, or the late Aglar Turn's estate, where his brother Forsyth would maintain the responsibilities of Master while Kin enjoyed the luxuries with which he'd been raised.

If Kin stopped, that would be it. There would be no room in Kintyre Turn's life for a Bevel Dom, his questing partner, sword-mate, and dogsbody. And a life for Bevel Dom with no Kintyre Turn in it is a life I'm afraid I might not actually have the strength to live.

I know with the surety of a man who has been in love for half his life with someone who will never be aware of it that I will die of heartbreak, or maybe by my own hand, the day Kin marries someone else.

And Writer, that sounds melodramatic as bloody anything. More fit for my scrolls than my thoughts, but there it is. I jam my fists down harder in my pockets and hunch, chewing on my bottom lip to keep from scowling.

And the bastard is *still* walking, just a few paces ahead, like his long legs can't be bothered to shorten his stride for the sake of anything as banal as a short companion. Fine.

So I do as I have always done: I put one foot in front of the other. I shove the weariness away, raise my chin, squint to keep the sun out of my eyes, and follow after Kintyre Turn.

The tiredness can be ignored.

***

He's unpleasant from the moment he dismounts, is how I introduced Kintyre Turn in the epic scroll-series that documents our adventures. But that's a much kinder way to think of it than how I really felt.

"What an elfcock," was what actually came out of my mouth. The twat had wanted me to drop what I was doing to replace a thrown shoe on Stormbearer, which was both arrogant and entitled. And he hadn't even been willing to pay extra for the inconvenience.

Now, watching the way Kin's swagger increases the closer to the village we get, the same sentiment rolls between my ears.

Though I'm not annoyed enough to admit that the thought of finding a nice warm bed with a nice warm woman does sound appealing, but for reasons different to Kin's. I torture myself with it, I know, the thought of finding a way for it to be okay to reach out, to touch, to stroke . . . damn Dargan anyway!

All the same, my own swagger is probably just as pronounced, so I say nothing about it. The view from a few paces behind Kin is a nice one, after all. Kin's customary leather trousers seem to be especially tight today, and his Sheil-purple jerkin leaves very little to the imagination.

I catch myself licking the road-dust from my lips and decide to be optimistic. A bed tonight, shared sleep rolls for the next three, and six days on the road with just Kin for company, except for the taverns or inns we'll stay at. No battle stress, no strategies, no deadlines nor swords looming over our throats. No insidious plots, no villains to roust, no blood.

Just nice, calm, congenial conversation, honestly earned sweat, and at the end of all that, Turn Hall with its feather mattresses, large copper tubs, and fresh baked bread waiting for us. Even the adventure Forsyth proposed in his missive seems more like a walking holiday than a quest—escort damsel in distress from Turn Hall to her far-off home? Easy!

Maybe there'll be some bandits en route, which will keep my sword arm from getting too rusty. Maybe there'll be some fancy politics and fast talking when we get the damsel in question to where she's meant to be, just to make it clear that we weren't the ones who took her in the first place—that will keep my wits from atrophying. But most likely it will be boring, easy, and finish in a feast. We'll have forged yet one more ally, have one more community in which we'll be welcome, maybe even one more castle from which we can draw supplies.

And, if the damsel in question is amenable, the nights of the journey will be warm for other reasons. I like the adventures like that.

Either Kin will try to seduce her first, or I will, but neither of us leaves the other out. Hard to, when you're on the road and there are no walls between you. I do like *that* about traveling with Kintyre—everything we have, we share. The burdens, the battles, the packs, the blood, the joys, the feasts, the wine, the women, and sometimes, though we never talk of it, the nightmares. *That* is something I will never grow tired of. The sharing. Not the nightmares. Those can just go right back on whatever Shelf the Writer pulled them off of.

By mid-afternoon, we've reached the outskirts of a small market village. The sign by the side of the road depicts a festival of sorts, something with fire and foliage, as well as the place's name.

"Gwillfifeshire," Kin reads, carefully parsing out each of the tangled syllables.

"Gilsher," I correct, the side of my mouth quirking up at his gaffe.

"But there's—"

"It's pronounced *gil-sher*, Kin," I insist.

Kintyre points indignantly at the sign.

"Yeah, I see it," I say mildly, determined to hold on to my self-imposed good mood. I hook my thumbs into my belt and nod. "But that's how they pronounce things 'round this area."

The wind goes out of Kin's sails when I refuse to rise to the verbal spar and his shoulders slump. Instead, Kintyre readjusts his pack, head high and fingers curled lightly on Foesmiter's pommel, and leads the way toward the small square as if he actually remembers being here before. He doesn't. I know he doesn't, because he never does.

The square is the only open space amid the cramped, close buildings of the village. There are three or four layers of buildings separated by cobbled streets spreading back from the square, which get progressively smaller, made of more wood than stone, and finally give way to an open meadow. In the distance there's a knoll, and atop the knoll is something gray and crumbling, probably an old monument, or the remains of a castle. Many of the house walls are made of that same gray stone, so it was probably dismantled for building materials a century or two ago.

There isn't much use in statues and monuments, I guess, when there are houses and barns to build and hewn bricks already on hand. I approve of the sensible repurposing, but Kin, who grew up in a manor house with a wing to himself rather than amid a pile of brothers in a three-room cottage, is always vaguely upset that the beautiful architecture and statues have been pulled down.

He'd never own to it, of course, but Kin is secretly a great admirer of the arts. The deep well of his affection for anything creative always raises froth and waves when something beautiful is destroyed—more so if it was vandalized or dismantled so long ago that there's no way to even know what the original art looked like.

Kin is predictably glowering at the top of the knoll, huffing in indignation. He gets that wrinkle between his eyes, and he fingers the small whittling knife he carries in its own leather sheath alongside Foesmiter, and chews on the outside corner of his mouth. He looks like a drakeling. It's hilarious.

Just once, I gave in to the urge to reach out and press my thumb against that swollen, abused lip, but Kin didn't meet my eyes, didn't look up, didn't lean forward, so I've never done it again. Doesn't mean I don't want to, though. Resisting the urge, I say, "Draw it for me. The way you think it looked." He usually does, when I ask him, and it makes him feel at least a little better about it all.

In the seventeen years we've been traveling together, Kintyre has acquired a sword, a questing partner, maidenheads and titles, prize purses and scars. But I firmly believe that the most important thing Kin ever picked up in all that time was a pencil. He's always so much calmer, so much more content when he's had the time and tools to draw. There is no better way to distract Kin out of his agitation and worry than to put him in front of a blank piece of parchment.

Maybe tonight, we'll forget finding someone to seduce and go out to that knoll with a torch and our stationary cases. Kintyre will sketch the statue as it once was, and I can lean back against him, spine to spine, our ribs pressing together warmly with each of Kin's inhalations, sharing support and warmth as I compose the tale of *The Eerie Eyes of Estagonnish.*

The scene I create in my mind fills me with a hot swell of yearning, as appealing as my little domestic fantasies from earlier, and no less ridiculous. I can almost feel the cool night breeze on my cheeks, the backs of my hands, the hollows of my wrists—along with the ache in the small of my back from carrying this ruddy pack all day and the pain in the bottom of my feet from the walking. I'm north of forty now, and yeah, the Doms are long-lived—Da is going on seventy soon—but that doesn't keep us from feeling our age. Still, I can almost smell the pine pitch, the grass, and the special butter soap that I hoard and only dole out in small shaved curls for scrubbing away road-dust when we can hire a proper tub. There would be graphite and stone, and the crisp spring of grass under us. If I close my eyes, block out the harsh sun and the reek of the open gutters, I can *just* feel warm skin, a wet mouth as we both lay aside our tools, a hot push against my stomach, and . . .

Stop, I snarl at myself, and open my eyes. Kin is nearly around the next bend, all but lost to sight. I've been dawdling as I daydreamed and rush to catch up, moving as fleetly as possible to hide that I was ever gone. Secret. Shamed.

As the fantasy ebbs, I feel both empty with want, starving for touch, and at the same time, strangely at peace. I can't deny that I desire what I do: the small domestic instants, the quiet, the stars. Dargan was right—things that didn't seem important fifteen years ago, ten years ago, Writer, even three years ago, seem as vital as water and bread now. But these small, stolen moments will have to feed me. I consume them greedily, stockpile them carefully, and turn them over and over in my mind on days when things are bad.

And if I'm honest with myself—I should be, it's the least I owe me—if I'm really, truly *honest*, I *know* that this is all I'll ever have. The small moments, and the horded memories, and the oblivious companionship of Kintyre. I will never have more.

At least until we're old enough to stop adventuring and settle in one place. If we settle together at all. I think back to that croft, that cottage, that estate I've been building in my imagination, but instead of a hearth with a rocking chair, surrounded by puppies and babies, a wife in the chair opposite me placidly cross-stitching, I conjure up Kintyre with his pencil and sketching book. Maybe Forsyth will take pity on a graying old adventurer and let me live out my retirement in Turn Hall. No babies. Maybe puppies. And wouldn't that be a sight: three old bachelors, sniping at each other until we die, heirless and cranky, surrounded by slobbering dogs.

If we *live* to retire, of course.

I rub my wrenched wrist and frown. I may fantasize about the domestic life, but I also have no illusions about the sort of life I lead. I stretch out my arm, circling my left hand under its bandages.

A few paces ahead of me, Kintyre stops so abruptly that, lost in my wool-gathering, I nearly run nose-first into his pack. He's peering up at a painted sign, hanging above a large, clean window of lead-mullioned glass cut in the shape of diamonds.

"What about this one?" he asks. His gaze drops to the window, and he smirks, then throws a smug look over his shoulder at me. "Seems perfect to me."

"The taproom?" I ask with a chuckle. "Or the truly spectacular tits behind the bar?"

***

The tavern is called Pern, probably after the someone's beloved nag or something just as sentimental, but it's the cleanest one on the thoroughfare. Even better, it lets beds above the taproom. Good enough for me. The perfect tits behind the bar turn out to belong to our landlady, and she brings them over to the booth we settle in to take our food, ale, and rooms.

Kin is scratching idly at a wood block, scraping away a careful layer of shavings into a tidy pile on the tavern table. It's a terrible habit. But I'm sick to the teeth of asking him not to do his carving over our dinners. I've lost that battle for seventeen years running. I have no illusions that I'll be winning it today.

Instead, I crane my neck and try to figure out what the picture is supposed to be.

"What's that, then?" I ask around a mouthful of a really, *really* tasty savory game pie. I'm going to have to ask the Goodwoman what herbs she used. There's an unexpected, spicy sweetness clouding up the back of my nose, and I *love* it. Spices make all the difference when foraging on the road. They can make each meal taste like something else, something new and interesting, especially if you have to keep using the same boring old road rations. And they absolutely make up for the fact that I currently have to eat with the wrong hand.

Kintyre holds up the block, and I can make out the beginnings of a reversed image—Foesmiter, and some sort of craggy outline that could be either a cliff or the beginnings of a forest. I cast my mind back over what I saw Kin smudging into a piece of vellum a couple of nights ago, right before we went into the Dark Elf's cave. Ah, yeah. It's the maw of an entrance, and the beginnings of figures that are probably supposed to be us standing in front of it. He always draws me too short, the twat.

"Oh, ah, that's for the eyes story?" I ask, sitting back.

Kin nods. "If you decide to write it up."

"Of course I'll decide to write it up," I say. "You're already illustrating it. I have to now, don't I?" I shrug, trying to sound jovial about it. It's not like I wasn't already working on it anyway.

Kin grunts, his mouth twisting into an aggravated line, and he sets down the block with a thunk that rattles my fork against the metal tureen. He picks up his own fork and stabs at the center of his pie, rich brown gravy oozing from the wound.

"Oh, come on, Kin, I didn't mean it like that—" I cut myself off when Kintyre just shovels a steaming heap of lunch into his mouth and turns his blue, blue eyes out the dirt-streaked window. "Fine then, be a snit," I say, and reapply myself to my own pie. "Not like you can't actually see that I've been writing."

Kintyre grunts and holds out his hand. I would like a "please," but I know I'm never going to get one, any more than I will ever get him to stop flicking curls of wood shavings into my cooking. I gave up on that a while ago, too.

I hand over the scrap of paper I've been scratching at between bites.

I've also long since stopped being precious about my writing. When I first met Kin, I was as illiterate as every other title-less peasant in my Chipping; he'd taught me to read and to write. He'd helped me craft letters back home, letters that my mum still needed to pay a scholar to read to her, and to reply for her. But I had kept my first, coltish forays into fiction—a sort of sensational journal of our adventures—to myself. I never liked to share anything but my best work when I was a blacksmith's apprentice; I had felt the same about my writing. But Kin found the first of the story scrolls and had sat with me, patient, for many long nights as he taught me story structure and punctuation, and coaxed description and depth of narrative out of me. I'd been ashamed of my work, but he had likened it to smithery. I had the tools, he said, now that I could read and write. I just needed to work on the skills, the little tricks and shortcuts that masters knew, the muscle memory of the thing. I just needed practice.

Kin drops his eyes to the parchment and reads, chewing thoughtfully. His praise made me a writer, and his diligent generosity made me a *great* writer, and that is as close to divinity as worn-out, tired old Bevel Dom is ever going to get. So I can't help but watch his expression, my stomach twisted into knots, as he reads.

My work is recited in salons all over the world, and every one of the royal libraries has leather-bound, gilt-edged copies on display. I never pay for drinks in taverns and public houses where I read my scrolls. And I always have company to bed when I'm done.

But it's different when the subject of your stories is reading your descriptions of their own adventures. I want Kin to like it so much. I study every eyebrow twitch, every swallow, every motion of the left corner of Kintyre's mouth, seeking out the approval that the crinkles in the corners of his eyes signal, or the confusion that comes from the corner of his lip. It all *means* something—boredom, amusement, that he thinks the prose is too purple, or that he's found an error in the way I wrote the events. It's torture, and now that I'm published and out of his tutelage, he rarely says anything beyond "s'good" when he's done.

For all that Kin has a deep and intense love of the arts, he keeps his opinions held close to his heart, and doesn't like to speak out against errors or interpretations. I've always guessed that it's because of the way his father believed that real warriors had to leave the feminine pursuit of artistic knowledge to women. Patient enough to teach me but dismissive in praise, Kintyre is a study in juxtaposition when it comes to his father's beliefs, and how they clash with his own passions.

Kin is a man imprisoned by the expectations of a mean drunk ten years in his grave. I sometimes wish that I'd broken Algar Turn's nose when I had the opportunity. It's too late now, unless I want to spend an hour shoveling first.

Instead, I settle on reading the parchment upside down, my eyes following my own messy first-draft scrawl along with Kin:

The cavern reeked of mold and leaf-rot, and the faint tang of whatever liquid was in the preserving bottles around us. The air was both humid, close, and yet oddly stale. The cobwebs in the high corners surged and bobbed as air passed through the tunnel, like a giant's faint snore was disturbing them. They were tattered and collected dust, silvery in the half-light of our lanterns, hanging like a fop's silver-laced cuffs spilling from his court robe sleeve.

And the shelves, oh, the shelves. Gleaming clean, they were, not a speck of dust allowed to fall and remain on this beloved, morbid collection.

We kept along silently, Kintyre Turn and I, and as we did, I ruminated on why it is that the terrible, most possessive, and creepy practitioners of the Dark Magicks prefer, above all other things, the eyes of a person.

Sometimes it's literal, like when they try to claw you in a fight. I would pass judgment and call it unsporting, but when it is a contest of life and death, then all the rules hang.

Heed me in this: there is no such thing as unmanly fighting. There is winning, and there is dead. And I tell you, my listener, that the Golden Hero and I both agree as to which side of that coin we'd rather be on.

But more often than not, it is one's eyes that they, in the most physical and literal sense, wish to own. Perhaps it is because eyes are the doorways to the soul? Possess the eyes and you own the soul?

In the stale chill closing in around me, fetid and foul, I shudder, for I cannot help the surge of disgust at the thought of my own soul cradled in the foul, soiled hands of the Viceroy.

With Kintyre's attention on the parchment, I think about the lines that I *hadn't* written down, the confession that had been on the tip of my pencil, but had seemed too personal to invite the rest of the world to read. I grind the heel of my hand against my right cheek, doing my level best to dispel the ghost-memory of Bootknife's blade sliding clean and neat along the wrinkle of my bottom eyelid. There's a scar there, just a small one, and it has mostly become lost in the folds of skin I've seemed to acquire with age. It goes unseen by any who don't already know to look for it, and that's as small a mercy as I can hope for, really.

I'm not vain. I know I am sort of bland, and short, and going gray, especially compared to Kin. But I'd feel ten kinds of ashamed if I knew Kin was looking at my face and seeing only the scar. I don't want him to remember my fear and pain. Or to only see the blood, and sweat, and— yeah, I'm not too proud to admit it—the tears that my terror had wrung out of me when I thought, when I *realized*, that Bootknife was going to put out my eyes.

Kintyre grunts and stops reading when he catches me scrubbing at my face. He looks up, his fork suspended between tureen and lips, and dammit, I haven't been subtle enough. He *is* looking at the ruddy scar now.

At least he's still got enough of his Turnish manners not to mention it, though. He taps the parchment with the butt-end of his fork, slopping a bit of gravy on the edge—*twat*—and says, "I've never understood why you write like this. You never sound like *you*. Sometimes, it's like someone else's got control of your quill."

"It's called having an artistic *voice*, Kin." I sneer back gamely.

"S' weird." He taps the parchment again. But he doesn't add anything else.

The strange antagonism from earlier flares back up, making my shoulders tight and my belly burn. I take back my scrap and swipe away the gravy. Bugger him, then, if he doesn't like it. I don't write for him, do I?

We pass the next long moments saying nothing to one another, too used to each other's tempers to know that speaking right now would just make it worse. I have enough manners to not lick the tureen clean, at least, unlike the lord's son sitting across from me, and after the Goodwoman clears our table, I sit back and pack my pipe with the sticky herbal mash I learned how to make on the decks of *The Salty Queen*. I light it with a long match and suck in a white, fragrant mouthful, reveling in the heady, soft taste.

It floods my lungs, burning at first and then becoming prickly, soothing, and I blow it out of my nostrils, feeling playful and dragonish. I like the way it makes my nose hairs singe.

"That's a disgusting habit," Kin says with a grunt.

"You pick your teeth," I point out, jabbing at the air in front of his face with the stem of my pipe. I take another deep puff in defiance.

"But it doesn't make me smell like the ass end of a tannery when I'm done."

I clench the stem of my pipe between my teeth, hard enough to make the bone mouthpiece creak. "It's an orange-blossom hash. How is it even *remotely* like boiling urine?"

The Goodwoman laughs behind her apron as she delivers another round of her excellent ale and says, "You sound just like my parents. You must be very much in love."

Kintyre snorts and says nothing, eyes turned out the window, and I work very, very hard to beat down a blush. *Bloody buggering hells*, I think. *Is the whole of Hain determined to see Kintyre and I Paired and rogering each other stupid?*

"We're not," I blurt. "Trothed, I mean."

"*But I am in love*" remains unsaid.

The Goodwoman cuts a glance between the two of us, and a quick, short look of pity flickers in her gaze when she turns it back to me. "Well," she says, and I'm grateful to hear that her tone has turned formal and brisk, backing away from the uncomfortable topic. Good. She *should* feel bad. "Perhaps at the festival, then."

"Festival?" Kin asks, reaching for his ale and turning his light eyes to the Goodwoman. She wears a marriage bob in her ear, but that doesn't stop him from turning on the charm. His smile is warm and luminous, and my stomach twists, my heart lurching to the side.

Bastard.

"Oh, aye," the Goodwoman says with an actual, honest-to-Writer *titter*. "The Fire Flower Festival? It is why you're here, isn't it?"

"Just passing through, actually." Kin smiles wider. "We stopped for provisions—and lucky we did, for *Pern* has the most delicious ale and pie we've had the honor of tasting, and we've supped at the table of King Carvel himself, haven't we, Bev?"

I nod as the Goodwoman giggles, and do my best not to roll my eyes. Maybe Kin should have been a theatre-player instead of a hero. He certainly seems to come by his ridiculous charm naturally. Writer, Kin is laying it on thick. Is he really so desperate for a warm body between us tonight that he'll pounce on the first woman who flutters her eyelashes at him?

Well, she *does* have really perfect tits. It seems a shame not to even try for them, I suppose.

"But now that we know it's a festival night, we'll have to stay," Kin says, as if we weren't planning to do exactly that anyway. Writer.

I don't protest, though, because Kin seems to be making strides. The Goodwoman's cheeks flush and she says, "Aye, well, then why don't you and your, um, friend, join my family's fire circle tonight? Wouldn't do to have you outside a circle. And in the meantime, why don't I fetch you both a bit of sweet cheese?"

"That's very thoughtful of you, thank you," Kin says, and I scoff and grin down into my ale, because of course the only time Kintyre Turn remembers his "pleases" and "thank yous" is when he's playacting the gallant. And he only playacts the gallant when he wants to get a leg over. Arse.

The Goodwoman bustles back to the bar, and I level an unimpressed look at my friend. "She's married. Look, she's got a little boy behind the bar wiping the mugs."

"I see no spouse," is all Kin says.

"Writer preserve me," I sigh.

"Speaking of," Kintyre says, reaching across the table to pull my hand toward him. He turns it over slowly, unwinding the bandage that wraps around my wrist. His touch is dry, and warm, and absolutely does not send lightning skittering up my skin. Kintyre bares my swollen joint to the air and I gasp at the light touch of his fingertips against the very sensitive underside of my wrist. "How is this? Do you need some of the pain tea?"

"Not mixed with my ale, I don't," I say. All the same, I let Kin massage my arm gently, soothingly, discovering all the places where the pain lingers, inspecting the ligaments and the bones.

I should pull back. I should keep my distance. I should bloody well stop *torturing* myself with this.

Kill. I am going to *kill* Dargan. It will be violent. I will *enjoy* it.

"Not broken," Kintyre murmurs, golden head bent over his task. The tail of his hair brushes into the pile of wood chippings and some tangle into the ends like cockleburrs. It shouldn't be endearing. It is.

"No," I agree. "Barely even sore anymore. I'll be pure as unicorn piss come Turnshire."

Kintyre chuckles at my crassness and grins up at me. His eyes are crinkled around the corners in new ways, ways that speak of our long years of friendship, of the sun and the wind and the salt spray we've both endured, of the cold and the heat, of the pain and the laughter. There are small white hairs in his eyebrows and at his temples, but luckily his hair is light enough to disguise them. Kin looks simultaneously aged and ageless, still like the brash young man I first met, swinging his well-formed thighs across Stormbearer's back to dismount before my Da's forge. And yet he also looks like a man who is well into his middle life, the way I know we both are. His eyes have not changed, though. They still sparkle like northern ice cliffs in his mirth.

Bastard. It's not fair.

I look my age, scarred and weather-rough, hair sprinkled with a dirty white, the corners of my eyes crinkled like a lady's badly-closed court fan. Blast and bugger Kintyre Turn for remaining gorgeous while I age. Bastard. Twat. Arse.

Kin sits back, and I leave my wrist unwrapped. I tap the ash out of my pipe and repack it. The Goodwoman returns with another tureen, and this one is fragrant with the scent of baked apples, onions, and cinnamon. Kintyre perks up and sends her another one of his beaming smiles, and, deciding that I like his plan, I offer up a grin of my own, reaching out slowly to brush the backs of my fingers against the edge of her apron, just casually enough for it to look like an accident.

Her eyes follow my hand, and I curl my fingers up, close to the apex of her thigh, suggestive without being too lewd.

"Sorry," I say, but I wink to show her that I'm not, not really. Her ears flush pink, very sweetly.

If I can get her into bed, then I can touch Kintyre, kiss him, *have* him, and then maybe get this madness out of my blood, strangle the weed that Dargan planted behind my ribs.

The Goodwoman, flustered, thumps the tureen onto the table, slaps the plate of cinnamon-infused flatbread down beside it, and scuttles away. Kintyre meets my eyes with a pleased smirk. I lift the lid off a pot of melted goat's cheese mixed with stewed apples and onions, and file away the flavor combination to try in one of my own dishes when we're on the road later.

We take our time with the sweet cheese. Kintyre returns to his carving, and I scribble some more of the story, enjoying the fragrant smoke that curls around my head, and we have several more tankards of ale. We both flirt and charm the Goodwoman whenever she returns to the table, arousal slow and syrupy in my limbs, and she blushes but does not avoid us, or scold us. To my mind, this is as good as a "yes." Lovely.

In this drowsy, golden-sweet way, the afternoon passes.

We have nowhere pressing to be. We bought all our cold rations for Miliway, and it seems as if we're attending a festival tonight. Two festivals, if things with the maybe-not-really-married Goodwoman goes our way.

When the dinner crowd begins trickling into the taproom, the Goodwoman comes back.

"Your rooms are ready," she says. "Were you wanting dinner, or did you want to go up?"

"Up," I say. I'm tempted to add, "*and will you join us?*" But it's too soon for that. Don't want to tip my hand just yet. "And if we're off to your festival tonight, then perhaps we should bathe as well. Can you ask your husband to bring up your tub for us?"

"Husband!" The Goodwoman snorts. "I reckon not. The hall boy took it up an hour ago. Figured you'd want it as soon as I caught a whiff of you both. My son will fill it now, if you like."

"No husband, then?" Kintyre asks, and under the table, I step down hard on his foot, warning him not to be so obvious so soon.

The Goodwoman snorts again and crosses her arms under her breasts, which makes them even more plump and . . . yeah, I can't wait to bury my face between them. Writer at His desk, they look so *soft*.

"No husband, nor wife, neither," she says. "Not no more." And she nods once, firm, and leaves it at that. "Now, up the stairs with you both. You're stinking out my regulars."

Kintyre and I laugh and go. She's not wrong, is the thing. Our last bath was in Estagonnish—we *do* reek. Splashing around in a river will never replace what hot water and good soap can do.

"There's only the one tub," the Goodwoman says, as a parting shot, and then seems to think better of it and hesitates. Kin waves her concern away.

"We've shared before," he says.

The Goodwoman smiles, nods, and then cuts another curious glance at me. I resolve then and there to ask her what she meant by "*Perhaps at the Festival.*"

***

Thinking about sex, and thinking about domesticity, and

thinking about murdering Dargan, has led me to thinking about marriage. Never a good place for my imagination to go, especially lately. All the same, sitting in this room and watching Kintyre disrobe, I figure that if I were to exchange promise tokens with Kin, I'd like the tokens to be clothing.

Swords and weaponry are traditional for soldiering Pairs pledging a troth, but Kin has Foesmiter, and I've got my compact bow and my own sword, and after seventeen years, we don't really need any other weapons. Our kit is already perfected, comfortable. It would make no sense to change it. Likewise, we already buy each other pipes and quills, carving tool wallets, boots and tack. We've always bought each other the kind of gifts that trothing Pairs do, not to show our dedication but because, inevitably, somebody's money purse will get left behind in the middle of the night, or accidentally slide down some monster's gullet, or get stolen by a conquest. And then we'll have to share coinage until we have the chance at another reward, or can swing through Turnshire or Kingskeep for more. Because of that, anything else we'd buy (or craft) one another wouldn't be, well, as meaningful.

But clothing, clothing would be good. Neither of us can *make* clothing, so the purchase would mean something. And frankly, I hate that Kintyre still wears the color of his mother's House, as if everyone doesn't know that he's a Turn. Seventeen years ago, when Kin was running away from home to join the border guard, it made sense. Now it just seems forgetful, and gives him the air of being ashamed of his family.

True, the only time I met Algar Turn, he was a drunk-flushed, boil-covered, pus-weeping elfcock. And Forsyth is bossy and skittish and annoying. But the Turns have done great things in their history. It's a grand legacy that Kintyre has augmented honorably, and he should be proud of his lineage. He should be wearing Turn-russet, even if only to make it clear that he is a member of a Seated House when we're on the road. Preferential treatment is nothing to be frowned at. It's dead useful if you've been in a fight with some horrible monster and the master of the estate has a beautiful, grateful daughter.

And of course, I wouldn't mind being able to wear Turn-russet myself, to declare myself part of that same great House, that same honorable lineage, to tell the world that I love and am loved . . . to be a part of Kin's *family*.

Uhg. I'm so sentimental I'm making myself sick.

And, yeah, I can admit that I'm a possessive little bastard. I'd like to see Kintyre wearing the same colors as me, to be clad in the same shade, so that when we walk into a room together, it's obvious that Kin is taken. And that I'm the one that took him.

But the thought is fleeting, even though it's complex, and drops right out of my head the moment Kintyre finishes unlacing said Sheil-purple jerkin and drops it onto the end of his bed. The flex of Kin's shoulders through his thin, much-abused shirt is momentarily distracting, and I have to swallow hard to banish the dryness in my mouth.

By the Writer's left nutsack, this is torture.

Two bloody decades of torture, and still I can't seem to walk away, or put myself out of my misery. My fingers twitch with the desire to touch. Instead, I hook them into the laces of my own shirt and turn my eyes away.

The Goodwoman's son comes into the room, without knocking first, to dump another kettle of boiled water into the travel tub. I'm suddenly grateful that I didn't give in to my urges. That would have given the boy more of a show than I think he would ever want. It's the fifth kettle of hot water, and the boy is dawdling so much that I figure the whole lot will be cold before Kin and I ever get the chance to get into the tub. A flutter of fabric in the corner of my eye catches my attention again, and I turn to watch as Kin strips his shirt off over his head. It is yellow with sweat and grime. Once we're done with the bathwater, I'm going to throw our clothes in it for a good scrub. I'd ask Kin to do it, but he's never got the hang of scrubbing laundry. He grew up with maids to do it for him, and had no desire to learn on the road because he always knew I would get annoyed enough to just grab it out of his hands and do it for him. I'm a fool, and I've spoiled the great lump.

We've both got spare trousers and shirts in our packs, so I slip out after the Goodwoman's son and pop back over to my own room to fetch mine. I come back to Kin's room, where we both plan to bathe so the Goodwoman doesn't have to move the tub, and spread it out on the drying rack. I have a vague hope that the lavender-scented steam might help pull out the wrinkles and give the cloth the illusion of freshness. When Kin doesn't seem to catch the hint, I grumble and rummage through his pack to lay his spare shirt and trousers beside mine.

Half naked, and in no rush to strip any further, Kin stands by the window, watching the procession of villagers as they head down the main road with garlands and wreaths and bouquets. He lounges against the sill in just his leather trousers. His skin, though scarred, still glows gold from years of living under the sun, his shoulders broad as a ship's masthead, tapering to battle-trim hips and an arse that fills out his trousers like a ripe peach. He looks appetizing, and he knows it. It's probably for the benefit of the lovely lasses on the street below. Or the Goodwoman. Or both.

The sight of his bare feet against the wooden floor nearly does in my self-control. I distract myself by stripping out of my own short-robe, jerkin. Writer, my shirt's in no better state than Kin's.

The boy lingers in the doorway, gawking at Kin instead of heading back down to the kitchen for another kettle. The Goodwoman comes up the hallway with a tray of ales we didn't ask for. I'm chuffed to see them all the same. My mouth is horribly dry. The Goodwoman shifts the tray so she can swat the back of her son's head with a free hand.

"Layabout!" she snaps, but her tone holds affection and exasperation. This isn't a blow from an abusive parent, but one merely at the end of her tether. I've seen innumerable swats delivered by my own sisters-in-law to my abundant nieces and nephews in just the same way. "Stop staring and go."

"But Ma—"

"But nothing," she cuts him off.

"But it's *Kintyre Turn*," the boy interrupts in reply.

Ah, so that's the problem, I think. Hearing his name spoken in that tone of awestruck worship, Kin stops being outwardly annoyed by the delay and instead turns and offers the boy a dazzling, white-toothed grin.

"Let the boy—" he starts, but then the Goodwoman is glaring at him, too.

"I've already told my son that he can pester you *after* his chores are complete. Don't undermine me, Master Turn," she says.

Kintyre blinks, startled by her forthrightness and his complete failure to charm her into obedience. Her twitterpated blushes from downstairs are no match for motherly chagrin. I snicker, amused by this reversal.

"As for you," she says, rounding on the boy, finger poking his nose playfully. "You finish your chores, or no festival for you."

"Aw, Ma, no!" the boy whines.

"Aw, Son, yes," the Goodwoman replies. "Get on, now, or I'll have you off to the ghost!"

The boy's whole posture goes rigid, his face turning white as milk, and he flees down the hall with the empty bath kettle at speeds I'd say he normally saves for running toward sweets.

"A ghost?" I ask, as the Goodwoman hands out the ales. There's a nice sharp bite of condensation against my palms as I take the offered tankard. "Surely not a real ghost."

"Oh, aye," she says, setting the tray down on the hearth and fussing with the towel rack until it is close enough to warm the bath sheets, but not so much so that they'll singe.

"A real ghost?" Kin asks, attention well and truly caught finally. I can tell because Kin's looking the Goodwoman in the face, and not elsewhere. "And you use this as a threat for good behavior?"

"Why not?" the Goodwoman says, hands on her hips as she leans over to peer up the flue, opening the hatch a bit more to allow the fire a little extra air. Her perfect tits sway perfectly. "A mother uses what weapons are in her arsenal. You'll learn that when you have sprogs of your own, Master Turn."

"But a *real ghost*," I say, and meet Kin's ice-blue eyes over the Goodwoman's head. We conduct the same sort of silent conversation we've had a hundred times before through grimaces and waggling eyebrows.

This could be a problem, I communicate.

Kin's tiny head-jerk means he agrees. *We should look into it, see if we can rid the town of this monster.*

A sniff and a nose wiggle: *Agreed. I'm especially concerned that she doesn't seem concerned about it at all.*

Me too, from a seemingly idly scratched cheek.

"So, where would we find this ghost?" I ask, voice a study in nonchalant interest. I hook my thumb into my belt and rock back on my heels, as if I were no more than a curious farmer passing a lazy afternoon in idle chatter, then sip my ale.

The Goodwoman laughs over her shoulder, eyes crinkling in what appears to be genuine joy, which makes my guts clench with horror.

"In the old well, o' course. Where else would a ghost be?" She jerks her head vaguely south.

"Of course," I murmur, and shake my head when Kin opens his mouth to ask for more details.

Don't get her suspicions up, I communicate with a tug of my trousers. *Ask the boy*, I mouth, because we haven't devised a signal for that one.

The boy, Kin agrees. "Your, er, your son, will he back up soon?" Kin asks.

"Oh, aye, he ought. We have two kettles we swap around. You'll get your warm bath, Master Turn, no worries. Fear o' goin' to the ghost is a good motivator for boys like 'im. Sometimes it takes the children," the Goodwoman says, smoothing her hands down her skirt and fetching the empty tray up. She sighs; it fluffs the locks of hair that have escaped from under her mop cap. "But only when they're naughty. If that's all, gentlemen?" And then she has the chilling *gall* to smile at us, as if all was still level with the world.

"No, no, that's . . . thank you," I say, too stunned to say any more. The Goodwoman bustles out. She seems so *blasé*. And about a ghost that takes away naughty children, presumably back to the old well where it . . . well, in my experience, it probably drowns them. Possibly in punishment; possibly because it's lonely and looking for ghostly playmates, and thinks murdering village children is the best way to gain them.

Kin and I have twin expressions of carefully contained horror aimed at the now empty doorway.

"Bloody buggering hells. That was creepy as all get out," I breathe, breaking the silence. I shiver despite the hot steam curling through the air, making the tips of my hair limp and sag. Everything smells of lavender and butter soap, and I think I might never be able to smell the combination ever again without feeling sick to my stomach.

"Do you suppose they've been bespelled to be so calm about it?" Kin asks, voice low in case someone's in the hall.

"Possibly." I run my hand through my hair, scrubbing the goose pimples away. "Writer, if Tallah ever spoke that way about the twins—"

Kin presses one square palm against the nape of my neck, reassuring. He loves those boys too. He sends them little drawings in my return letters, and carved them wee swords from willow switches last time we were through Bynnebakker.

They're children. Children are meant to be loved. Cherished.

Protected.

We perch on the end of the bed, lost in mutual contemplation of what it will take to slay a ghost. I rotate my wrist, testing it, becoming familiar with the stiffness, the burning pull, stretching it where I dare. Kin whispers Words of Healing under his breath, and slowly the soreness fades. The Words always help, but they're magic's never strong enough to heal a hurt entirely and immediately, more's the pity.

In silence, we prepare. In silence, we make careful ready. We exchange head jerks and long stares, plotting, planning, and all the while keeping the air free of whispers that can be overheard. We're well practiced at this, too.

When the boy comes back with the kettle, Kin leans down to meet his wide brown eyes. "My boy, I have a proposition for you."

"You do?" the boy asks, readjusting his grip. Kin takes the heavy kettle from him and passes it off to me. Not wanting to waste the bathwater, I dump the kettle into the tub, but keep my attention on the conversation. I pour the water out slowly and from a height, causing splashes to muffle Kin's voice from any eavesdroppers. My wrist twinges, but I ignore it.

"I do," Kin says. "How about, after you finish all your chores and we finish our baths, the three of us go on an adventure?"

The boy's eyes and mouth become comically round. "Yes, sir, Master Turn, sir. Yes, please!"

"Excellent," Kin says, straightening and rubbing his huge paw against the top of the boy's head, scruffing up his dark curls into a disarrayed nest. "Meet us back here at sundown. Wear sturdy boots."

***

We take turns bathing, and dressing, and then fill the idle time between that and sundown with more writing and carving. My teeth are clenched tight around the stem of my pipe, but for once Kin isn't bitching about the smell. He's seated by the window, which has been opened enough for my smoke and his whittlings to get out, and the noise and conversations of Gwillfifeshire to get in. Both of us are silent, ears attuned to the chatter of the festival-goers walking past the inn, listening for any other tidbits about the ghost which might give us an advantage. So far, no luck.

I'm only halfheartedly scratching at the story, to be honest. My blood is singing with the possibility of adventure and danger, and it's making me fidget. I always get squirrelly when we're forced into inaction, knowing that a fight is just on the horizon. Kintyre is the fussy one in daily life, but when it comes to camping out and waiting, he has the ability to sit still and quiet for long periods. His little brother is the same. I've never asked, but I get the feeling it has something to do with their arsehole father.

I praise the Writer again for being born into a family where I didn't have to be scared of my own Da, where I didn't feel the need to be still in an effort to be overlooked. Brain cramping with the futile wish to sock Algar Turn in the nose again, I force myself to focus, to pay attention to the pencil and parchment under my hands.

It feels as if the shelves of crystal decanters are watching us as my companion and I slip past, I write. *Luckily, the eyes—all shaded between teal and emerald, grass and old copper—can't actually see us. Or, at least I pray strongly that they cannot.*

A few paces ahead of me, Kintyre pauses. He raises the Wisp lantern slightly, throwing rainbows of illumination against the cavern wall as the light reflects from the facets of the decanters. They splinter against the rough rock ceiling and glisten in the moldering deadfall. It occurs to me just then to wonder how the leafrot got into this cavern, for there are no trees in this subterranean hell to drop them.

"What is it?" I ask, my voice ratcheted down to a harsh, hushed whisper, palms sweating on the leather-wrapped pommel of my sword. I want nothing more than to sheathe my blade and wipe my hand on my short-robe, but I know better than to put away my weapon now.

Seventeen years of adventuring, and I've learned this lesson above all others—the moment you put away your sword is the minute you're going to wish you hadn't.

"This decanter is different," Kintyre says, and his powerful voice is a soft boom against the barren stone rocks. "Different color."

"Liquid?"

"Eyes."

Before I am certain of his next action, he has plucked that decanter from amid its shelf-mates, and has tucked the neck of the bottle under his wide leather belt. The angle at which the shadow of his arm now falls across the bottle means that I cannot make out what, exactly, is singular about it. "Maybe it's a favorite. Could be leverage."

I suppress a shudder, and instead of shaking my shoulders, it crawls down my spine like a drop of cold sweat.

"Kintyre?" I ask, voice a hush, and he hums to show he's heard me. I read the last few paragraphs to him. "And then what did you say?"

Kintyre looks up at me from his carving and grins with that wicked boyishness that always makes my heart lurch. That same damnable grin that made me trot after him when I was done shoeing Stormbearer all those years ago, a witless blacksmith's son trailing like a tugboat in the wake of a lad determined to make a name for himself outside of his great House, and with enough arrogance and charm to get whatever he wanted.

"Ah, I think what I said was, 'The Dark Elf can suck my cock. Let's just kill the creepy bastard and be done with it.' Then I suggested we smash a few decanters to see if that would bring him running, but you reminded me that we promised to give them back to the families."

I snort, swallowing down a chuckle. "Kin," I admonish in a whisper, grinning back, "I can't put that."

"Well, then I don't know why you asked me," he says. "Make up something."

"I don't know what," I say. I can't help the frustrated sigh. "Maybe I won't write this after all."

Kin frowns, holding up his woodcutting, and I nod.

"I know, Kin, but I just . . . the *eyes*." I touch my scar. My eyelid twitches and jumps at the memory, my eyes suddenly watering, and I squeeze them shut, hard.

"Oh," Kin whispers. "I didn't think about . . . huh. Well. I mean, if you don't want to . . ."

I shake my head, bare my teeth once, and then run my free hand across the back of my neck to banish the goose pimples. "Right. Blast. Right. I just . . . I'm really, *really* not comfortable here, my friend."

"I know."

"The Viceroy—"

"I *know*." Kin lays a comforting hand along the back of my neck, filling the space mine has left, and it almost feels as if we're holding hands, our fingers deliberately tangled instead of by accident. I ache with the want of him.

I push the story aside and stand, shrugging Kin off before I can do or say something that I'm going to regret later—or worse, *he* might regret.

Luckily, that's when the boy knocks on the door.

Our shirts are still slightly damp from the steam, but there's no time to let them toast by the fire any longer. We throw them on, and I open the door for the lad. The sun has set, and Kintyre has been muttering about the Witches' Hour since the twilight slipped from orange to soft gray. If we're going to confront this ghost, we both know that it will have to be before midnight, when the monster's power would be at its apex.

The only blessing of the damp is that the shirts no longer cloud the air with the reek of long travel. Instead, the scent of lavender-soap and hearth-fire curls under my nose, and I do my best not to be revolted. I wasn't jesting when I thought I'd never be able to stomach the herb ever again. I've already packed my hip satchel with all manner of potions and talismans. Some are tricks and trinkets I've picked up over the last two decades of adventuring, some are from a standard set that I replenish through Mother Mouth with each return trip to Turnshire. I rummage in it now, pulling out my small brocade bag of healing ungents. I swipe some lemon cream along my upper lip to mask the smell of lavender.

We lace up our jerkins before the fire, sealing in the last of the warm air. The boy is wearing sturdy boots, as instructed, but only a pair of black trousers and a thin, wine-colored shirt that his mother clearly chose for him to wear to this Fire Flower Festival. His wee waistcoat is furled with intricate embroidery picked out in brightly sparking copper thread, and I make him take it off and leave the fine and flashy garment behind. It will attract too much attention. Instead, I have the boy don my own short-robe of Dom-amethyst, so travel-grimed now that it's practically mud brown, just so he won't freeze. It's not horrifically cold outside, but cold enough that, with the window open, Kin and I had been able to see our breath.

As we finish kitting up, the boy gleefully introduces himself as Thoma, and then proceeds to tell Kin all about the adventures he has with the other children of Gwillfifeshire while pretending to act out the tales in my scrolls. He has a small sword, made of two sticks tied together with twine, shoved into his belt and, beside that, a more sensible kitchen knife. I'm torn between taking the knife from him so Thoma doesn't accidentally cut his own leg and leaving it so that the boy has some sort of protection, just in case this little adventure gets out of hand. I don't intend to leave the boy in any sort of situation where he'll need the knife, of course, but sometimes plans don't work out as they are, well, planned.

Better to let him keep it. He seems sensible enough not to cut himself, and it's always better to have a weapon when none is needed, than to *not* have one when it *is*.

It's easy enough to slip down the stairs and out the back of the building. Thoma is an excellent guide, having grown up in the *Pern*; he knows all her secrets—like the servant's hall tucked away in the shadows, and which treads on the delivery stairway squeak. He thinks all the skulking and sliding is great fun, and he turns a bright grin to us each time we round another corner. Kin and I let him continue to have his glee—there's no point in frightening him now, not when we need him as a guide.

There will be time to make him understand how deadly serious we are later.

Thoma leads us to the back kitchen door, and out through a small cobbled courtyard where the laundry is hanging and raised boxes cradle his mother's herb garden. On the way back, once we've dealt with this creature, I fully intend to indulge myself in cataloging everything she's growing.

A bustling festival mood has gripped the main street, where villagers in what appear to be their celebration best travel in pairs and family groups toward the ruin on the hill. It covers the sound of our footfalls as we slink down the alley between the *Pern's* small stable and the neighboring row of shops. In the distance, over the wooden roofs of Gwillfifeshire, I can see that they've lit a bonfire at the apex of the knoll, and as we slide past yet more revelers on our way around a corner,

I realize that each household seems to be carrying with them an unlit torch wreathed in fresh meadow flowers.

Fire Flower Festival, I remind myself. *For whatever it is that means.*

We take more back alleys and squeeze through fence slats, following a circuitous route that only makes sense to the boy. Finally, we arrive in an older, crumbling part of town where the houses lean against one another like limping beggars and the square is frosted with the refuse of what appears to be a butcher's market. The breeze gifts us with the odors of old meat and blood, spilt marrow and bowels. Mixed with the lavender of my shirt, it is bile-inducing. I clamp my mouth shut against the taste of it, absurdly glad for the lemon cream.

If Kin is nauseated, I can't tell. Dammit, I should have offered him some of the ungent. Thoma doesn't seem to even notice the smell. Kin scans the square, but all the houses appear empty. The festival has pulled away all the residents. Hmph. That's an unexpected blessing.

In the center of the square, bathed in auspicious and melodramatic moonlight is an ancient yew tree. Its circumference is at least twice the span of Kin's arms, and the light from above filters through its creaking branches, casting the well tucked into the lee of the thick trunk in ominous shadow. The wall is crumbling, lopsided, and rough. It would come to Thoma's waist if he was standing beside it, and it seems the roots of the tree have crowded it so bad that the ground around the yellowed stones has buckled and heaved, shoving the well into a motley array. A small pulley-rack is planted into the ground beside the wall, a fresh rope threaded over the wooden block and attached to a slim, clean bucket.

"Of course it's right out in the open," Kin grumbles.

We stop in the last patch of shadow afforded by a narrow alleyway before the exposed air of the square. Kin leans against the wall of the building and scratches the back of his head, thinking. I settle in beside him, watching the well warily while Kin is distracted, as I always do. Someone has to remain alert and ready.

"She's in there," Thoma says, rather pointlessly, as that much is already obvious. He steps out of the slice of shadow and thrusts his finger at the well.

"Yes," I hiss, and drag him back. "Thank you, Thoma. You should head home now."

"What?" the boy yelps, eyes large and wounded. Writer, I do not want to wrestle with a child having a tantrum right now.

"You've been very helpful," I say quietly, crouching down to meet the boy's eyes. "And we thank you. But things are about to get dangerous, and I think your mother would be happier if you were not here with us when they do."

Thoma's brow wrinkles, and he frowns fit to resemble the arches of Kingskeep's gates. "Dangerous?" he repeats, incredulous.

"There's a ghost about," Kin says, and he speaks with the tone that makes it clear he thinks Thoma is a stupid child. Thoma is grown-up enough to take umbrage with being spoken to in that way, though, and puffs out his chest.

"I ain't afraid," he insists. "She ain't scary."

Kin makes a sound at the back of his throat that I know is muffled disbelief, and then covers it with a cough. "All the same, young Master Thoma," Kin says, without turning to the boy, "you'll go now."

"No, I won't!" Thoma brandishes his twig sword. "I'm a *hero*, and I ain't scared of nothing!" He waves the toy in a wide arc and I have to duck to avoid its swing.

It's stupidity and bravery like this that gets people killed, and I'll be damned if I'm going to watch it happen to a *child.* It's dangerous work, adventuring. And it's not for the innocent, the uninitiated, the small, and the weak. I have stood beside too many graves and attended too many wakes, mourned for more of our companions than I can count on both hands. I will *not* attend one more.

As the boy flails, chest thrust out and chin forward, I grab his wrist. It's harsher than I should have been, but I'm annoyed. The boy yelps and drops his wooden sword. It clatters against the cracked flags and both Kin and I suck in a breath at the volume of the sound.

The world goes quiet. Thoma whimpers. Kin and I scan the area, ears open, eyes darting. When nothing jumps out at us, I uncurl my fingers one by one, slowly enough not the startle the boy. As soon as he's free, Thoma yanks his arm out of my reach and cradles it against his chest. The skin's red, but there's no bruising. He looks betrayed.

"You're mean," Thoma hisses, whispering because Kin has raised a finger to his own lips. "You're not nice, or smart, or courageous, or anything like the stories. You're terrible, and you're stupid, and I want you to go away."

"We'll go when the ghost is destroyed," Kin hisses.

Thoma gasps, eyes bulging, and takes a step back so swiftly that his narrow shoulders slam into the brick wall behind him with a muffled slap.

"No!" he says.

The word is freighted with such horror that I whip around to spot whatever is coming up behind Kin. But I find only empty air over Kin's shoulder, and turn back to look at the boy, wondering if it is something only he can see. That's when I realize that his gaze isn't trained on some invisible creature, but on Kin himself.

Thoma sees a monster. But it isn't the ghost.

"No," Thoma says again, and this time he takes a step forward, glaring. "I won't let you!"

"*Let* me?" Kin snorts. He looks as if he's about to palm the boy's forehead, to hold him away and out of punching range like a schoolyard bully. I shoot Kin a warning look and Kin heaves a sigh, crossing his arms over the pommel of Foesmiter instead. We share another conversation of facial twitches and almost-gestures and agree that whatever spell this ghost has cast upon the Goodwoman of *Pern*, it must also have cast on her son.

Monsters often enchant their human slaves into loving them. Love means that the slave will sacrifice themselves to save the creature, or betray the people who have come to rescue them. And that means Thoma can't be here.

"Go home, Thoma," I say. "Please."

Thoma crosses his arms in deliberate imitation of Kin, mulish. "No. I *like* Mandikin, and I won't let you hurt her."

A sharp blast of grave-cold air rushes through the alley. I groan. Kin runs his hand through his hair, puffing out an irritated sigh.

"Perfect," I mutter. "You said her name."

Another chill blast rushes past, and this time the origin direction is clear. Kintyre spins around and faces the well, Foesmiter leaping into his hand. I press my back to my partner's, feeling the slide and bunch of muscle, reading Kin's readiness and wariness in the shift of balance and the heat of his skin. Kin will watch my back as I try to drum some damned sense into Thoma and get the little brat to hide.

"Thoma," I hiss through the rising wind, pushing the strands of hair flapping into my eyes out of the way. It stings.

"You should never name a ghost so close to its grave, or midnight."

"It summons them. I *know*," Thoma says, and peers at me as if *I'm* the one who's the idiot. When he realizes how worried I am, Thoma's grin grows wide and his eyebrows pull down into the eternal expression of a child willfully about to throw himself into mischief.

It is so like one of Kintyre's expressions that I'm momentarily poleaxed. I raise my hand, to silence, to muffle, but my surprise makes me too slow.

"Mandikin, Mandikin, MandikinMaaaaaandikiiiiin!" Thoma calls. "Mandik—*umunf!*"

I slap my palm over the boy's mouth. But it's useless. The wind, pulsing with half-hearted blasts, grows steadily stronger, and cold enough that my next exhale hangs in front of my mouth like a specter itself. Thoma digs his fingernails into the back of my hand, whining high and shrill between my fingers, but I grit my teeth and hold on.

The alley is no longer a defensible position. Too many shadows. Too many walls that a creature of air could corner us against, with too few handholds for climbing away.

Without me even needing to say it, Kin gallops forward into the open air of the square. I wrap my free arm around Thoma's shoulders and drag the gagged brat into the square behind Kin, once more taking up my position at Kin's back, facing out, waiting.

The boy kicks my shins and swears under his breath, but I hold on. The last thing I'm going to do is let the boy wriggle away and run. He'll be cut down by the creature. Or worse, join it and turn himself into a hostage, leverage, a shield and a distraction.

The breeze is freezing. It grows into a gale, and my fringe cuts at my eyes. I squint, unwilling to let go of Thoma until

I know which direction is safe to push the boy toward. The freezing wind turns the lingering dampness of my shirt into an icy punishment.

And then the gale stops. Just like that, our clothing and hair drop limp, the night air suddenly unmoving. It's like those summer nights when it's so hot that even the breeze can't bear to stir, but it's *chill*. Wrong, in every and all ways.

Goosebumps march up my spine, and I take a deep breath, forcing myself to ignore the eeriness around me and focus. I narrow my eyes, watching the debris and mist kicked up by the wind slide slow and molasses-like through the butter-thick air. It coalesces, dancing like dust motes in a library sunbeam that's cold, so cold.

"There," Kin says, but doesn't point. Doesn't need to. Didn't even really need to speak, except that our world is too quiet, all of a sudden. It needed shattering.

Thoma goes still. I spare him a glance, worried that the boy will be limp or statue-like, eyes glowing, mouth parted in a grimace, or any of the other horrid things I have seen humans become while under spells of compulsion or Words of Obedience. But the boy seems fine. Irritated, fuming, but otherwise fine.

Carefully, I release him, my free hand curled, ready to shoot out and nab the kid by the back of the collar if I need to. Thoma shuffles a few steps away, but doesn't seem inclined to throw himself at the ghost, or on Kin's sword, or at me. He only glares mutinously, tiny jaw thrust out, thin arms crossed over a skinny chest. He seems to have totally forgotten that he has a kitchen knife threaded into his belt, and for that I'm grateful. I don't need a child flashing around a blade on top of everything else. I should have taken it away at the inn. Fool.

I risk looking away from Thoma and at the monster.

It's a woman, or at least, it's womanish-shaped. I get the sense of white, white, and white—long hair, long scarf, full-length sleeping gown, all of it trailing into frosty mist, flakes of the ghost breaking off and falling like a never-ending drift of sparkling snow, but never piling up at her feet. Fingers of ice crawl out along the paving stones toward us. The wall of the well grows rimed with ghost-frost.

It seems, at first, as if the ghost cannot, or does not see us adults. Kin's grip on Foesmiter shifts as two tendrils of frosty mist reach out toward Thoma. They don't grab, they just . . . reach. Invite. It's not seductive, or dangerous, it's . . . maternal. Parental.

Terrifying.

My stomach tries to crawl up my throat, and I swallow hard, my heart fluttering. The pose is the exact same one my brother takes when he's beckoning the twins over for cuddling. And nothing *dead* should look so *inviting*.

"Back, wretch!" Kin snarls, rocking up on the balls of his feet, Foesmiter held at its most menacing angle. Starlight tumbles down Foesmiter's keen edge, a threat and a promise both. The ghost startles, straightening a bit and scowling. It beckons again, agitated. Thoma inhales, obvious and indicative. I dig my fingers into the back of Thoma's coat seconds before the boy tries to break into a run.

"Mandikin!" he squawks, when it's clear that I have no intention of letting him go.

Only then does the ghost straighten fully. She scowls harder, fierce and furious, hair lifting, scarf and nightdress whipping about in a hurricane wind that neither I nor Kin can feel. She reaches for the boy, arms out and issuing ghostly tendrils that remind me of the menacing tentacles of a kraken.

They writhe and reach. Foesmiter cuts, but the mist only parts like pipe smoke, coalescing again as soon as Kin's blade has passed, unharmed.

"The phials! Bevel, the Words!" Kin prompts, but I don't have enough hands to hold Thoma and my sword, *and* root into my pouch.

"Writer's calluses!" I snarl, and shove Thoma down hard, hoping the daft brat will have the presence of mind, or at least the willpower, to stay where he's put. The boy cries out, a sharp yelp that seems disproportionate to the mild pain of landing arse-first on cobblestones, and I belatedly remember the knife.

If the kid's been hurt . . . no, worry about the ghost first, I scold myself.

Sword up, I keep an eye on the ghost and Kin, and get Thoma flipped onto his hands and knees with one foot, putting enough weight on the wriggling little brat's back to keep him pinned in place. The ghost hisses in displeasure, probably annoyed that I keep manhandling its slave instead of letting the boy go to her, and I duck quickly to tug the knife out of the boy's belt.

I lift it by the pommel, point down, looking for blood. There isn't any on the blade, and neither Thoma's clothing nor flesh looks slashed. There's no dark stain on his trousers, thank the Writer. I take my boot off the kid.

And that is when the ghost *howls*. It points a finger that's slowly growing sharp at my face, at the knife. The sweet, womanish face transforms into twin black pits and a sucking, terrifying wound of a mouth.

"I'm fine, Mandikin!" Thoma yells from the ground. "I'm fine, see?" He kneels up and holds out his palms. They're scratched and dirty, but there's no blood.

The sharp finger, the accusatory point aimed at me, curls into claws and suddenly, immediately, I *understand*.

Mandikin's not trying to hurt Thoma. She's trying to *protect* him.

Protect him from Kin and me.

I look down at the knife in my hand, at the boy, then up at the ghost.

"Oh *hells*," I mutter, and fling the knife away. "Kin, stop!" I yell, but it's too late. Kintyre is already lunging at the thing, muttering Words of Repellence. He's rat-arsed rubbish at Speaking Words, always has been. The ghost wavers and shifts a bit back toward the well, but is otherwise unaffected.

"Get the boy to safety!" Kin shouts over his shoulder, lunging again. Is he really trying to make himself a human shield between me and the specter? Apparently, he is. It would be so easy for the ghost to cut through him, to *step* through him, hells, to even just step *around* him, and . . . I'm reminded very suddenly why I'm often the one who has to do the planning in this partnership.

"Kintyre!" I call again, but Mandikin's howling has risen to such a pitch that I doubt Kin can hear me. "Kin, stop it!" I lunge forward, sheathing my sword and grabbing on to Kin's bicep, only to be shrugged off as Kin whips Foesmiter through the ghost's non-existent skull. "Kin, stop! Writer, for once, will you *listen* to me?"

Just as I guessed she would, the ghost smokes through the gaps in our bodies and reforms behind us. Thoma stands and smiles, but Mandikin doesn't go to him. Instead, she turns to the hill outside of town and rushes away along the cobbles, down the main thoroughfare. Her hair is whipping around behind her, loose and flapping with the trail of her scarf, the fluttering hem of the modest, incorporeal nightdress diffusing like smoke rings against the starry sky.

"Follow!" Kin growls and, being the faster of the two of us, pelts after it. As always, I follow. And if I fall behind, I'll follow Kin's footprints.

"No, wait!" Thoma cries, and I can hear the clatter of the boy's boots fall away behind me. Thoma is a smart boy—smarter than me, it seems—he'll catch up.

I shoulder through the rough, narrow gap between two wattle-and-daub houses, and suddenly I'm in a muddy field. The sky bursts into full radiance above me, deep indigo and black splattered with a cornucopia of constellations, and in the distance, capping the hill, the firefly wink of torches.

The Fire Flower Festival, I realize. *Mandikin's not running from Kin. She's going for help!*

The ghost flees up the hill, and I catch up to Kintyre just as he begins to climb it, Foesmiter slashing wildly and stupidly at her trailing scarf. We're perhaps a giant's stride behind when the ghost stops. She is standing beside someone, female, but beyond that, the finery of the lady's festival attire makes her difficult to recognize.

"Ma!" Thoma cries from somewhere behind us, voice sharp and loud for such a small pair of lungs, and the woman beside Mandikin turns to its source. The ghost points at Kin and me, steaming up the hillside, Foesmiter naked in the starlight.

"Mandikin? What are you—good gracious! Thoma!" the Goodwoman of *Pern* hollers. "Master Turn, Master Dom! What*ever* are you doing?"

"Back!" Kin roars, skidding to a halt and menacing his already-proven-to-be-useless blade in the ghost's face like the dumb lump he is. "Stay back, away from that thing!"

"Kin, wait—" I try again, reaching out to grab for my partner's bicep a second time. Kin actually smacks my hand away and I dance back, both my knuckles and my pride smarting.

Kin again mouths Words, and a fission of terror shivers down my spine. Words of Banishment, and, with Foesmiter so tuned to the ghost . . . no wonder Kin was cutting through the fog. He wasn't trying to hack at a specter, he was aligning Foesmiter to the ghost's energies.

"Writer, Kin, stop!" I shout.

Then Thoma barrels past both of us. At first, it seems as if the boy is heading to bury himself in his mother's skirts, but he swerves and throws himself at the ghost instead.

Mandikin is just solid enough for the boy to puff against, like diving into an overfilled feather pillow. Her skirts flare and curl around his shoulders and head like protective fingers.

Kin stutters to a halt, tongue tripping over the final Words of the destructive phrase, and the world goes horribly, breath-stealingly silent. Foesmiter glows gold in the starlight, lit from within by the Words it waits to cut at their foe.

"Move," Kin hisses at the boy.

"No!" Thoma spits back. "I won't let you hurt Mandikin!"

"Hurt Mandikin?" another voice roars, and a man with mutton chops and a sash stretched across his rotund belly shoulders his way to the front of the increasingly horrified-looking crowd that has begun to condense around us. The town's lord, I'd guess, and then I dismiss him to focus on my stubborn friend.

"No one's hurting anyone!" I shout, but my voice is lost under the sudden wave of protests and noise from the people of Gwillfifeshire. Bodies shove forward, getting too close to Kin's blade, and I wriggle myself between them. Kin's broad hand lands on my back, using me to shepherd the incensed bystanders back, like I'm better for nothing but acting as his shield. Humph. Arse.

Shouting rakes against my ears, pierced by Mandikin's ghastly wails. I want to clap my hands over them, but instead, I shove my arms out to the side, taking on the role of human barricade that Kin has foisted on me.

Thoma is crying now, clutching at Mandikin, and other children have begun to wail as well, one little girl screaming over and over, "Don't kill her! Don't kill her! Don't make her go away like Daddy!" The town's lord is trying to bully his way to Kin, and Mandikin is no help— the more the children cry, the more she screams.

"Enough!" I roar. This is my battlefield voice. "By the Writer's left nutsack, that is *enough*!"

The expletive is harsh, but it works. Everyone on the hill falls silent all at once, the adults blushing and glowering furiously, the children muffling sobs or giggles behind their hands. Mandikin offers me an expression so poisonous I wonder vaguely if I'm now cursed to die at dawn, or something. She primly lays partially opaque hands over Thoma's ears.

"Finally!" Kin bawls, puffing up his chest like he's just killed a dwarven pimp.

I spin on my heel, duck under Foesmiter with extremely practiced ease, and stab my finger against Kin's sternum. "I was talking to *you*, you thick-skulled *tit*!"

Kin gapes at me, blinking rapidly, Foesmiter wilting in his grasp. The Goodwoman of *Pern* applauds slowly, loudly. No other sound except the crackle of the nearby bonfire shreds the quiet.

"Now, what is this about harming Mandikin?" the lord blusters, and Writer, he sounds like a satire of a lord, all jowly vowels and burring consonants puffing out from behind his soup-strainer moustaches, like something from a play.

"It was a misunderstanding," I say, taking a step back from Kin and waiting until my partner has caught up enough to sheathe Foesmiter. Then I make a very humble, very simple, but very low bow to the official. Not my court bow, not the one that I save for King Carvel, but the one that I really mean. "We apologize most humbly."

"They were going to hurt Mandikin!" Thoma snarls, wiping tears from his flushed cheeks with the cuff of my short-robe.

The lord puffs up his own impressive girth to match Kin's and rocks forward on his feet, ready to have a fight.

"We were, it's true," I jump in, hands up and placating, before Kin can open his mouth and doom us to another night on the road. Or to a lynch mob. "But you must understand, sir, that with our, um, extensive experience with malevolent spirits, we might have, ah, made some hasty assumptions. We now stand corrected and offer no ill will to, ah . . . Miss Mandikin. Or Gwillfifeshire."

"Extensive experience?" the lord asks, eyes narrowed in suspicion.

The Goodwoman leans over and hisses, in a deliberate stage whisper, "That's Kintyre Turn and Bevel Dom, Lord Gallvig."

A ripple of murmurs and suddenly craning heads spreads back over the crowd.

Oh, thank the Writer, I think as I feel the last of the tension that had crackled in the air break and crumble away amid the buoyancy of the town realizing that they have *heroes* in their midst. Write a few dozen scrolls, and suddenly you can do no wrong. I try not to take too much advantage of our fame (Kin's head is big enough without drinking and getting favors from brothels for free), but sometimes, just sometimes, it's welcome.

"And you were after the ghost?" another woman calls out, startled.

A man raises his arm and makes a sort of panicky hand gesture over the heads of the crowd. "But Mandikin is the town *babysitter*. You can't *banish* her!"

"We need her!" says another. "She's one of us!" More voices join in, a chorus of parents as desperate not to lose Mandikin as the children.

That deflates Kin a bit. "We apologized," he mutters.

"*I* apologized," I correct, under my breath, just enough for Kin to hear. Kin ducks his head and nods once. My friend is stupid sometimes, but he can learn, too.

"I am deeply sorry for my mistake," Kintyre says, using his Eldest Son of Turnshire voice and executing the matching bow. It's a bit showier than mine was, as befits his station and fame, but it's not *his* peacockish court bow, either.

Good, I think. *At least he's taking the apology seriously*.

Kin turns to Mandikin, taking a deep breath for another formal apology. Thoma puffs out his chest in defiance of the hero's attention on his friend. Kin is wounded by the boy's lost worship. It manifests as a small twitch in the corner of Kin's mouth, but only I see it because I know him so well. Gutted, Kin swallows back the flowery words I know he would have said and simply bows again. Mandikin nods solemnly, slowly, just once.

When she raises her head, it is wreathed in smiles, and the chill of ghost-breath seems to have warmed into a summer breeze, rather than the sharp snap of winter. A spill of children push past and around us. They all crowd around her, and their parents seem happy to let them go.

"Well then, back to it, back to it!" Lord Gallvig roars, belly shaking with the force of the laugh that follows as he ushers people back toward the bonfire and the food stalls pitched haphazardly against the walls of the ruin.

Mistress *Pern* sidles close enough to pluck my short-robe off her son. She shakes out a bundle of fabric that proves to be the waistcoat we'd left behind in our rooms, wraps it around him, and then sends him off after Mandikin and the other children. She pats down my short-robe, a motherly gesture that I've seen women everywhere perform, and then hands it to me.

"Thank you," I say.

"Thank you for wanting to protect him," she replies. "Even if it was misguided."

I scratch the back of my neck and fight the flush I can feel trying to crawl up my cheekbones. Usually I'm the one making other people blush, and it's a nice change. It's also a nice change to come out the other end of an adventure unhurt, unbloody, and unbruised for once. I nod to the Goodwoman, feigning humbleness at her gratitude, and she cants a hip at me. Oh, she's *flirting*. With me. That's lovely.

That is very good, indeed.

Kin cuts a look between us, and his eyes widen fractionally. Realization is followed by a small smirk of anticipation and triumph. Oh. He expects me to share.

After all of this? After everything that could have been avoided if Kin had just *listened* to me? Not bloody likely.

"Thoma left one of your cooking knives in the square," Kin says, abruptly charming again. "I'll fetch it back to the tavern." He jogs down the hill to give me space in which to work, dodging around a group of pretty young women and men trying to get his attention. Followers of my scrolls, most likely. Adoring youths like these are always pie-eyed in Kin's presence, cooing and making offers that they're all too young to really understand.

I take a deep breath, taking a moment to watch Kin go, giving myself time for my face to cool.

"So," I venture, playing at harmless and polite. I reseat my sword in its sheath to give myself an excuse not to meet the Goodwoman's gaze. Acting a bit nervous makes women want to coddle and protect, which are feelings that are more easily translated into "taking care of me in bed" than those engendered by approaching them with overconfident arrogance. I duck my head, look up at the Goodwoman through my lashes, and fiddle with my pouch, rearranging things so they're all laying correctly. "A ghost?"

"That's both supremely unsubtle and a fair bit more narrow-minded than I expected from one as well traveled as you," the Goodwoman replies with an unladylike snort. Startled at having my ruse caught out, I look back up. And I only now notice that her mop cap has been replaced with a crown of intricately braided golden hair and wildflowers. The smile lines beside her eyes deepen as she grins at me. "You'll not be charming me with your wiles and your false coyness. I know you, Master Dom. And I know your habits. If you want the story, just ask. Your scrolls say you've consorted with nixies and sirens, nagas and ogres. You should know better than to assume. You've taken dinner with wolves."

I snort and resist the urge to shove my hands in my pockets like a truant child who's been caught out. For I absolutely have been caught out. Instead, I shrug on my short-robe and roll my eyes theatrically, willing to banter. It seems I should focus on a more forthright, mature approach with the Goodwoman. Fine by me. I prefer it when no one needs to be persuaded. "It was bloody."

"It was still dinner."

"True." I look over at the ghost thoughtfully. "She's sweet with them," I decide. I'd trust her with the twins.

"She was in life, also," the Goodwoman says softly, taking the whispered confession as an excuse to step closer, to brush the tips of her fingers against the inner curve of my elbow. "She wanted nothing more than to be a mother."

I obligingly tip my head down toward her. "How did she . . . if it's not impertinent to ask—?"

"Childbirth."

I nod grimly. "The babe?"

"Gone to rest on whatever shelf the Writer places our books when our story is over. Or not quite begun."

I nod again, brushing my nose against the shell of her ear, the one that earlier today had a marriage bob. Which is now missing. "And the father?"

The Goodwoman grimaces slightly. "You know as well as I that fauns don't mate for longer than a season."

Oh. *Oh.* I sigh slowly. All the excitement of the adventure drains out of me, leaving only hollow, empathetic sorrow. That poor woman. "So, he's likely forgotten her name by now."

"If he ever knew it," the Goodwoman agrees. "It was a good love, though. A solid love. And Mandikin had no illusions, no imaginings that what she had was other than what it was: just a season."

"You knew her well, then?"

"My grandmother was her sister. I know her better than most, but not from firsthand experience."

"Still a treasure," I say. I reach into my pouch for a pencil and some scrap parchment, and then pause. "Before I . . . do you mind? I mean, do you think the gh—*Mandikin* would mind if I wrote her story down?"

The Goodwoman's eyes shine. "Mandikin's tale told by Kintyre Turn's bard? I think all of Gwillfifeshire would be quite, quite honored, Master Dom. So long as you tell it honestly."

I chuckle as I retreive my writing tools. "So, making a fool of Kin and myself, am I?"

"Aye, Master Dom, that you will be. Come, I haven't forgotten that I offered you two a place in my family circle." The Goodwoman pulls me off to the side of the festival fairway, where people have begun to clump and cluster on the grass. There is a blanket there, and Thoma has already deposited his stiff, formal waistcoat in a crumpled heap on the knitted wool. The Goodwoman sighs fondly, scoops it up and refolds it, and then seats herself. I sit beside her, deliberately pressing my side against hers. She doesn't move back. Progress. Excellent. I lay the scrap of parchment against my knee.

"Very well. Go ahead, please," I say.

The Goodwoman's tale enchants me, and I take every opportunity to encourage her to rest her cheek against my shoulder and whisper it into my ear. I turn my face only a few times, when I want clarification, and make it seem as if brushing my lips against her nose or chin is an accident. If she wants to kiss me, she will—I'll let her initiate that.

I don't know how long it is before my notes have filled up both sides of the sheet, and she's placing her hand on my shoulder and saying, "Ah, Master Turn has returned."

I twist to look. Kin is climbing the hill slowly. He's still wearing Foesmiter, but he's carrying my writing box under his arm. As he passes stragglers carrying torches, the light gilds his hair and the embroidery on his jerkin with gold. Writer, Kin looks edible—flushed from the earlier adventure, windblown and confident. And better than all of that, my pipe is in that writing box. Now *that* is a true hero.

"He's handsome," the Goodwoman admits, clearly admiring the view as much as I am.

I feel my guts twist with the small jealousy that always curls there when someone else openly admires Kintyre the way I can't.

"He is," I say carefully. The last thing I want to do is reveal the extent of my wounded heart to a woman who is, by virtue of her occupation, probably the proud spider at the center of Gwillfifeshire's gossip web.

"You're a lucky man," the Goodwoman say guilelessly, and it takes a second for me to remember what she said in the taproom. She thinks Kin is my *lover*. We're not wearing the same colors, so it's clear we're not trothed, which means she must think . . . Writer, what a scandal that would be, if Kin and I were carrying on like that, the eldest son of a lord and a blacksmith's boy.

Yet, we're both knighted, both men of titles and wealth now. Both men of renown, and to be frank, the bedsport we engage in with women is already extremely close to actually making love.

I feel my cheeks go hot. I lower my face, making a show of putting my notes away in my pouch to avoid having to answer. The Goodwoman clears her throat expectantly, and I have just enough time to murmur, "He doesn't love me," before Kintyre reaches us.

Her face slips into an expression of shock, which, for his sake, she quickly shutters. Then she stands, and my whole side feels suddenly cold. I try not to take that as some sort of portent.

The Goodwoman is formal and polite when she offers Kin a seat on a second blanket that she shakes out next to her own; the flirting and the geniality has stopped. She is still kind and warm while the three of us chat idly, and I realize that she was never really flirting with me. She was just trying to see if she could get a rise out of Kin, see if he and I might . . . might what? Put on a show? Reveal ourselves?

As lovers? As husbands? Maybe goad me into pledging my troth now, before the whole village, in a romantic gesture inspired by battle and burning flowers? The Goodwoman must be one of those faithful readers who seems *sure* that there is more happening between me and Kintyre than I put in my scrolls. Of course.

What an absolute minx. *I'm* supposed to be the charming one who talks people into things they didn't realize they were agreeing to.

I refrain from pinching the bridge of my nose and dig through my writing box for my pipe. I clench it between my teeth and try not to hiss as I pack the bowl; adrenaline spent, my wrist is throbbing again. Kin has edged closer to the Goodwoman, mistaking her warmth for genuine interest, the same way I did. When his hand edges up the pool of fabric that is her gown to brush one questing knuckle along the Goodwoman's ankle, I take a breath to stop him. Before I can, the Goodwoman shoots to her feet and crosses her arms under her bosom, taking a step back.

"Shame on you, Kintyre Turn," she says, glaring first at Kin, and then shooting a meaningful, sympathetic glance at me.

What, does she think he's going to take that as an opening for a love confession? Absolutely *not.* I take a puff of my pipe and blow out a ring, trying to figure out how to command my brain to say any sentence that doesn't start with "*Come back to the inn with me, Kin. Just us.*"

Uhg! I'm a stupid, foolish, desperate, hopeless *sop*, and

it's really starting to infuriate me. *Murder. Death. Killing Dargan. Killing him slow.*

"Where's she going?" Kin asks, eyes trailing after her like a puppy left tied up in the yard. There is actual *petulance* in his tone. "I thought that you—"

"No," I interrupt.

"But she—"

"No!" I can feel the rage rising from the knot in my chest, sliding up my face like mercury in a thermometer. "And to be quite frank, Kin, I'm not really in the mood tonight."

"But you said—"

"Well, that was before you made a fool of us in front of a whole town, wasn't it?"

Kin splutters and his face crumples into that calculatingly adorable look of surprised hurt. "Before *I* made a—"

"Oh, Writer, just *stop*!" I slam my pipe down hard enough against the ground that the embers scatter all over the dew-damp grass and splutter out. I toss my pipe into my writing box and stand. I haul Kintyre to his feet, and this time, Kin goes with me when I grab him by the bicep and drag him far past the back of the festival stalls, out of the ring of firelight to where the din of the people will cover the shouting match we're about to have.

I wouldn't want to sully Kintyre's reputation by screaming at him in public, after all.

"How is any of this—? Where is *this* coming from?" Kintyre asks with a pouting mutter. "What's wrong with you?"

"Wrong with *me*?" I snarl. "My problem is that you never bloody well *listen* to me!"

"There's no need to be womanish about it!"

"Did you really just . . . ?" I gawp. "Womanish? Really? When you know Captain Isobin, and Cassiopith and . . . by the Writer's balls, Kin! You don't really *think* like that, do you?"

"Like what?" Every line of his body screams defensive and deliberate ignorance.

I throw up my hands. "*This*, Kin. *This right here* is why I'm mad at you! You pretend to be so stupid; you don't *think*, you just *react*! You just wave Foesmiter at something, and you think it will fix everything! Either one or the other of your swords needs to be unsheathed and that's it, isn't it! That will solve all the problems! Never mind Bevel Dom, it's not like you trust *his* judgment or advice or his Writer-be-damned *friendship*!"

Kintyre does exactly what he always does when I try to confront him, to pin him down, to stake him to the spot and *force* him to absorb truths: he deflects. "Well, I wasn't wrong. It was a ghost, and it *sounded* like it was—"

I rock back on my heels, mouth hanging open in stunned fury. "Do you even hear yourself?"

"It's not our fault that—what did they expect, a hero hearing about a ghost? They should have *told* us . . . "

I stab a finger against Kin's sternum. "It's easy to be a hero when you're born to all the advantages, Kin. Wealth enough for a good horse, and fine gear. Wealth enough to have grown strong on good food, to have training masters to hone your body, and scholars to teach you the paths and secrets of the world. But have you stopped to consider what it *means* to be a hero? What it means to be the idol of that little boy? Thoma looks up to you. The twins worship you. Even Forsyth looks to you for clues on how to live his life. We must cast our names carefully, Kin. We must *think* before we act. And we can no longer be unaware of how our actions read. Whom we shun, whom we throw our support behind, this *matters*."

"It was a mistake!" Kin shouts again. "It wasn't our fault!"

"It's entirely our fault!" And I'm sick of it, just *sick of it.* Kin just can't be wrong, can he?

"We weren't to know—"

"We could have *asked*!" I snarl.

"You never asked either!" Kin bawls back.

"More the fool, me!" I shout. "Why, *why* do I never learn? Why do I always, *always* go along with you? Why do I always follow, unquestioningly, un*thinkingly*, like a stupid spaniel? And why am I always surprised when you *kick*?"

"I don't kick you!" Kin says, and every line of his body, every blink, every breath is suddenly desperate. His entire demeanor changes, becoming contrite and needy. He fists the shoulders of my short-robe in his hands, scrunches down to meet my eyes, blue to blue. "Bev, no, I don't hurt you. I never want to hurt *you*."

"But you do! *Writer*, Kin, you do!"

"I don't mean to—"

"That's not the *point*! I am tired, Kintyre. *Tired*!" I roar. The truth that has weighed on me since yesterday comes falling out of my mouth like a cannonball, crushing the air out of my lungs. I gasp for another breath. "I'm sick of the road, and I'm sick of the travel, and I'm sick of fighting, always *fighting*. If I'm not fighting monsters, then I'm fighting with *you*. I'm sick of waking up sore and cold. I'm sick of having nothing, and I'm sick of you not . . ." I trail off and stop, biting down hard on the tip of my tongue to keep the words trapped behind my teeth.

I can't say it. *I can't say it.*

It would ruin everything.

He would never agree. He will never say yes. If I say it, he will leave, and it will be all over. And I would rather be tired, and sore, and cold, and be fighting monsters and bickering with my truest friend than be *without* Kintyre Turn.

Kin blinks, icy eyes wounded, chin tucked in shame. "Sick of me?" His voice is so small.

I sigh lustily, a gusting burst of irritation drawn from my very guts. "That's not what I meant."

"You said—"

"I know what I—! Kin, please, you don't . . . you don't *understand*."

Kin lets go of my robe. His hands slide upward, palms skimming over leather to cup the thin flesh of my throat. His thumbs circle, just once, along the edge of my jaw, calluses rough against my larynx. I swallow hard. His hands are *warm* in the chill spring air. My flesh tingles.

I want to either grab his hands and kiss him, or punch him. I ball my hands into fists and rest them on my belt, refusing to allow myself to do any of those things. I can't . . . Kintyre has to make the first move. He has to do it first. He has to *want* it.

He feel my own eyes growing wide, and I can't seem to stop them, can't *blink*. I don't dare look away.

"Kintyre?" I ask, and I can't seem to get my voice to go louder than a croak. I want. I'm shivering with *want*, and Kintyre has to say yes, doesn't he? This is a yes. It has to be a yes. I just might die if this isn't a yes.

Kin licks his lips, tongue sliding against the bottom first, corner to corner, and then the top, disappearing again and leaving a shimmer of wetness, and Writer, how desperate I am to chase it back into Kintyre's mouth with my own. We exhale as one, inhale, and we are so close together that our chests bump as they inflate. The moment stretches, stretches.

And then it snaps.

I surge forward and throw myself on Kin's mouth.

It's probably the stupidest thing I've ever done. But I can't, I absolutely cannot *stand it* anymore. I can't *not* be kissing Kintyre Turn.

I dig my fingers into the hair behind Kin's ears and yank him down. He's such an infuriatingly tall bastard. I mash our mouths together, biting, *devouring*, taking first one of Kin's lips and then the other between my own; wet, hot, wonderful. Breath puffs against my cheek, a surprised snort, and Kin grunts. I toss my arms around his neck, hold on, and think dazedly that breathing? Breathing is for suckers.

"Let me show you. Writer—" I pant against Kin's mouth, peppering words between kisses. "I—what I—for so long."

And then there are hands on my shoulders, and Kin is holding me, massaging, pushing. . . . Pushing?

Pushing.

I freeze. Shame splashes down my spine. Ardor turns to ice in my veins.

"Bevel," Kintyre whispers. His breath is hot on my ear, and still it turns my limbs to frost and snow and isolation.

With one word, Kintyre the basilisk turns me to stone.

"You beautiful, beautiful idiot," I moan, and my voice crackles over each word like a winter pond crumbling beneath my feet. I hope Kintyre thinks I'm talking about myself.

I turn away, press my hands against my face and scrub. Because if my cheeks are flushed from chaffing at them, then Kin can't possibly believe that it's from the way I'm desperately, desperately swallowing back tears.

"Bevel," Kintyre says again, and I both do and don't want to turn, to see which expression his face has twisted to house. Disgust? Pity? Fear?

Never love. It will never be love, and hope, and joy, and

affection, and if it can never be those, then I don't want to see it.

"Look, I didn't mean it," I say, softly. I offer it up, just like that—an escape route for Kin. "I'm feeling . . . I'm just tired, you know? I'm muddled. Just . . . go back to the blanket. I'll . . . I need a walk. I'll clear my head. Then I'll meet you back there."

"I'll buy us some ale?" Kin whispers. His voice is tremulous, low, and I don't allow myself to believe that it's because Kin is as affected as I am. It didn't mean a thing to him. It was just weird, something strange, just Bevel Dom having one of his breakdowns. Something to get drunk over and laugh about, and then forget. Like always. "Something to . . . I can get you, I don't know . . . do you want some honeycomb?"

"Sure, Kin," I sigh. *If you think I'm some simpering maiden whose good humor can be bought with treats and booze and gewgaws . . . oh, Kin, how are we getting this so wrong?* "I'll be along soon."

"As you wish," Kintyre says. "Just . . . follow me soon?"

I make no response. I just keep my head down, my hands firmly at my sides until I hear Kintyre's boots on the grass shuffling away, out of hearing.

Only then do I raise my face to the moon and wrap my arms around myself. "I'll follow. I will always follow you. And that's the real problem, Kintyre Turn. I was made to follow you. And I'm so sick of walking one step behind."

***

I'm gasping for a few moments of quiet time with my pipe. Without Kin. Just to drown this buzzing, itching desire and the horrific shame that flares under my skin, in the base of my spine, lingering on the back of my tongue. To numb all the places and patches where Kin has touched me before, where I want him to touch me again. But my pipe is in my writing box, and that's on the blanket with the Goodwoman of Pern, and I don't have the guts to look her in the face right now. Not yet. So instead, I walk the perimeter of the festival.

It makes me feel better, one eye on the people, one eye on the darkness beyond, like I'm patrolling. It makes me feel like I have a purpose.

On the far side of the massive bonfire from the Goodwoman's blanket—and presumably Kin—Lord Gallvig is standing on a small, knocked-together wooden platform, accepting strips of cloth from a line of people. Some of the cloth looks new, some worn, and some even looks like it was torn from wedding finery or funeral shrouds. I lean against the pole of a pastry tent and watch the lord wrap the cloth around and around a long length of pine, until the end is absolutely bulbous. Some children offer up string to tie it all in place, fussing over their knots and bows, tongues poking out and eyes squinting in their concentration.

When it's done, the lord walks twelve circles around the fire with the cloth-stick held aloft. Every time he passes the ruins side, the children squeal with delight and shout the name of a month. When a whole year's worth of laughter has been counted out, a woman who must be the lord's wife wreathes the head of the torch with a garland of dried flowers and fruits, herbs and winter wheat.

Together, her cheek resting on his shoulder, fingers intertwined, they touch the ball of fabric to the flames. It catches slowly, sweetly. Deep beneath the layers of cloth there must be pitch. The torch, once lit, doesn't smolder or flicker out.

The lord plants the torch into a hole bored into the side of the ruin wall. The scent of sage and clary, rosemary and golden roses, weeping martins and forget-me-nots perfumes the clearing as the fire licks at the wreath. It is the bouquet of mourning and remembrance, of filial love and neighborly admiration, and gratitude.

I breathe deeply and am filled with shame.

***

Judging by the fall of the moon, over an hour passes as I wander the stalls and impromptu dances that have erupted wherever someone has thought to plant themselves with an instrument. In that time, I have drunk more than one tankard of ale that was pressed into my hands, and swung about two fair young lasses and a youth just old enough to know what he likes and how to ask for it with the coy tilt of a chin and a look up through his fanning lashes.

But it is not his company I want tonight.

There is only one man, one person I want to talk to and touch, to smell and laugh with, and even though my heart is a little more broken tonight than it was when I rose from my bedroll this morning, Kintyre Turn is still the man I want to spend the rest of my life with.

My miserable, masochistic, foolish life.

In whatever way Kintyre dictates, I am his.

So I find the Goodwoman's knitted throw among the throngs of families picnicking on the grass. Kintyre sits alone on one corner of it, slightly removed, contemplative looking. There is a small basket with a packet wrapped in oilcloth by his knee.

"Hello," I say, and drop down beside him on the ground, sprawling as if I don't have a care in the world. The posture is very carefully put on, and it makes Kin look all the more tense and nervous, sitting upright with his legs folded under him.

Kin blinks, and then looks as if he's screwing up his courage. I lick my lips again, a quick flicker, and draw in a breath. I can't stand it. If Kintyre tries to explain, or deflect, or blame away, I'll *scream*. So instead of letting him talk, I pull back the oilcloth on the basket and inhale.

"Oh, a spinach and cheese roll. My favorite."

"I know," Kin says, deflating. He reaches into the basket and pulls out two of the steaming buns.

I take mine graciously, prop myself on one elbow, and go about the very important business of *not talking about it.* I nibble and people-watch, quiet and companionable. Slowly, the tension bleeds out of Kin's posture. As the buns vanish, the silence becomes comfortable and familiar again, and the storm is over.

Thank the Writer, it's over, I think. *And Kintyre is still my friend.*

When I have licked all the crumbs off my fingers, I retrieve my pipe, my wallet of sweet herbs, and matches from my box of writing tools on the blanket beside us. Kintyre takes one of the matches from my hand, strikes it against his own belt buckle, and holds it out for me. The gesture is intimate, and I watch as Kin brings the small sliver of wood to his crotch, and then offers it toward my mouth.

I nearly forget to inhale. Just before the flames can lick the tips of Kin's fingers, I remember that I'm meant to be lighting my pipe.

Kin's breath, when he leans in close to cup the bowl, betrays that he has somehow acquired mead or honeyed ale. When he withdraws, he tugs a dark drinking skin off his belt and takes a swallow. He offers the skin to me, fingers loose around the neck as he brings the rim to my lips. I hold the stem of my pipe to the side to accept the sip without needing my hands.

It's silly, but I'm suddenly in a silly mood: giddy with relief, skin starved, both of us wanting to reassure ourselves that we are still the most important person in all of Hain to the other. Even if we aren't . . . *that*. When he lowers the skin, Kin turns and leans back-to-back against me, as if we are about to do battle. Close, without being intimate. He pushes a bit, playful, and I shoulder him back and take a deep, soothing draw of sweet herb.

It tastes and feels like forgiveness. Or at least a desire to return to the way things were three hours ago, over dinner in the *Pern*. Which is close enough.

Kin is warm. Kin is always warm. It's one of the things I like best about him, unless we're in the hotter climes. Then Kin is clammy and sticky, and clings like an octopus when he's irritable and uncomfortable, which just makes me irritated in turn. But now, in the cool night breeze, with the fire at our front and Kin mapped against the constellations of my spine—stars of shoulder and muscle, bone and cloth, the dips and swells—I'm comfortable. I'm content. It is not all that I've ever wanted, but it is close enough. Close enough. I can live with this.

I'll have to.

I tap a finger over the bowl of my pipe and relish the sweet smoke that sifts up my sinuses. A deep breath in clears the smoke from my head, and brings me a hint of my friend.

Kin smells of sweat, and the faint hint of butter soap and lavender water. He smells of man. He smells of Foesmiter's whetstone and polishing oil, petrichor and musk, leather and road-dust, horse and hard work. Kin.

I turn my face to the flames, resting my cheek on

Kin's broad shoulder. In return, Kin sighs and arches his neck, settling the vulnerable curve of his skull against my cheekbone.

All around us are families, most sitting on woven throws of every dye color, embroidered with flames and flowers and bursts of glittering metallic thread that could be Urlish Fire-rockets or the cold glitter of the full moon reflecting on the Sunsong Sea, or the distant twinkle of the Sky Lights above Erlenmire. Flasks are passed among the adults, wineskins and steaming glass bottles of what appears to be hot chocolate and tea. Children's mittened hands reach up to snatch, sliding on the smooth sides, fingers wiggling unseen beneath patterned yarn. Some of the skins are held up to cupid's bows and sticky mouths, and the adults laugh when the children make horrified faces as the wash of whiskey or tart wine dribbles against their lips and they realize that the adults aren't drinking anything desirable after all.

Beside the old ruin, the ghost of Mandikin crouches low, her skirts dissolving into the night-cool grass like dew mist. Her fingers fly as she tells a tale to the rapt audience of toddlers that have piled around her like sleepy puppies. Her eyes shine silver; her smile is wide. She is happy. She must feel my gaze on her, because she raises her head to me and winks, charming the children around her into a crescendo of high, sweet giggles.

Over the crackle of the bonfire, I can hear some sort of fiddle being brought into tune. There are tin pipes in the muddle, too, and the deep strum of what might be a harp or a large guitar, but the players are on the far side of the flames from us, and I can't see through. A tinkling chime rings out, and then suddenly everyone's attention is on the half dozen couples who are mingling between the families and the fire.

Pairings, I realize. Yeah, they must be.

Standing stiffly, closest to the flame, is a career military man. The fellow to his left, with a matching bearing, must be his new shield-partner. Next to him, a shy couple very obviously in love blush and flutter at one another, only their pinkie fingers entwined. He has bright red flowers woven into his dark beard, and she has the same woven into braids hanging from her temples.

Next to her, a woman about the same age as my oldest sister-in-law is grinning slyly up at a tall, slim, nude fae creature, all onyx eyes and ebony skin, and an unashamedly bare phallus.

The Pair next to them consists of two sweet young girls who keep kissing and giggling, tucking each other's hair behind their ears, righting ribbons, only to fall back into each other's orbits, to grab and kiss again as if their lips were iron and magnets. And beside them stand another pair of young lovers, this time both young men. One is talking incessantly, his hands flying, and the other cradles his cheek close to his own collar, indulgent and attentive.

And lastly, slightly off to one side, is a sturdy couple. They are a man and a woman, clearly farmers, and are surrounded by nearly adult children with two very different hair colors, eager to finally be one family.

Each pair carries a broom, the birch-twig skirt of it woven with pitch-soaked ribbons, the handles carved smooth and intricate with a hundred little knots and whorls, chains and images, symbols that must speak of love, fidelity, promise, and those little moments and secrets meant only for the Pair. I wish I could get a closer look at the brooms. What stories they must tell.

Kin sits up and I shift, strike another match and tamp it in the bowl of my pipe as I wait. Another ringing skirl of string and pipe, and, one by one, the partners join hands on the broom handles, fingers twined. A third flourish of music, and they turn their backs to us, and touch the tips of the brooms to the flames. The pitch catches, the birch twigs crackle, and a flash of magic flares, containing the fire to the broomhead, sealing the flames away from the handle. A fourth and final skirl, and the partners plant the ends of the brooms into low stone pockets that hold the flame just high enough off the grass that they won't sputter out, but not so high that when the Pairs entwine their elbows, brush back their beards, ratchet up their skirts, and leap over the flame, no one catches fire.

One of the young girls, one of the the kissing ones, shrieks in surprise as a trailing ribbon from her hair sparks up, but Mandikin is there quickly. She douses the flame with her wet hand, and the girl's yelp trails off into embarrassed laughter before I have even really registered the cry. Mandikin scolds the girl, and then kisses first her forehead, and then her new wife's, fond and a little sad. The ghost probably minded both girls when they were young.

Kin's hands are on his thighs, curling and flexing in a way that says he clearly wishes there was enough light to sketch by. Instead, he swigs more mead, and I wonder if he intends to get drunk tonight. Not that a nice little festival isn't worth celebrating, but it's me who'll have to haul him back to the inn, who will have to strip him out of his clothes, have to dunk his head in a cold basin and dry his hair, have to tuck him in and . . . I shift, suddenly glad that the firelight is low enough that Kin *can't* sketch. Because if he had enough light to draw by, he'd also have enough light to see the tent I'm pitching.

Bloody hells.

Instead of doing anything about it—it'll go down on it's own, and I'm not feeling particularly inclined to handle it any other way—I tap out the ashes of my pipe on the heel of my boot, repack the bowl, and relight the herb. We watch the revelers in companionable silence.

Kin is lax in the aftermath of adventure and a few good swigs from his skin, not to mention an argument forgiven. Pliant and nonverbal, this is my favorite version of my friend. This Kin lets me touch, lets me run my fingers through gold-threaded locks, lets me rest my palm on his wide thigh, lets me wrap around him in our bedrolls, lets me bury my nose behind an ear.

I take a breath to speak, lick my lips, and then abruptly freeze, my brain tripping to a stunned halt at the question my tongue was just about to push from between my teeth.

No, I think. I can't say that out loud. Can I? No. No. Kin wouldn't . . . *I* can't. Could I? Can I?

"What?" Kin grunts. "Just say it."

I release my breath in a rueful chuckle, forcing my spine to un-fuse, my shoulders to lower. I should be startled that Kin knew I was building up to something, but . . . seventeen years. We know each other well.

Well enough that Kin knows when I'm biting down on words. Well enough that my request might actually go unmocked.

I'm a brave man. I've faced down dark elves, Bootknife's blade, hungry sirens, and vengeful barrow wights. And yet, I can't directly say it. Instead, I decide to take the flank, to test Kin's shields and how drunk he is, how . . . amenable.

"Looks fun," I venture, slipping the stem of my pipe out from between my teeth and pointing the stem at the Pairs now dancing around the Fire Flower torches.

"Mmm," Kin grumbles, which isn't an agreement. It's not an evasion either, though.

I lick my lips again, tasting mead and smoke, herb and possibility. "We could do that."

Kin swigs, seeming to be processing what I suggest. "Dance?" he asks, half in jest. "Set you on fire?"

I'm feeling loose-jointed and warm, and ever so slightly drunk myself after those few ales and the honey mead. I screw up my courage and blurt: "Jump a broom."

The guffaw is half out of Kintyre's mouth before he seems to realize he's even laughing. He doesn't even bother to raise his hand to cover his mouth.

I can feel my face going cold, all of Kin's lovely warmth pulling away as he curls over the mead skin and giggles. Shame surges in its absence.

Stupid, I think. I'm not sure who that's directed at. Both of us, maybe.

"Forget it," I snap, climbing to my feet, shaking the ash out of my pipe with a hard swing that smacks against my thigh and is nowhere near as satisfying as, say, punching Kin in the nose would be.

"Aw, no, Bev!" Kin chortles and paws at my arm. "Come back, you daft bastard, come back."

"Let go," I snarl, feeling more embarrassed and angry with myself than I think the situation warrants. It's not like I'd even *wanted* it particularly badly. It's not like anyone else overheard my awkward, awful proposition.

"Hey now," Kin says, sitting up and looking instantly sober. Whether or not he really is, I can't say. Despite seventeen years of companionship, Kin can still keep things from me when he wants to. "What's this?"

"I said forget it. It's nothing." I turn my face back toward the center of town, toward the *Pern* and the bed that's waiting for me—probably clean, but definitely cold.

Writer, I'm a stupid, *stupid* fool.

Kin squints, tugs the hem of my short-robe, and says, "Bev. We don't *need* to jump a broom together."

"Yeah, right, sure," I say and tug my robe out of his grip.

Kin scrambles to his feet. "Bev, stop, I mean it. We don't need to jump a broom together."

"Why, because we're already Paired?" I sneer. I jam my pipe into my pouch before I end up snapping the stem in my rage—a pipe Kin had given me, sure, but not as a Pairing gift. Kin's never, even after everything I've done, even *thought* about me like that.

Yeah, he'll lick, and touch, and kiss—when there's a woman with us. Sometimes he'll even sheathe himself in me, or allow me to sheathe in him when we are out of our minds with passion. But to *declare* it, to even *admit to it* . . . no. Never. Not in front of my brothers and sisters-in-law, never in front of the children, the people of Bynnebakker. Never where Forsyth Turn, Lordling of Lysse, or Sheriff Pointe, or anyone from Turnshire could hear. Never even in front of his damned *horse*.

Never even when it was just the two of us, alone in a shared berth or bed, on the hundred and one nights where we were jammed together for warmth, or because the room was too small, or because we were imprisoned together, or because the make-shift lean-to or snow-hutch we'd constructed had been too narrow. Never when we were sharing breath, and spit, and tears, and blood. Never *once* has Kin even acknowledged the humid air between our mouths, the way the whorls of our fingertips lock together, the flutter of eyelashes, the scrape of stubble, the peaked nipples, the stained smallclothes.

Never.

Except tonight. And only then to push me away.

And that is not a Pair. That is not what it *means*.

Kin rocks back on his heels and goes absolutely still, absolutely silent. It takes a moment for me to register through the harsh hiss of my own breath slithering through my clenched teeth, to hear the silence for what it is. For what it *isn't*.

Finally, when I have ahold of my temper, when I've managed to unclench my fists and wiggle my toes in my boots, I look up. Kin's face is a well-carved expression of carefully considered blankness.

"Aren't we?" Kin asks, and his voice is low, barely audible above the crackle of the great bonfire, the giggles and shouts of laughter, the yelling children, the cheering adults, the music on the far side of the flames. His shoulders are a straight, unreadable line against the bright aura of firelight, his arms loose at his sides—neither tense nor prepared to fight, nor actually as relaxed as he's trying to appear.

He is so tense, so prepared to be hurt, so ready to just take this blow on his stupid, perfect cleft chin that I can't... I can't. I crumble.

"We are," I lie, hating myself for every syllable of it. "Of course we are."

Kintyre relaxes, happy, oblivious, satisfied. I take the mead skin and drink heavily.

***

As we depart Gwillfifeshire the next morning, packs weighted down with supplies enough to see us through Miliway, my heart is as heavy as my load, my feet plodding. I can't tell if the regret I'm carrying is from what I did last night, and what I said... or from what I didn't have the stones to say.

But Kin looks like he's carrying air, the great prick. He raises his face to the sky and grins. He folds his hands on the back of his neck, mischievous. It makes him look so young again, so carefree, that my heart lurches. And my head throbs; I've got one troll of a hangover.

As I work to unstick my fuzzy tongue from the roof of my mouth, Kin offers me a drink—the last of the mead. It must be stale by now, and certainly warm, but the best cure for a bite is the hair of the dog that bit you, so I accept it with both a grimace and a small nod of gratitude.

There's just one mouthful left when I pass it back.

"Do you suppose there'll be time to find someone in Lysse?" Kin asks, eyes bright as he fists the flask. He tilts his chin up to glug, but his eyes remain on mine. It's not a challenge, not really, so much as a silent plea to keep things as they have always been.

Change nothing, that look begs. *Leave things as they are.*

And I, living in terror that each day will be the one where Kintyre Turn realizes the true depth of my affection for him and departs in a cloud of offense and disgust, give him the closest thing to a nod I can muster.

"Possibly," I answer. "We may have time. We're headed straight there, and Bossy Forssy didn't want us for a fortnight yet. I'd say that's plenty of time."

Kintyre lowers the flask, licking syrupy golden liquor from his lips, and claps me on the back. "Good lad! You'll find me someone good, eh? Maybe this maiden in distress we're meant to be rescuing will be grateful!"

"We can hope," I allow. I swallow hard. It tastes like ash, but I arrange my face into a mask of pleasant blandness all the same. I check our direction by the sun, squinting to spare my eyes. And my throbbing head. I wish something could spare the agonizing squeeze of this damned seedling Dargan planted behind my ribs. I wish I could yank the weed out of my heart.

"Well, to Lysse and Turnshire, then?" Kin asks, twisting the cap of the flask back into place and running his wrist along the underside of his cleft chin to catch any fleeing droplets.

"To Turnshire," I agree, and do as I have always done. As I will always do.

I put one foot in front of the other. I walk.

And I follow Kintyre Turn.

Also by J.M. Frey

The Dark Lord and the Seamstress, a coloring storybook
"The Promise" in *Valor 2*
"Whose Doctor?" in *Doctor Who In Time And Space: Essays on Themes, Characters, History and Fandom, 1963–2012*
"How Fanfiction Made Me Gay," in *The Secret Loves of Geek Girls*
"Time to Move," in *The Secret Loves of Geek Girls Redux*
"Bloodsuckers" and "Toronto the Rude" in *The Toronto Comic Anthology vol 2*
"TTC Gothic" in *Amazing Stories vols 1-4*
Triptych
City by Night
The Woman Who Fell Through Time

The Accidental Turn Series
The Untold Tale
The Forgotten Tale
The Silenced Tale
The Accidental Collection
shorts and novellas from the series

The Skylark's Saga
The Skylark's Song
The Skylark's Sacrifice

About the Author

J.M. Frey is an author, screenwriter, and professional smartypants. She's appeared in podcasts, documentaries, and on television to discuss all things geeky through the lens of academia. Her debut novel TRIPTYCH was nominated for two Lambda Literary Awards, and garnered a place among the Best Books of 2011 from Publishers Weekly. Since then she's published THE ACCIDENTAL TURN SERIES, a quadrilogy of meta-fantasy novels, and THE SKYLARK'S SAGA, a steampunk adventure duology. Her Wattpad-exclusive queer regency historical fiction novel THE WOMAN WHO FELL THROUGH TIME was honoured with a Watty Award in 2019. Her life's ambition is to step foot on every continent – only three left!

www.jmfrey.net

CPSIA information can be obtained
at www.ICGtesting.com
Printed in the USA
BVHW041440201020
591412BV00011B/706